Dead Ground

Justin Warren

Copyright © 2017 by Justin Warren
All rights reserved. This book or any portion thereof may not be reproduced or used in any manner whatsoever without the express written permission of the publisher except for the use of brief quotations in a book review.

Printed in the United States of America.

First Printing, 2017. This edition 2020.

ISBN 9798560170912

Buff Burn Publishing
Christchurch
New Zealand

Website: www.justinwarren.org.nz
Facebook:www.facebook.com/justinwarrenauthor/

For

Melissa, Payton, and Deacon

CHAPTER 1

Dylan Harper was awake. Woken by what, he didn't know. As the fog of sleep lifted and his conscious thoughts fell into their rightful place, he began to sense something was wrong. It was a gut feeling more than anything else. A sense that something, or someone, was closing in on him. Trouble made a habit of chasing Harper. Maybe it had finally caught up with him.

He turned his head to read the digital display on the bedside clock. In a room starved of light, even its dim green glow hurt his eyes. Four thirty-three a.m. Sitting up in bed, he listened. Except for the shallow whisper of his breathing, there was only silence. Even the traffic hiss coming from the nearby western bypass had relaxed, if only temporarily.

Harper dragged himself out of bed and moved to the window. Opening the curtains a crack, he peered out onto the sleeping street. The narrow lane that cut between the rows of houses lay still. The windows of neighbours, black. No signs of life. No hint of movement. All seemed normal. But Harper knew better than to trust first impressions. Complacency will get you killed, he told himself. He needed to be sure.

Eyes straining, he scanned the shadows, searching for anything that might explain his growing unease. With dawn's creeping light more than an hour away, the only illumination came from a lone streetlamp, its intermittent flicker made the dew-covered footpath shimmer like a ribbon of steel.

A car parked three houses away caught Harper's attention. Late-model, dark in colour, navy blue or black, Japanese in design. Silver rims shod in low profile tyres, an after-market spoiler bolted to the boot, tinted windows shielding whoever was inside. He couldn't remember seeing the vehicle before and was confident it didn't belong to anyone on the street. It looked out of place. Was that what had woken him? Closer inspection seemed to rule it out. The cars metal skin was stippled with dew, the glass misted, no wiper marks on the windscreen. Probably been parked there for hours.

The rest of the street appeared perfectly ordinary. A typical scene of suburban bliss. But Harper felt something was off. His instinct for detecting danger was finely tuned and right now his radar was sensing multiple threats. With no clear targets outside, there was only one place left to check.

Harper released the curtain and turned around. It was too dark. Nothing could be seen. His eyes needed time to adjust. But he knew precisely where everything was. This had been home for the past three years, by far the longest he had remained in one place. That bred familiarity. Navigation could be achieved from memory. Step right, avoid the end of the bed, three paces forward, turn left, three more straight ahead, flick the lights.

Trouble was, stability made him easier to find. Three years in one location and he'd become a stationary target. Sooner or later they would track him down. Maybe they already had. Maybe they were already inside. It was time to find out. He crept forward, bare feet softly padding the carpet, each step somehow deafening amid the silence.

That's when it struck him. The silence. It was unusually quiet. Way too quiet. It felt like the city was holding its breath. Like it was waiting for something. Waiting for what?

That's when he heard it. Faint, but growing louder, drawing in on him at incredible speed. A rumbling like a jet aircraft on full reverse thrust. He was already at the bedroom door but an inner voice told him it was too late. He would never make it. The time wasted standing at the window had sealed his fate. Panic obliterated rational thought. He decided to run for it.

In the microsecond it took for the decision to travel from his brain to his legs, the noise had intensified tenfold, now so loud it reverberated through every muscle, the speed of its arrival breathtaking. As his foot hit the floor, it crashed into the house like a rogue wave slamming broadside into a ship.

EARTHQUAKE

The building groaned as the earth heaved. Harper found it difficult to stay upright. The roar enveloped everything. It came from above and below, from all sides at once. It was impossible to tell what was up, down, or sideways.

Using the walls for support, he lurched forward. When his foot came down to where the floor should have been—nothing. The unexpected free-fall hit him in the stomach like a sucker punch. The drop was violently arrested when the floor came surging back up to meet him. The sharp sound of shattering glass punctured through the thunder, objects toppling, wallboards cracking, the structure twisting.

He came to the bathroom, its open door swinging wildly. Losing his footing, Harper tumbled to the floor. The bathroom door slammed into his shoulder sending a bolt of pain down his arm. He shimmied away, seeking refuge by the bathtub. The earthquake was now in full force, shaking him like a rag doll, making coordinated movement impossible.

As the carnage thundered on, a calmness fell upon him, a hopeless acceptance that nothing more could be done. His fate lay in the hands of a higher power.

Seconds seemed like minutes as the chaos roared through the darkness. He waited for the sounds of nails tearing free, wood splintering, beams crashing to earth, the house falling in on itself. But those sounds never came. After what seemed like an eternity, the noise and shaking dissolved into the night like a train rumbling off down the line. The swaying subsided. The house gave a final groan and settled back onto its foundations. As quickly as it had begun, it was over. All was still and calm once again.

Harper hit the light on his watch. Four thirty-five. The earthquake had lasted thirty, perhaps forty seconds. His heart was beating out of his chest, adrenaline coursed through every vein and artery. He sat for a moment, unsure of what to do.

DEAD GROUND

The earthquake was over, but he still needed to convince himself that the house had stopped moving. A dull ache in his left shoulder grew into a throbbing pain that spread down his arm, rendering the limb almost useless.

He had been through worse pain. Years of contact sports had seen him accumulate an impressive array of injuries ranging from concussions to dislocations and a few broken bones thrown in for good measure. The pain he felt now was nothing more than a minor inconvenience. His body was built to take these knocks and merely shrug them off.

At six-foot-three and a shade over two hundred pounds, his rugged physique was that of a honed athlete. Broad shoulders framed a defined chest that tapered to a lean waist and powerful legs. Dark hair, closely cropped in a military-style cut, was easy-care and showed he meant business. His hazel eyes were sharp and piercing, but also gave a hint of the sorrow that lurked within. Overnight stubble shaded his angular jaw, the flecks of grey it bore made him look older than his thirty-two years.

It wasn't until he dragged himself to his feet that Harper realised he was naked. A split second later he remembered the woman he'd meet in the bar, the one who had made it clear she was coming home with him. What was her name? Something starting with R. Rebecca? No. Rachael? Yes, that was it, Rachael. Dark hair, tight dress, smoky eyes, legs that went on forever. How could he forget? Hot needles of guilt pricked his skin. He'd left her alone in the bedroom. How could he have been so stupid? Wait. That's right. He remembered now. She had left as soon as she got what she came for. A cool breath of relief made him shiver. He needed to get dressed and get out before the next aftershock.

Harper stood up, his legs unsteady like he'd just spent six months at sea. Amazing how a few seconds of ground movement could make a man forget how to walk. He made it to the bedroom door and felt for the light switch. It was found after some fumbling but the power was out.

'Fuck,' he muttered.

He stumbled into the bedroom and immediately slammed into something. This generated more four-letter words which, if nothing else, helped distract him from the pain. Blind and wounded, he felt around and found the culprit, a set of drawers toppled against the bed. He heaved the fallen furniture upright, dug through the drawers and threw on some clothes. Back down the hall he found his car keys hanging on a hook by the front door. He opened the door and made his escape into the safety of the night.

A quick canvas of the neighbours revealed minor bumps and bruises along with one woman who had cut her hand crawling through broken glass. The mostly single-story neighbourhood seemed to have well and there was no obvious structural damage, at least none that was visible in the dark.

The first aftershock hit as Harper backed his car out of the garage. The Ford Ranger rocked lazily and Harper held his breath. Compared to the first earthquake this was just a baby. It would be the first of many. He better get used to them.

Harper turned on the radio. The pre-programmed selection was a nation-wide station based in another city. Oblivious to what had just happened, it cycled through the usual medley of music, ads and station promos. Harper searched through the dial but all the local broadcasts were spitting static. After flicking through five more channels, he found one still on the air.

"We are getting reports of extensive damage in the central city. Numerous reports of buildings down but no word on casualties at this stage. Roads are blocked by fallen debris, High Street and Latimer Square are badly affected, and there is widespread liquefaction in the eastern suburbs. So, just to repeat the main facts as we have them at this time. Shortly after four-thirty this morning, a seven-point four magnitude earthquake struck Christchurch City. The epicentre was thirty kilometres west of the CBD at a depth of just ten kilometres. It has been felt as far south as Dunedin and Masterton in the north. Power is out in much of the region and phone coverage is intermittent. At this time we have had no official comment from the mayor or Civil Defence. We will keep you up to date as more comes to hand. You are listening to Radio New Zealand. It is four forty-five, Saturday, September the tenth."

The radio cut to a station promo so Harper turned it down. He reached into the driver-side door pocket and grabbed his police radio. He flicked to the emergency channel and it sprang to life with a squeal and a burst of static. What followed sounded like a pre-recorded announcement.

"… please report to the central station as soon as possible. This is a general recall for all sworn police personnel. Once you have made sure you and your family are safe, please report to the central station as soon as possible."

The announcement repeated on a loop, so he shut it off. Harper had no family, no blood relatives. At least none that he knew of. The police were his only family. He re-engaged reverse and backed out into the street. It was obvious where he needed to be.

CHAPTER 2

Six months later

The Criminal Investigation Branch occupied the entire eleventh floor of the Christchurch Central Police Station and housed the detective unit assigned to investigate violent crime, and in particular, homicide. On any regular Tuesday the floor would have been filled with the orderly drone of detectives at work. Staccato tapping of keyboards, whirring Xerox, phones ringing, and conversations conducted in hushed tones. But this was no ordinary Tuesday. Today, all hell was breaking loose.

The bombshell had come at just after nine that morning. Structural engineers had determined that the 6.3 aftershock of February 22, while less powerful than the main quake of the previous September, had further weakened the thirteen-storey building, making it unsafe to occupy the upper levels. Everyone, regardless of rank, had to pack up and move to the bottom four floors, and they had until midday to do it.

But Harper was in no hurry. He was already set. Word had spread that his partner, Joe Gardella, had staked out a space. Gardella had been prowling around the staff lockers on level three when he was heard to say, 'Harper and I will be working from here.' From that moment on, no one dared tread on that sacred turf. Gardella was not a big man; Harper had a good three inches on him, but he was tough as nails and had a never-say-die attitude. He was mid-forties, with greying hair and eyes like a leaden sky just before it rains.

By the time Gardella made it up to the detective bureau, Harper had made no attempt at moving.

'I may be mistaken, Detective Harper, but shouldn't you be doing something other than sitting on your arse?' Gardella said.

'Joe, I was just waiting for you,' Harper replied, hands up in a surrendering gesture.

'You know what pisses me off? You think you know it all. You stick with me and you're gonna learn real quick that it takes hours of grunt work before you break a case. Look at you. You ever broken a sweat?'

'That's why I'm working with you, Joe, I'm learning from the legend,' Harper replied. He knew his caustic attitude was not the most conducive to a harmonious working relationship. In his time with the department, he had already been bounced by two partners who failed to get his sense of humour. He needed to tone things down. As Gardella was about to unload another verbal tirade, the phone rang. He checked the caller ID and saw it was an internal call.

'It's from upstairs, top floor. Looks like the boss. Jesus, Harper, who have you pissed off now?'

Grinning, Harper replied, 'No one, except you.'

Gardella shot back with a steely stare. The phone rang twice more. Neither man moved. On the fourth ring, Gardella reached down and lifted the receiver, never taking his eyes off Harper.

'Gardella, CIB.' There was a short pause. Gardella nodded. 'Right, we're on our way up.'

'What's going on?' Harper asked, trying not to let any concern creep into his voice.

'Seems we have a case. Didn't say what it was, just that we need to get up to thirteen and he'd brief us personally.'

'Who'd brief us?'

'Bones.'

'What? You mean the DC?'

'The one and only.'

District Commander Trevor Jones was the top cop for not only Christchurch but the whole Canterbury region. He had been in the police for longer than anyone could remember and looked like a walking skeleton.

'Why would Bones have something for us? He doesn't normally get his hands dirty breaking cases down for the rank and file.'

'How would I know? He just said he had something for us, and to get our arses upstairs, pronto.'

Harper leveraged himself out of his chair and followed Gardella through the maze of desks and boxes, arriving at the elevator just as the silver doors slid open. A heavyset woman came charging out, breathing heavily, shunting an empty luggage trolley. Harper took evasive action and barely avoided being run down. He glanced at Gardella, who only shrugged.

Even before the doors closed Gardella was stabbing at the button as if this would somehow speed up the process. The doors eased shut and the elevator lurched upwards but then slowed to an almost imperceptible crawl. Finally, the lift halted and the doors peeled back to reveal an unexpected scene.

The foyer that typically welcomed new arrivals with a flourish of corporate smugness was eerily abandoned. Harper flicked a quizzical look at Gardella, who returned it in kind. An elegant reception desk, lonely and unmanned, a row of filing cabinets, their open draws like hungry mouths. An overturned chair and a fallen picture, its glass a spiderweb of cracks. The top brass usually stalked these corridors wearing crisp uniforms and sullen expressions as if the burden of running the city fell solely on their shoulders. But not today.

Harper and Gardella paced past the desolation and pushed through the frosted double glass doors that separated the foyer from the inner sanctum. As they moved down the corridor, Harper peered into each office. Cleared desks, empty shelves, bare walls, and a general mood of despondency. At the end of the hall, the entrance to the District Commander's office waited. Unlike all the other doors, this one was closed. Harper and Gardella stood and looked at each other, not knowing what to do. Standard protocol dictated that a secretary would escort them in. However, her office was unoccupied, except for a half-filled waste paper basket and a wilting potted plant.

Somehow sensing their presence, Bones called out. 'Come in, detectives.'

As Harper entered, he spied Bones loading personal effects into one of three cardboard boxes crowding his desk.

'Thank you for coming so promptly, detectives. I know you're busy downstairs. Take a seat.'

There were no seats nearby so Harper retrieved a pair of chairs from a stack by the wall and set them down in front of the District Commander's desk. Bones hefted the boxes onto the floor and eased himself into his leather armchair, leaving only a manila folder in front of him. The veins on his bony hands bulged in grotesque purple-black lines that looked as though they would burst at any moment. Wireframe spectacles outlined the tired, sunken eyes of a man whose fire had long ago burnt out. Thin strands of snowy hair were doing their best to conceal a mottled scalp. To Harper, Bones looked like a captain preparing to go down with the ship.

Behind Bones, a row of picture windows framed a scarred city where hagged grey clouds spewed from demolition crews as they dismembered the worst of the earthquake-impaired buildings. They operated like surgeons removing a cancerous tumour while trying to leave the healthy tissue untouched. But the cancer was everywhere. It would be years until they would rid the city of the disease. The sorry scene outside mirrored the feeling in the room. Christchurch was being gutted, and so was police HQ.

'I see the top floor got a head start,' Harper said. 'Where are you relocating?'

'Off-site, to temporary offices on St Asaph Street. We'll operate out of there until things settle down. It looks like we'll be there for a while.'

Nice for some, Harper thought. He wondered how many other police personnel would prefer to be out of this building. But this was not the time to raise the issue. He held his tongue and waited to hear about the case.

'Detective Harper, you're from Westport,' Bones said, more as a statement than a question.

'Yes. I grew up there.'

'You know the region well. You know the people, the community, the culture. Correct?'

'You could say that, yes.'

'Good. In that case, I might have something for you.'

'You're saying you have a case for us in Westport?'

Bones gave a thin smile. 'That's precisely what I'm saying.'

Harper glanced at Gardella.

'Correct me if I'm wrong,' Gardella said, 'but isn't Westport on the other side of the South Island? It's not even our jurisdiction. Why send us over there to work a case that belongs to another department?'

Bones turned a raised eyebrow toward Gardella like he had just become aware of his presence and glared over the rim of his glasses before he turned his chair so he could look out at the city below.

'Look out there, detectives. Look at what is left of our city.' Bones extended his arms like a minister preaching to his congregation. 'That is the reason I am sending you to Westport.'

Gardella and Harper glanced at each other, both with the same confused expression.

Bones went on. 'You see, after the earthquakes, two things changed. First, a state of emergency was enacted. That allowed us to call on every resource we might need. Do you know what our most crucial resource is, gentlemen?'

Bones swung around, glaring like a teacher expecting a wrong answer. When no one took the bait, he answered his own question. 'Personnel. Typically we're so thin on the ground that we struggle just to keep our heads above water. But after the earthquakes we've got every cop in the South Island here. Hell, we even have reinforcements from Australia. Every police officer in the country wants to be in Christchurch. They're volunteering by the busload. So many we don't know what to do with them all. They're all out there, working the cordons, preventing looting, patrolling the red zone, keeping order and so on. Now, that's great for us, but it means the other districts are short-staffed. The Tasman Police Department would normally take this case, but they're on a skeleton crew. Half their officers are here, meaning their detectives are forced to dust off their uniforms and walk the beat. They don't have the manpower for this investigation.

'The second factor at play here is crime rates. With so many police running around, crime is at an all-time low. You can't go two blocks before you run into a patrol. The gangs aren't stupid; they've seen the signs. They've up and left. So now I've got a thirteen-storey building full of detectives, all twiddling their thumbs. I can keep them occupied only so long.'

Harper agreed. In his experience, detectives were like sharks. They needed to keep moving. Hunt to survive. The minute they stopped, the trouble started.

'So that leaves me with a problem,' Bones continued. 'What the hell to do with all of you? Then this Westport thing comes across my desk. I go through the personnel records and see Detective Harper is from the West Coast. He knows the area. He's the obvious choice. You, Detective Gardella, are his mentor. You're there to make sure he does things by the book. That means you go, too.'

Harper folded his arms and Gardella leaned back in his chair. It was clear the decision had been made. There was no point in pushing the matter.

'So what are we dealing with here? What's the case?' Harper asked.

Bones leaned forward and placed a contorted hand on the manila folder. With unusually deliberate care, he opened it to reveal a single sheet of paper. Then he nudged his glasses up the bridge of his nose and said, 'What we have is a missing person. Fifty-three-year-old male, married with two adult children, works as a reporter at the local newspaper. Wife is an artist. She called it in. She went up to her studio for the weekend and when she came back, no husband.'

'When was the husband last seen?' Gardella asked.

'Wife last saw him Friday morning. She spent Friday at the art gallery that she runs then left for a small township up the coast called Karamea, spending Saturday and Sunday at her studio. Monday morning she returned to town, opened her gallery and worked all day. She got home Monday afternoon expecting to have dinner with her husband. He never showed up. She reported him missing around eight-thirty that night.'

Gardella shook his head in disbelief. 'So no one has laid eyes on this guy for four days. Anything could have happened. He could be anywhere. If he's dead, the killer has had more than enough time to cover his tracks.'

Bones lowered his glasses to look at Gardella. 'It is was it is Detective.'

'What are the names? The husband and the wife?' Harper asked.

Bones ran a crooked finger down the page. 'Jonathon Hayes. Wife is Samara. Those names familiar to you, Detective?'

'Yes.'

'What was your impression of the family?'

'Seemed fairly normal, middle class, no issues that I was aware of. But I didn't know them that well. There could have been things going on behind the scenes. You know, domestic problems.'

'Now let's not jump to any conclusions, Detective,' Bones said. 'I want you to deal in facts, not suppositions. You must approach this case with an open mind.'

Without warning, a violent shuddering surged up from below. The building began to rock. Bones grabbed his armrests while Harper and Gardella simply froze. A few seconds later, the movement died away. A cord of dust trailed down from a crack in the ceiling. Bones eyed it nervously. 'Christ!' he exclaimed. 'I will never get used to those.'

Harper did his best to appear calm. 'Look on the bright side, Joe,' he said. 'At least this trip will get us away from the goddamn aftershocks.'

Gardella ignored the comment. 'I'm guessing you want us in Westport this afternoon?' he said to Bones.

'Correct. I want you to make arrangements to leave before one o'clock. It's a four-hour drive so you should get there around five. Out of courtesy, I want you to check in with the locals, let them know you're there, see if they have any other details, and then interview the wife. Because you will be out of the district, I have authorised you to be armed. We can't have you at the mercy of the Westport Police now, can we? Any questions?'

'You've let them know we're on our way?' Harper asked.

'Yes, they're expecting you. Now get moving, gentlemen. I expect daily updates.'

As they made their way back to the elevator, Harper could sense something was bothering Gardella. It wasn't until the lift doors closed that his partner opened up.

'Why is this coming from Bones? This is a missing person case. Why is the boss getting involved?'

'Maybe Westport didn't want anyone sticking their noses in. Probably took a little extra influence to convince them.'

'I don't buy it. The senior sergeant could have made the same moves,' Gardella said as he punched the button for the eleventh floor. 'And what's with the firearms? Unless there's a specific threat, it's not procedure to be armed. What's he not telling us?'

'I think you're reading too much into this, Joe. We're going to be a long way from home and if things go bad we can't just roll into the armoury and grab a piece.'

'It still doesn't make sense. Not for a missing person's case?'

The elevator coasted to a halt and the doors parted. Harper went to his desk and gathered his laptop, a notepad, torch, evidence bags, rubber gloves and an assortment of other articles. After a few minutes, he and Gardella proceeded to the arms office where they each received the standard-issue Glock pistol and two seventeen round clips. They agreed to head home and pack their bags and rendezvous at midday. Harper climbed into his Ranger and pulled out onto Hereford Street. On the drive home he was finally alone with his thoughts. Why did it have to be Westport? Anywhere but there.

CHAPTER 3

Harper chose to eat at Dimitri's, a Greek place that made arguably the best souvlaki in the city. Before the earthquakes, they had a bricks and mortar restaurant on the corner of Cambridge and Gloucester, just near the river. But like most places in the CBD, it had been damaged beyond repair and was awaiting its date with the wrecking ball. Dimitri's now operated out of a small blue and white caravan on the northern edge of the red zone, catering mostly to demolition crews and the police who patrolled the cordons. The food was as good as ever, despite the temporary facilities. Gardella didn't seem to be enjoying the food and hadn't eaten a bite. He picked moodily at his plate until Harper had finished. Harper knew not to disturb him when he was like this. Nothing good ever came of it. After eating they got in their station-issued Holden Commodore and began the long journey to the West Coast.

An hour later and Gardella still hadn't said a word. Harper cracked open his window to let in the crisp air of the Canterbury Plains and the car filled with the aroma of clover from the surrounding fields. It was a refreshing change from the dust-choked urban smog of the city. This region had traditionally been sheep country. Flat open fields of pasture stretching out either side of the highway, only interrupted by the occasional grove of trees or scruffy hedgerow. In more recent years much of it had been converted to dairy due to record-breaking milk prices. Cows had replaced the sheep and today their hulking bodies wallowed lazily through the fields, chewing their cud and swinging their heavy heads in the mid-afternoon sun. Lush farmland flashed by as Harper gunned the Commodore down the straights.

Harper was enjoying the feeling of effortless speed as the road coiled left and plunged through a plantation of pines. The bright sun filtered through the canopy leaving dappled patterns on the road. It was then that Gardella finally broke his silence.

'So, you're a West Coast boy?'

Harper gripped the wheel. 'Yep,' he said sharply, hoping his curt reply would kill further questions on the topic.

'What was it like growing up in the sticks?'

Harper had been paired with Gardella for three months and in that time it had been all business. His partner had never once asked a personal question and that suited Harper just fine. As far as he was concerned, the less said about his past, the better.

Harper answered with another short response. 'It was okay.'

They were now approaching the alpine pass. The road began to snake as the mountains closed in around them.

'That's not what your NIA file says,' Gardella said.

Harper kept his eyes locked on the road and gripped the wheel a little tighter. The NIA was the New Zealand Police database of reported crime. It contained a wealth of information on individuals who had committed a range of offences or had a watch placed on them by the New Zealand Police. It also cross-referenced the details of witnesses and their statements along with records of the evidence collected in cases. Harper knew his name was in the NIA database. What he couldn't figure out was how Gardella had found it.

'What are you talking about?' Harper said.

'Don't play games, Dylan. I've read the file. I know all about you.'

The hot prickle of anger washed over Harper. He reached for the climate control, buying enough time to formulate a response. 'If that's true, you've breached protocol. The NIA database is strictly for investigative purposes. It's not there for snooping.'

Gardella laughed. 'What are you going to do? Report me?'

Harper sank into the driver's seat. Gardella had somehow accessed his file and probably knew the worst. He had no choice but to come clean.

He slowed the car, knowing there was a lay-by around the next bend. He flicked the indicator and turned off the tar-seal onto the gravel. Roughly the size of two basketball courts end to end, the lay-by was surrounded on three sides by tall beech trees, the fourth by the road and a mountain range that towered like a deserted grandstand at a sports stadium. Quiet, secluded, empty. Just the right environment to get a few things off his chest.

The tyres made a satisfying crunch as the car came to rest in the natural amphitheatre. Harper killed the engine. The grumble of the V8 extinguished, replaced by a chorus of birdsong wafting from the forest canopy. Harper thought he heard the distinctive song of the Kokako; its organ-like call seemed fitting in this forest cathedral. For a moment, they sat in silence and drank in their surroundings. Then Harper spoke.

'Let's talk over there,' he said, pointing towards a lone picnic table. They climbed out of the car and walked the short distance. Harper sat with his back to the road, Gardella facing him. Somewhere high above, the early afternoon sun shone, succeeding only in sending the occasional shaft of hazy light down through the trees.

'So, Detective Harper,' Gardella said. 'What was it that gave you this sudden desire to become an officer in the New Zealand Police force?' A bland enough question, but not with Harper's history.

Harper leaned forward, elbows on the table, hands clasped high, chin cradled by thumbs. He didn't know where to begin.

'The death of your girlfriend?' Gardella prompted. 'Tell me about that.'

Harper bristled. The memory still stung. 'You've read the file. You know what happened. What more do you want?'

'A file only contains so much. It explains what happened. What I need from you is why. I need to understand it from your perspective. If we're going to work as a team, trust each other, I need to know.'

Harper turned away, staring into the depths of the forest where the sunlight could not pierce as if escape into the darkness would make it all better. Only it couldn't. He had spent too long in the shadows. His only hope was to come back into the light.

'You're right. You need to know. But for the record, it starts much earlier than that night. You know about my mother? Was that in my file?'

'Yes,' Gardella said, his eyes narrow. 'She died when you were young.'

'I was eight. What it won't say is how she was found.'

Gardella shook his head. 'Not according to the police report. It says the body was discovered by a social worker. She came to the house, knocked, but got no response. The front door was wide open, she found your mother and called for an ambulance. Unfortunately, it was too late. Your mother was already dead. Estimated TOD was some time that morning. You were at school.'

'Yeah, that's what it says, but that's not what happened,' Harper said. He drew a breath and delivered the next line dead cold. 'I was there. In the house. I found her.'

Harper thought he saw Gardella flinch. A flash of compassion, if that was even possible for the man.

'Shit,' Gardella said.

'I skipped school and came home. Found her on the kitchen floor. Thought she was asleep and tried to wake her. That's when I saw her eyes. I'll never forget her eyes. They were open, staring vacantly at nothing. I freaked out. I didn't know what to do. I was only eight. I should've called for help, but I didn't. I just ran. That was why the front door was open. The cops picked me up wandering the streets. They notified me of the death, or so they thought. I already knew. The autopsy found she died of an overdose.'

The sound of an approaching vehicle gave both men reason to pause. As the noise grew closer, it became apparent the car was not going to stop. They sat stony-faced until the intruder had passed and the sound had faded.

'So that's what sent you off the rails?' Gardella said without his usual biting tone.

'It messed me up pretty good, yeah. I remember thinking that it was just not fair. I was full of anger and bitterness, which I took out on people who tried to help me. I was a real arsehole for a long time. I regret it now, especially how I treated my foster parents. I couldn't see it at the time, but I was lucky they adopted me. They took me in, put a roof over my head. I stayed in Westport, in the same school and everything. If not for them, I would have been shipped off to some home God knows where. But at the time I was just too messed up to know any better. That's when I started getting into trouble, drinking, shoplifting, tagging, stupid stuff really.'

'Tell me about the girlfriend.' The biting tone was back in Gardella's voice.

'Sara,' Harper muttered almost breathlessly, the mere act of mentioning of her name, difficult. 'I was eighteen when we started seeing each other. She'd been around before but had dropped out of school so was off my radar. I started noticing her in bars and at parties. She had this look about her, like a lost child or something. Maybe that's what drew me to her. Maybe I saw a bit of myself. I guess I felt like I could rescue her. I don't know. Anyway, in the end, I couldn't save her. I was lucky to save myself.'

'Tell me about her.'

'She was into some messed-up stuff, drugs mostly. Started with weed, but soon progressed to meth. I shouldn't have let myself get involved, especially after what happened to my mother. Sara had no job, and I was working part-time, so we had no money. So she started dealing. It meant easy access to the shit and some extra cash, but it brought all sorts of problems. When she was late with payments, the supplier would go crazy. One night they came around and smashed up the place where we were staying. It was meant as a message. Anyway, by this stage, I'd had enough. I wanted out. That night, I tried to convince her to snitch. When the cops showed up, I told them it was drug-related. I didn't know any names; she never told me their names. I think she was trying to protect me. They needed that detail from her, but she wasn't ready to give them up. She told the cops she needed to think it over. Somehow, it got out that she was going to talk. There must've been someone on the inside, a source within the Westport Police. That's when it happened.'

Harper paused, knowing he had reached the point of no return. Gardella eased back on his seat and waited.

'We decided to move back in with my foster parents,' Harper continued. 'They lived up on the hill overlooking the town. It was a lifestyle block, but without the lifestyle, if you know what I mean. We thought we would be safer there. It was just empty fields, hedges and the odd farmhouse. But Westport is a small place. It took the supplier a couple of days to figure it out. They sent an enforcer. A guy they called Bozo. Supposed to scare us into keeping our mouths shut. Except, Bozo fucked up. He broke into the house one night with a rifle, a .22. The cops said it was most likely meant as a final warning. Unfortunately, he went into the wrong fucking room. I woke to the sound of my mother's screams. Dad kept his .303 by the bed and probably reached for it. Bozo must've seen the gun and panicked. But rather than cut his losses and get the fuck out of Dodge, the idiot started shooting.'

Harper paused once more. The memories still fresh.

'My parents were killed in their bed. Dad first, then Mom. Our room was further down the hall. Sara and I were at the bedroom door as he came out. Sara made a run for it. I reached out and tried to grab her and pull her back into the bedroom. My fingertips grazed her T-shirt. She was wearing one of my old shirts. That memory will never leave me. I'll always wonder what if. What if I could've pulled her back in? But I didn't. Sara made it a couple of steps before he shot her in the back of the head. She was dead before she hit the floor. I was just inside the bedroom door. I heard him coming down the hallway. I didn't know what to do. I froze.'

Gardella brought his arms up and laid them on the table, palms facing down. He leant forward and calmly asked, 'Then what?'

'Footsteps, slow and deliberate, like he was stalking his prey. He was coming for me. He was coming down the hall. About three feet from our bedroom door, there was a creaky floorboard. If you knew where it was, you avoided it because it could wake the dead. He stepped on it. It must've spooked him because it went quiet. No sound. Nothing. Just him and me, separated by a few inches of wall and an open door. I was doing my best to control my breathing, but I was sure he could hear me. Then, I saw something.'

Harper closed his eyes. As he did, the sounds of the forest seemed to dissolve away. His body was still sitting at a table, but his mind was back in that room.

'A black barrel. A silencer on the end. It came through the door. Slowly. Floating. It seemed like it hung there in space for a lifetime. It was then that I knew what to do. I grabbed it. Yanked it hard. He stumbled forward, into the room, still holding the gun. He fired. Off behind me. Off to the left. I lunged forward. Rammed my head into his. He screamed. Dropped the gun. Staggered backwards into the hall. A light was on. Must've been the light from the end of the hall. Anyway, I saw his face. Blood streaming, broken nose. Eyes wide with surprise.' Harper paused, teeth gritted, and opened his eyes. 'I fucking decked him. One punch! Snapped his head around and knocked the fucker out cold. He dropped like a sack of shit. I stepped over him and went to Sara. She was lying face down. There was almost no blood. I rolled her over. Her eyes were open. She had the same vacant stare that I had seen on my mother. I knew she was dead. I went into my parents' room. They were still sitting up in bed like nothing had happened. But they were dead too. That's when I heard a groan. Bozo was coming around. I went back down the hallway and found his gun. I chambered a round, stuck the barrel up under his chin. He woke up and blinked. Our eyes met. I waited. I waited to make sure he was fully conscious. I wanted my face to be the last thing he saw. And then I pulled the trigger.'

Gardella had barely moved, his gaze firmly fixed on Harper throughout. Study the subject and watch for anything that hinted at a lie. Harper knew he had given nothing away because everything had been the truth. But the look on Gardella's face suggested he needed more convincing.

'In your statement to police, you said that the intruder entered your room, fired once and missed. He then attempted to reload. Before he could, you rushed towards him. There was a struggle. The muzzle of the rifle was pushed up and towards the face of the gunman. During this struggle, the gun went off, killing the intruder. The coroner's report said the .22 calibre round entered through the vomer bone at the base of the skull reducing some of its energy, before passing vertically upwards through the brain until it hit the top of the skull. It bounced off the skull and came back down, finally coming to rest inside the brain. No exit wound, no blood spatter. The weapon was found next to the deceased. The lead investigator concluded the physical evidence, including the prints on the gun and the injuries sustained, were consistent with an act of self-defence.'

'That's when I decided,' Harper said.

'Decided what?'

'My purpose in life.'

Gardella raised a tell-me-more eyebrow. Harper narrowed his stare and clenched his jaw, steeling himself for what came next.

'I'm not a religious guy, Joe. I don't believe in divine intervention or instant karma or whatever you want to call it. There isn't a higher power working to protect the weak and punish the guilty. There's just too much evil in this world for that to be true. There are only guys like you and me, people who are prepared to stand up for what is right.'

Gardella eased away, sliding his arms across the table until his hands came to rest on its edge. He pushed himself up into a standing position. 'We need to get moving or else we'll be too late to check in with the locals.'

With that, he headed back to the car, leaving Harper alone. For a moment, Harper sat there, not sure what to make of his partner's reaction. Eventually, he walked back to the car and lowered himself into the driver's seat. Gardella had returned to glaring out the passenger window. Then, without turning his head, he spoke.

'If I were in your shoes that night, I would've done the same thing.'

CHAPTER 4

They emerged on the western side of the Southern Alps as the waning sun began to stretch its shadowy fingers across the landscape. Harper eased off the gas and let the car coast down the bush-clad foothills to the coastal plains below. For the first time in hours, they could see out across the flatlands to the ocean beyond. Golden rays of sun sparkled as they caressed the blue waters of the Tasman Sea. Gardella sat up to get a better view. It was a welcome sight after the torturous twists of the Lewis Pass.

Since their heart-to-heart, Gardella's mood had softened. He had even made an effort at civil conversation. Granted, Harper had done most of the talking, but at least it was a change from his standard passive-aggressive demeanour. Harper used the opportunity to bring his partner up to speed on this region of New Zealand.

Westport was home to around five thousand blue-collar, hard-working folk. The rest of the country referred to them as "Coasters". These people were fiercely loyal to one another; a bond forged in the coal and gold mines where fortunes were made and lives lost in an instant. While outsiders were generally regarded with quiet suspicion, outwardly they were welcomed with a degree of warm hospitality and good-natured banter that you would normally only expect from a lifelong friend.

The township itself was nestled on a sliver of land between a five thousand foot mountain range to the east, and the Tasman Sea to the west. Living here was a double-edged sword. On the one hand, the mountains protected Westport from the cold winds blowing up from the Southern Ocean, making the climate mild year-round. The downside was that those same peaks caught moisture-laden clouds sweeping in from the west, forcing them to release their burden before they could pass. The high annual rainfall fed dense sub-tropical forests that cloaked the surrounding mountains in a thick green coat for as far as the eye could see. It made you feel like you had come to the ends of the earth, and in a way, you had. Once you found Westport, there was nowhere left to go.

They were now on the outskirts of the town. As they turned onto the Buller Bridge Harper gently stroked the throttle as they traversed the waters which it spanned. The Buller River was broad and deep and back in the days of the gold rush, it made an ideal port for the tall sailing ships of the era. The flat coastal plain and the unimaginative thinking of the early settlers had resulted in the town's streets being laid out in a traditional grid pattern.

Palmerston Street was the main road. It ran north-south for twelve blocks, two kilometres of old town architecture spanning its length. One block east of Palmerston was the river which flowed parallel with the main street. Next to the river a railway line fed into shunting yards and an industrial corridor of warehouses which separated the rest of the town from the docks. In more prosperous times, trains laden with coal would rumble into town and hulking steam cranes would pluck the sooty carriages from their bogies and deposit their loads into the holds of cargo ships.

By 2011 the last remaining coal mine was still profitable, but only barely. Ships occasionally docked, but mostly the port lay idle. These days the main street was lined with shops, banks, restaurants, bars, offices and various other amenities to cater to the growing tourist trade. Some of the buildings dated back to the 1800s and aside from a fresh coat of paint they could have passed for something out of a Wild West frontier town. But these were gradually being replaced by newer constructions. Boutique hotels were springing up here and there as more visitors came to experience the fishing, hunting, hiking, and history of the region. But Harper and Gardella weren't here to enjoy the sights. They had a job to do.

'You wanna check into the hotel or go and make ourselves known at the station?' Harper asked.

'Better give the boys in blue a courtesy call. Would hate to piss them off before we even get started.'

Harper nodded and steered the car towards the centre of town. The police station and the courthouse stood just metres apart but couldn't have been more different in appearance. The courthouse was a grand old wooden affair with a high-pitched roofline and French windows that extended from the eaves nearly down to the footpath. The police station, on the other hand, was a low-slung grey cinder block construction, almost devoid of windows, that could have easily passed as a toilet block. A narrow strip of grass and a few small shrubs did nothing to disguise the ugliness. Harper pulled into an empty park directly outside.

'You'd never get a park like that in Christchurch.' Harper said.

'Tin-pot town,' Gardella added with a snigger. 'Most people probably don't even own a car.'

Harper smirked. Humour was another good sign.

The two men strode through the double glass doors of the main entrance. It had been twelve years since Harper had left Westport, but he was still considered a Coaster. This gave him a distinct advantage. The locals were more likely to trust one of their own, as opposed to an outsider. At least, that was the hope. For this reason they had decided Harper would do most of the talking. Gardella would step in if he felt Harper had missed something or needed to explore a particular line of questioning further.

The lobby was elevator shaft small with scarcely room to accommodate three vinyl clad chairs that looked like they fell straight out of the 1970s. There was a reception window cut into the opposite wall with a lip protruding from its base from which a ballpoint pen dangled on a beaded metal chain. A handmade sign read: Back in Five Minutes.

'Yeah right,' Gardella said.

Harper stuck his head through the opening. The office on the other side was deserted. 'Hey! Anybody home?'

No response.

On the wall was a red button with the instructions: Push for Emergency Assistance. Harper looked at Gardella, shrugged, and pressed it. There was no bell or buzzer or any sound at all. He tried it again, this time holding it for several seconds.

From somewhere inside the station, Harper heard movement. Someone running. Seconds later, a police officer in a powder blue shirt and dark trousers burst into the office. He was a tall, painfully thin man, who looked as though he would struggle to stay upright in a stiff breeze. He was followed a second later by a short, heavy-set officer, who had what looked like tomato sauce smeared on one side of his face. Both men were out of breath.

'What's the problem?' the fat one blurted out.

'Sorry to interrupt dinner, guys. I'm Detective Constable Harper. This is my partner Detective Sergeant Gardella. We're from Christchurch CIB. We're working the Jonathon Hayes case. We would like to speak to Senior Sergeant Snowden.'

A moment of silence.

'You pushed the buzzer.' the thin officer eventually said, still panting.

'Yeah,' Harper said. 'I called but got no response.'

'The buzzer is only for emergencies. Did you read the sign?'

'I noticed it. I also noticed no one crewing the desk. That's not supposed to happen either.'

Harper looked at their name badges. The fat one was called Bevan, the other was named Button. Neither seemed impressed. Eventually, Button, who appeared to be the ranking officer, instructed Harper and Gardella to wait as he left the office with Bevan in tow. Harper thought he heard the word arsehole and a few other expletives as they went.

Gardella shuffled over and found himself a chair. 'I thought we were trying not to piss off the locals,' he said as he leaned back in his seat, apparently trying to keep a straight face.

After an unnecessarily long wait, the door leading into the central part of the station buzzed and clunked and swung open. A man Harper recognised as Senior Sergeant Snowden emerged. Tall, with salt and pepper hair, wiry moustache, protruding jaw, and bushy black eyebrows. He stood shoulders back, chest out, like a pompous battlefield general surveying the troops.

Snowden had been at the start of his police career when Harper's mother died and was there when Harper became entangled in the drug scene. Snowden had also been the first officer to arrive at his foster parents' house on the night of the shooting. He had been assigned to Harper and had taken his statement. Harper was never sure that Snowden fully believed him. The final report suggested he did, but ever since, Harper always sensed a lingering sense of suspicion.

'Look what the god-damn cat dragged in,' Snowden said as he looked down his nose at Harper.

'Good to see you too,' Harper said. 'This is my partner Detective Sergeant Gardella.' Gardella stood up but made no effort to shake hands.

'So, we've got not one, but two hotshots to help us with our missing person. I guess you boys think you'll have this wrapped up by Friday so you can be back home for your weekend round of golf..'

Gardella couldn't hold his tongue. 'You want the case then be my guest. I would just as well get the hell out of here.'

Snowden eyed Gardella the way you do a fly buzzing too close for comfort.

'Ignore Detective Gardella,' Harper said. 'He's just grumpy because I wouldn't let him drive. Can we go on back and discuss the case?'

Snowden said nothing, his glare firmly locked on Gardella, contempt oozing out of every pore. Harper glanced at Snowden, then at Gardella, and back again at Snowden. Time to put an end to the cold war.

'C'mon ladies. Our missing person isn't likely to find himself now, is he?'

More silence. Harper shook his head. It might be easier to reason with a couple of preschoolers. Then, without warning, Snowden turned and walked back through the door, gesturing for them to follow. They all marched down a short corridor, Snowden's shoes clopping on the polished floor. Dim lighting gave the feeling of an underground bunker; a musty smell added to the subterranean feel. The walls of the corridor were lined with noticeboards, each burdened with scores of bulletins tacked loosely with multicoloured pins. Upon reaching the third door, Snowden stopped, pivoted, and held out his hand to shepherd them into a meeting room.

Seventies décor was evident here as well. Brown and orange carpet complemented a small Formica faux-wood kitchen table and matching chairs, upholstered in an obnoxious floral fabric. A pair of portable whiteboards stood discarded in a darkened corner alongside an ancient overhead projector. A strip of frosted glass stretched the length of the opposite wall, but let in little light. A fluorescent bulb blinked intermittently, producing almost as much noise as it did light.

'Good to see you haven't ruined the place with any tacky renovations,' Harper said.

'It serves its purpose,' Snowden said. 'In any event, we don't have the resources to update things, even if we wanted to.' Snowden found his seat at the head of the table and Harper and Gardella sat opposite one another.

'Okay sir, what can you tell us about our guy?' Harper asked.

Snowden let out a long sigh. 'Jonathon Hayes, fifty-three, works as a reporter at the Westport News. Married to Samara, forty-nine, a local artist. Two adult children, both live overseas. Wife made the notification last night. We did a bit of sniffing around. It seems no one has had any contact with our man since he left work on Friday and went for his usual beer with friends. He was last seen at the Black and White bar on Palmerston Street, at around ten-thirty Friday night. According to people who were there when he left, Hayes said he was heading home for an early night.'

'You have the name of the last known contact?' Harper asked. He had the impression Snowden was cooperating because he had been ordered to do so, not because of any great desire to help.

'Derek Graham. He also works at the Westport News. He prints the newspaper. He was the one drinking with Hayes. Graham said it was unusual for Hayes to leave the bar so early. Said Hayes would normally stay till after midnight. He told us that Hayes made a phone call before he left.'

'Let's get his phone records. See who he called,' Harper said to Gardella.

'We'll need the polling data from the cell company as well,' Gardella added. 'Hopefully, we'll get a fix on his last known location. Going to need a warrant for that.' Gardella produced a small notepad from his jacket pocket and thumbed its yellow pages until he found a blank one and began jotting. Head down and still writing he asked Snowden, 'I see the courthouse is next door. Is there a sitting judge who can sign warrants?'

'No. Not a local one at least. We bring one in from Christchurch about every two weeks to clear the backlog. However, it's your lucky day. The court was in session today, and also tomorrow. You should be able to get what you need. After that, we won't have a judge for a while.'

'Anything on this guy Graham?' Harper asked.

'He's no saint. He has convictions for DUI and possession. But from what we know, he's fairly harmless. No history of violence, no record of any problems with Hayes. We don't like him for this.'

Harper raised an eyebrow. 'Why is that?' he asked. 'Seems to me like he would be a person of interest.'

'Like I said, he has no violent history. Yes, he's got a drug problem. But I know the guy fairly well. I don't think he's capable.'

Harper glanced at Gardella and saw him write the name "GRAHAM" in letters big enough for Snowden to notice. Harper caught a flash of annoyance on Snowden's face. Time to move on.

'What about Hayes's relationship with the wife. Any domestic violence or other issues?'

'Nothing that has come to our attention. Nothing official that is.'

Gardella stopped taking notes and fired a look at Harper. But Harper didn't need prompting.

'Unofficially, what do you know?'

'Well, the word around town is ...' Snowden's eyes skimmed the room as if to be sure no one had snuck in without him noticing. 'It's not a hundred per cent, but word is Jonathon Hayes was having an affair.'

'Do you have a name?' Harper asked.

'Viki Waldron. Just married Nathan Munroe, a local mechanic. They live on the corner of Brougham and Russell, just opposite the Gates of Remembrance. Don't know the number but, hey, you guys are supposed to be detectives, I'm sure you can find it.'

'What do you have on Munroe?' Harper said, ignoring Snowden's cynicism.

'Nothing. He's clean. We haven't talked to either Munroe or Waldron. Didn't want to upset the happy couple or contaminate any potential witnesses. We'll leave that up to you.'

Harper cringed, sure Gardella would not be able to let the comment go. Gardella once again stopped writing. A cold silence descended, like a heavy mist on a winter's morning. The broken light continued to buzz, adding to the tension.

'Hayes is a reporter, correct?' Gardella said, his tone laced with contempt.

'Correct,' Snowden replied.

'How long?'

'As long as I've been on the force. Coming up thirty years.'

'Over that time, would you say that Hayes has pissed off a few people?'

'Of course. That's only natural in a small town like this.'

'Anyone in particular?'

'Only about half the town.'

'What about in the last month? Has Hayes written anything that might lead to him going on an unexpected vacation?'

Snowden thought for a moment, his brow furrowed. 'There was a piece about a conflict of interest within the local council,' he said. 'Something about a large contract going to one of the relatives of a council member. Caused a bit of an uproar. I can't recall the exact details. I don't even remember who the journalist was. Could've been Hayes, but you'd have to check. The only other one that springs to mind was about a doctor at the hospital. The doc was accused of malpractice. Hayes covered that one for sure. I remember because the doctor is currently suing Hayes for defamation. The paper published the defamation story two weeks ago.'

'Any names?' Gardella asked.

'Not for the council member one, but the doctor's an Indian guy, not local. Last name is Sharma, I think. First name Amar or Amala, something like that.' Snowden glanced at his watch, which looked too expensive, even for a senior sergeant. 'Now Detectives, I am a very busy man. Do you have anything else?'

When no one said anything, Snowden stood up and made for the exit. He had reached the door before Harper spoke.

'Will we have the full cooperation of the Westport Police in this investigation?'

Snowden stopped and turned to glare. 'I will instruct my officers to give you whatever you need. However, we are a small department with a lot of ground to cover so don't expect a police escort every time you want to go take a shit. I trust you can find your way out.'

With that, Snowden disappeared into the corridor.

CHAPTER 5

While Gardella parked the car, Harper checked into the hotel. The Westport Motor Hotel had once been the best place in town, but these days it looked in need of a refresh. Harper had chosen it because it had a restaurant and a bar, two things most of the other joints lacked. Another bonus was its conference room, which they hoped to use instead of setting up shop at the Westport police station. The woman at reception completed the paperwork and fetched the room keys.

' Mr Harper, you will be in room four. Mr Gardella will be in five. Is there anything else I can help you with this evening?'

'Yes. I understand you have a conference room?'

'Yes dear, we do. Would you like to use it?'

It was the first time anyone had called Harper "dear" since he had been a child, but he didn't mind too much. The woman, whose name tag read "Beth", appeared old enough to be his grandmother, despite her efforts to look younger. Her bleached hair had been permed into a ball of frizz, then lacquered with so much hairspray that it looked like steel wool. Bright red lipstick flaked from her cracked lips and her eyebrows were drawn on with a pencil.

'Yeah, but the thing is we don't know exactly how long we're going to need it. It could be a couple of days, or it could be a week or more. Is that going to be a problem?'

'Why of course not, dear. You can use it for as long as you like. I can't recall the last time we had a proper conference.'

'Also, we will need to restrict access. How secure is the room?'

'How about I take you down there and you can see for yourself, love.' Beth darted out of view and seconds later emerged from an adjacent door. 'Come with me,' she cooed, and Harper duly obeyed.

The receptionist escorted Harper through the lobby, past the restaurant and bar, before arriving at the door of the conference room. She produced a key from seemingly nowhere, slid it into the lock, and turned in one fluid motion. She opened the first door, flicked on the lights, and unlatched the bolts of the second door. With both doors flung open, she stood aside and made a broad sweep of the room with her arm as if welcoming a king into his palace.

The oval-shaped boardroom table appeared to have been carved out of a single piece of oak and was polished to a deep sheen. Ten chairs, tastefully upholstered in black leather, were neatly arranged around the perimeter and a modern data projector aimed at a white screen hung from the ceiling. Located on the adjacent wall was a whiteboard, which looked as if it had been borrowed from a school classroom, and in the far corner, a bulky Xerox machine.

'Is this what you're after?' Beth asked, her voice flush with pride.

A substantial amount of money had been spent on the room in the hope of attracting conferences and Harper felt he was doing them a favour by using it.

'This will be perfect,' he said. 'Now, access to the room. How many keys are there?

'The one I have, and a master.'

'I will need both of those keys. Is that going to cause any issues?'

'Fine with me, dear. Like I said, the room never gets used. We don't often open it up, except for cleaning.'

'Well, you can tell the cleaner to have the week off. We'll make sure the place is kept tidy.'

Beth gave a flat smile and motioned to turn away, but then something made her stop. 'You're here to find that missing man, aren't you?' she asked.

Jonathon Hayes had been reported missing less than twenty-four hours ago. Obviously, word had spread quickly through the small community. When Harper had checked in he had flashed his police ID. It made sense that Beth would connect the dots. He thought about giving her a lie but knew it wouldn't wash.

'That's correct. However, that's all I can say I'm afraid. Thank you for being so accommodating. The room will fit our needs perfectly. I'll grab those keys now if you don't mind.'

'Sure, love.' She handed Harper her key. 'Take a look around. I'll fetch the other one.'

With that, she marched out as quickly as she came and Harper was left alone. A moment later, Gardella found his way to the conference room.

'Told you this place would be great,' Harper said.

'It'll do,' Gardella sounded less than impressed. 'Let's get down to business. We need to get to the wife. Like we agreed, you do most of the talking. I'll make myself scarce, try to sniff around and get a feel for the house. You play it dumb. Ask if there is any reason for hubby to take off. Don't let on that we know about the affair. See if she fesses up. If she does, it's a sign she has nothing to hide.'

'And if she doesn't?'

'You ask her straight out. See if she denies it. If she does, we know that's where we go first.'

'What if she truly doesn't know?'

'In my experience, the wife always knows.'

Harper wasn't so sure. His experience with women had been limited to a few short-term relationships which hardly qualified him as an expert on the female psyche. Maybe he was naïve, but he wasn't ready to concede the wife knew about the affair.

Harper locked the conference room and proceeded to the lobby where he got the second key from Beth. He stowed his bags in his room and by the time he met Gardella in the hotel car park it had just ticked past eight o'clock. A full moon filtered through the veil of clouds and bathed everything in a silver glow. It was quiet for this early in the evening, just the occasional breath of northerly breeze stirred the trees of the hotel's garden and a light trickle of traffic brushed by along Palmerston Street.

After being confined to the car for much of the day Harper asked Gardella if he wanted to make the short trip to Samara Hayes' house on foot. Gardella agreed and they ambled through the mild evening air to the end of the block, making a right at the petrol station, then proceeding along Rintoul Street for eighty or so metres before making a left onto Russell. From there it was a short walk along a quiet residential street to the Hayes' house. The whole journey had taken less than four minutes.

The house was an unremarkable two-storey rectangular shoebox with a shallow peaked roof, clad in white weatherboard siding. The only departures from this simple Lego-block design were the main entrance which was set in from the front wall under a small porch. A small lean-to nestled against the back wall of the building at the rear of the property. The house occupied almost the entire width of the narrow section meaning the concrete driveway had been shoehorned between the boundary fence and the house and it ran the length of the section to a single car garage located at the rear. Next to the garage was a large dark coloured rubbish bin with a flip-top lid and two black wheels at its base.

'You sure this is the right place?' Gardella asked.

Harper checked the address. 'Yep. This is it. What's the problem?'

'I don't know. I guess it doesn't fit my vision of a house an artist would live in.'

'What were you expecting, frescos and French doors?'

'I'm not sure. Just not this.'

Harper knocked. He had barely finished when the door jerked open revealing a blonde woman with sad, wet eyes. Her make-up was tear-streaked and her shoulder-length hair hung dull and crumpled. Despite all of this, she was nevertheless attractive. Slim but strongly put together, her toned legs stretched the denim of her blue jeans while a figure-hugging white T-shirt emphasised her well-defined arms and shoulders. Prominent cheekbones framed sea-green eyes and a defined jaw-line tapered to a small chin. She didn't look a day older than thirty-five. Harper wondered why any man would want to cheat on her.

'Are you the detectives from Christchurch?' she said.

'Yes. Are you Samara Hayes?' Harper asked.

'Yes. Please tell me you're going to find my husband?'

'We will do everything we can to locate your husband, Mrs Hayes. I am Detective Harper, and this is my partner Detective Gardella. Do you mind if we come in?'

'Of course. Please, come in.'

Inside the front door a narrow stairway scaled the wall at a steep gradient, its carpeted steps faded and threadbare. Samara Hayes led them past the stairs and down a short passage and as he followed Harper caught the creamy vanilla scent of her perfume. At the end of the passage was a kitchen with wood-framed windows that overlooked a small backyard. The kitchen had been tacked on at some later stage and the builders had botched the job. Two circular stains on the ceiling betrayed water damage, long cracks in the plaster exposed where the poorly constructed addition had pulled away from the main building. The room projected out three metres from the rest of the house and ran the entire length of the rear of the building. It was lit by a single light bulb that hung from the ceiling on a long cord. An L-shaped kitchen counter occupied the far right-hand corner. At the end of the counter stood an art deco fridge that looked more at home in 1955 than the present. The linoleum floor was cracked and peeling while the paint on the walls was in only marginally better condition. Clearly, there was little money in this family. It brought back memories of the house Harper shared with his mother before she died.

'Would you like something to drink? I've just put the kettle on.'

'No thank you. We're fine,' Harper replied. 'We'd like to ask a few questions about your husband. The more information we get, the easier it will be to find him.'

'Sure, anything to help. I just want him back.'

Samara motioned towards the kitchen table. She and Harper took a seat while Gardella edged over to the counter. Harper pulled a notebook, laid it on the table, and flipped to a fresh page. Samara eyed Gardella, but Harper distracted her.

'So, you reported your husband, Jonathon Hayes, missing at around eight-thirty last night. Can you tell us everything you told the Westport Police?'

'Um, well, I left for work about eight on Friday morning. Jon was just finishing breakfast and getting ready to go to work. I reminded him that after work I would be going up to my studio for the weekend. That afternoon I shut the shop just after five, did a quick tidy up and left for my studio at around five-thirty. I worked up there all weekend. On Monday I came back to town and went straight to the shop. I left the shop around five, came home, unpacked, and put my clothes back in the closet. That's when I noticed some of his stuff was missing.'

'What exactly was missing, Mrs Hayes?'

'His clothes. Not all of them, but I could see most were gone. I looked up to see his suitcase was not on the top shelf where it usually is. My first thought was that he had gone on a boys' weekend or something. I waited, expecting him to be home for dinner. By eight he still wasn't home. I got worried and rang his phone. When he didn't answer, I started phoning his friends, but they hadn't seen him all weekend. Eventually, I phoned the police.'

'You mind if my partner checks out the closet for himself?' Harper asked.

'That's fine. It's up the stairs and down the hall. Last door on the left.'

Gardella nodded, then made his way back towards the stairs, leaving them alone in the kitchen.

Harper kept going. 'I'm just curious. Why didn't the newspaper call you when your husband didn't show up for work Monday morning?'

'He doesn't work Mondays. The paper cut his hours about six months ago. Said that profits were down or something and they couldn't afford to keep him on full-time. He wasn't due back at work until this morning.'

'Right. That makes sense.' Harper made a note of the new information. He wrote slowly, buying time for Gardella. 'So, is this sort of thing normal behaviour? I mean, has your husband done this in the past, gone off on a trip and not come back when you expected?'

'Ah, no, not at all. This has never happened before. We've been married for twenty-seven years and nothing like this has happened. That's why I'm worried.'

Her hand came up and began tugging the sleeve of her T-shirt. A sign of dishonesty. It was the first chink in her façade that up until now, had been very convincing. Maybe the whole grieving wife thing was an act. He let it slide for the moment.

'You mentioned that when you first arrived home on Monday evening, you thought he might have gone on a boys' weekend. You phoned his friends and they said they hadn't seen your husband during the weekend. Is that right?'

'Yes, that's correct.'

'Okay, so, was there anyone else who he might have spent the weekend with?'

'Uh, not that I can think of.'

She had turned away from him and was avoiding eye contact. She grabbed her coffee cup, took a sip, then placed it down between herself and Harper.

'Can you think of any reason he may have taken off without telling you?'

'No, none at all. Jon would never leave without telling me.'

'Were you aware of your husband seeing someone else, another woman perhaps?'

Samara's body slumped and her head fell forward. She wrapped her arms around her chest as if she was trying to hold herself together. Her shoulders started to shake as she began to sob quietly. Her bobbing head turned into a nod.

She knew about the affair. Gardella had been right.

Harper waited for Samara to compose herself. A minute later she stood up and retrieved a box of tissues from the kitchen counter. She brought them back to the table and dried her eyes.

'Do you know who he was having an affair with?' Harper asked.

'Victoria Waldron. But it was over. He told me it was over. She just got married. He told me it was over.'

'Do you think your husband wanted out of the marriage, Mrs Hayes?'

'No,' she said, sounding offended. 'He would have told me. He wouldn't just walk out.'

'You talk to him on the phone at any stage between Friday and Monday?'

'No. There's no reception at the studio. I like it that way. I can just work and not be interrupted.'

'Where exactly is your studio?'

'Just out of Karamea.'

Harper knew the town well from the endless school camps he'd had to endure as a kid. Smaller and more isolated than Westport, Karamea was a ninety-minute drive north up the coast. Home to artists, hippies, small farms, and alternative-lifers in search of even more peace and solitude than could be found anywhere else on the West Coast. It was where people went when they wanted to escape the stresses of the modern world.

'What sort of art do you do?' Harper asked, not knowing where he was going with this line of questioning but thinking it could help him understand his witness a little better. And give Gardella more time to explore.

'Mostly painting, landscapes, wildlife, West Coast scenes. The tourists like them. Also some sculpture, but that doesn't sell as well. I like to work on the weekends and try and sell a few pieces during the week.'

'How many do you sell?'

'Not enough. During the summer I just about break-even. But in the off-season, it's pretty slow.'

'You rely on your husband's income to pay the bills?'

'Pretty much, yeah.'

'So, financially it's been tough for you since his hours were cut?'

'Yeah. With the rent on the shop and the mortgage payments, plus Jon only working four days a week, it's been a stretch. But a couple of months ago he picked up some casual work. He was doing water testing or something. That's helped a bit.'

Harper noted this down and continued. 'You have any insurance, like mortgage protection or life insurance?'

'We used to have mortgage insurance. We stopped that when Jon's hours went down. We still have life insurance, but we were thinking about cutting that as well, to save some money.'

Past tense? Interesting There could be an innocent explanation. Or maybe she knew her husband would do no more thinking.

'Can you recall the amount of the life insurance policy?'

Sara looked up from her coffee. 'What has that got to do with anything?' She said. 'I hope you're not trying to say that I would do something to my husband?'

Harper raised a calming hand and tried to explain. 'What I'm trying to do is to find out where he is, and the best way of doing that is getting as much information about him as possible. I'm sure you want the same thing.'

In the dim light the rings under her eyes seemed blacker. Her jaw clenched, causing the muscles in her cheeks to knot in small fists of anger. After several seconds of considering her options, she relented.

'Well, I can't recall the exact amount. It was enough to pay off the mortgage on the house and the business, with some leftover. Five-hundred or six-hundred thousand dollars, but I could be wrong.'

Harper noted the amounts, then said, 'Does Jon have a car?'

'No. Well, he did, but we sold it a while back. He walks to work, or I drop him off.'

'So, if you're away on the weekends, how does he get around?'

'He has a work truck so he can do his water testing. He picks it up Saturday morning and drops it off at the depot on Sunday or Monday.'

'Tell me more about Jon's second job.'

'He tests the rivers to make sure no pollution gets into the water. He works for Solid Energy. They own the coal mine.'

'Have those tests ever come back with results the mine might not like?'

'No. They're hardly producing any coal at the moment. Jon's been doing the job for only a few months, but all the results have been clear.'

'So, he uses the truck to get around on the weekends?'

'Yes.'

'Can you give me a description?'

'It's white with blue writing on it, not words but numbers, like a serial number I can't remember the numbers. It has yellow lights on the roof, and big off-road type wheels.'

'You know what make it is?'

'Um, yeah, it's a Toyota … I think.'

'And where is the depot?'

'It's down the road from the Westport Motor Hotel, on Palmerston Street.'

'Okay, we'll check it out. Now your husband is a newspaper reporter. I'm guessing he would have written stories over the years that would have upset some people. Has he mentioned any threats made against him?'

'No, nothing like that,' she said, sounding startled.

'Were you aware of anyone upset with your husband for any reason?'

Sara's shoulders slumped as if her body was collapsing in on itself and her head bobbed faintly up and down. 'There's this guy, this doctor at the hospital who's suing Jon. We talked about it because it's been in the paper. Jon said not to worry because the paper would take care of it.'

'Your husband hasn't had any contact with this doctor that you are aware of?'

'No. Jon hasn't mentioned anything like that.'

'Have you had any strange phone calls, noticed anyone watching the house, unfamiliar cars parked in the street, or seen anything else that stood out as unusual?'

'Ah, no. I can't think of anything like that. Nothing that sticks out.'

Harper drummed his pen and thought of where to go next. 'Right. I think the next thing to look at is his bank and phone details. If he's still making calls and accessing his account we should be able to locate him quite quickly. Are you happy to give us access to those Mrs Hayes?'

'Um, that might be a problem. We got rid of the internet to save some money, so I can't show you online. We get statements in the mail, but once I pay them, I put them in the rubbish I'm sorry.'

'That's fine Mrs Hayes. We can get those tomorrow. I think that's all the questions I have for now. I'll go upstairs and check how my partner is getting on. If you don't mind, I've changed my mind and I'd love that coffee if you're still making one?'

'Sure. How do you like it?'

'Milk, lots of sugar.'

Harper didn't want a coffee. He just wanted to keep her downstairs and out of the way so he could discuss what he had learned with Gardella.

He went up the stairs and down the hall to the bedroom. It was sparsely furnished. A queen-sized bed, two small bedside tables and matching dresser with attached mirror. The top of the dresser was littered with perfume bottles, candle holders, jewellery boxes and assorted trinkets. The bed had been neatly made, the pillows puffed and tidily arranged. The sheets had been firmly tucked, leaving not a wrinkle in sight.

The closet that ran almost the full length of the room had three large sliding doors. You could open one or both sides by stacking the doors together like playing cards. The two outer doors had been pushed into the middle, revealing the contents of either side. The left side was mostly empty, with only two business shirts and a crumpled tie. Deeper in the closet hung a men's dinner jacket and matching dark trousers, the kind of suit that would only see the light of day for weddings and funerals and nothing else in between. On the jacket's left-hand breast pocket was a shiny silver tie-clip. In all, Harper counted seventeen empty coat hangers dangling from the galvanised clothes rail. The storage shelf above the rail was stacked with old CDs, VHS tapes and what looked like photo albums as well as two bulging shoe boxes. In the middle of all this clutter was a suitcase-sized block of emptiness. The right-hand side of the closet appeared to belong to Mrs Hayes. It was stuffed with dresses, skirts, jackets, jeans, shoes, scarves and belts.

'What are you thinking?' Gardella asked, startling Harper.

'Jesus, Joe! Don't do that to me.'

'Hey, just keeping you on your toes. So, what did you learn?'

Harper put a hand on the closet door to steady his rattled nerves. 'Well. It took a bit of coaxing. But she admitted the affair. Also, she's got her husband insured for half-a-mill. She played it coy with the bank and phone records. Said she couldn't access them. I didn't push it. We can get those later. The only other thing is this doctor. He's suing Hayes and the newspaper. Another angle to look at.'

'Did you get the impression he wanted out of the marriage?'

'It's a possibility, but I've been thinking about that scenario and I don't think it works. If he leaves without telling her, he's walking away from his job, the house, the car, everything. He just leaves it all to his wife? I'm not sure I buy that. If he wanted out, why not tell her, get a divorce and split the assets?'

'Maybe he feels guilty about the affair. Maybe the mortgage is worth more than the house. Maybe he secretly won the lottery and doesn't like sharing.'

'Okay, okay. We know he's gone,' Harper said. 'We're not sure why or where, but I think I know when.'

'I'm all ears.'

'Friday night.'

'How do you figure that?'

'Look at that,' Harper said pointing at the bed. 'He hasn't slept there. It's too tidy. That bed, the way it's made, I don't see him making it like that. She made it on Friday morning. It hasn't been touched since.'

'What about last night? What if she slept there and made it this morning?'

'I'm picking she didn't. Look at her. She looks like the walking dead. If I had to guess, I'd say she's been up all night.'

'We should ask her before we leave.'

'You see anything interesting up here?'

'Not a lot,' Gardella said, letting out a deflating breath. 'No signs of a struggle. No trace that I can see. Nothing that suggests foul play. I mean she could have cleaned up of course, she's had all weekend to do it, but on the surface, the place looks as it should.'

'Do you want to get the forensic guys in here and give it a once over?'

'Not yet. I can't see the wife giving us permission. We'd need a warrant. Trouble is, we haven't got probable cause. The judge would never grant it. We need to work things a bit more.'

For the next few minutes Harper and Gardella sniffed around the upstairs rooms but nothing seemed out of place or unusual. The drawers were empty, no aftershave or toothbrush, and they couldn't locate a razor or shaving gear. Everything seemed to suggest Jonathon Hayes had packed his things and left town. Eventually, they gave up and headed back downstairs.

In the kitchen, Samara handed Harper a steaming cup. Harper sipped it politely. It tasted about as good as a mouthful of cigarette butts. She clearly bought the instant crap the supermarkets sold by the one-kilo tin. After a couple more swallows, he put it on the kitchen counter and didn't touch it again. He tried again with more questions about anyone who might have a grudge against her husband, but she couldn't think of anybody other than the doctor. He did manage to find out that she had gone to a friend's place last night because she didn't feel safe in the house by herself. Harper got the address and wrote it in his notebook. Gardella used his cell phone to take a snap of Jonathon Hayes from one of the many family photos. Harper began to wrap up the interview.

'All right, Mrs Hayes, I think that's enough for tonight. We'll go away and process all this information and get back in touch with you tomorrow. We would like you to stay in town for the next few days in case we need to speak to you again. We would prefer that you not go up to your studio in Karamea. Is that going to be a problem?'

'No, that's fine. I need to stay in town to keep the shop open anyway. I just wanted to ask. What do you think has happened? Do you have any idea where he might have gone?'

'As I said, we've got a lot of information to look at. Once we've done that, we will let you know. Unfortunately, I can't say more than that.'

'Oh. I see.'

'Thank you for your help tonight, Mrs Hayes. If you think of anything else, give me a call.'

Harper handed her his card from the small stash he kept in his shirt pocket and Samara showed them out.

On the street, the air felt heavier. Harper could taste the moisture in it; rain was not far away. It made him quicken his pace as he and Gardella walked back down the quiet street. As they headed in the direction of their hotel, Harper began to feel a little uneasy. The feeling you get when you sense someone is watching you.

CHAPTER 6

During the night it rained hard. It was an angry, un-yielding rain that clattered at the hotel window as if it was trying to break into the room. Harper usually enjoyed the sound, the steady drum helped facilitate sleep But not last night. The rain kept him awake but for two fitful hours of sleep in which his mind churned with the nightmare he had left behind twelve years ago.

The previous night Harper had sensed eyes upon him. He hoped it was just his paranoia but instinctively he knew there were people in this town who would not appreciate seeing his face again. He would need to be on guard but could not let this distract him from the investigation.

At five o'clock he gave up on sleep and climbed out of bed and took a shower. The water had a soothing effect, enough to dull the tension and get his thoughts back on the job. Once out of the shower and dry he put on tan shoes, slim-legged trousers, a brown leather belt that matched his polished footwear and a long-sleeved fitted shirt that hugged the lean lines of his torso. This morning, in addition to this standard attire, he wore a cadet-grey windbreaker jacket, both to keep out the weather and to conceal his shoulder holster and gun.

It was still too early to bother Gardella so Harper flicked through TV channels, all of which were broadcasting infomercials, then read the tourist information in the hotel guide. After an hour of boredom he decided it was time to wake up his partner.

He opened his door and stepped outside, half expecting a small lake to be lapping at his feet. Instead, he saw a soggy rectangular grassed courtyard enclosed by the hotel on three sides. Dotted around the courtyard were raised garden beds from which jade-green native ferns grew, their thick feathered fronds arching heavily under the weight of last nights rain, the tip of each frond shedding water in fat droplets that fell in a steady patter onto the concrete path that hugged the frontage to each hotel room.

As Harper looked up he saw the milky blue of a washed-out sky and the retreating remnants of last night's storm. The air was thick and pure and you could roll it around the inside of your mouth to make yourself feel new again. To most visitors, it would be invigorating. But to Harper, it tasted bitter. It brought back memories of misery and suffering. It made him want to solve this case and get the hell out of town as soon as possible.

He walked the half dozen paces to Gardella's room and used the butt of his fist to thump. There was a muffled commotion and a minute later Gardella emerged rubbing his eyes and tucking his shirt.

They made their way to the restaurant for a quick bite of breakfast, then went back to their rooms, gathered their laptops and reconvened in the conference room. Gardella started typing up the warrants. The first was for the polling data from Hayes' cell phone. This would hopefully allow them to narrow down a last known location. To determine the phone's current location they would need the cell phone company to send out a ping so Gardella incorporated this request into the same warrant. The second warrant was for his text message activity. The third and final warrant was for his cheque account. In addition to a list of all the transactions Gardella knew that the bank could also set up an automated alert so the instant the account was accessed, the detectives would receive a message telling them the location of the terminal used to make the transaction. Twenty minutes later, Gardella had finished the paperwork and had sent it to the printer. Three sheets came out, one for each warrant.

It was now almost eight. Harper assumed the judge would not be in chambers until nine. They considered calling in early but decided they would have more luck if they didn't annoy the judge by interrupting breakfast. Instead, they locked the doors and made their way over to the Solid Energy office.

The mine that Hayes worked for was owned by Solid Energy and their office was directly across the street from the hotel. Thin morning traffic made it easy to cross to the other side and they walked up the short path and let themselves in through the main entrance.

A spacious reception area hinted that mining coal had once been a profitable enterprise. There was a quiet alcove to the left of the entrance where the lights had been dimmed and three leather couches had arranged themselves around an elegant glass-topped coffee table as if they were conducting their own private meeting. The walls carried photographs documenting various mining activities going back through the years. Most striking of these was a picture of an enormous yellow Caterpillar haul-truck, set against the dirty black background of a coal seam at an open cast mine. For scale, four men stood at the base of the gargantuan beast, the tops of their heads only as high as the metal rim of the front wheels. Straight ahead a curved reception desk bound in brass embellishments was sheltering two very busy-looking women who hadn't yet bothered to notice the two visitors. Harper approached the desk and flashed his credentials to the younger of the two women.

'Detectives Harper and Gardella, Christchurch CIB,' Harper announced in a voice designed to convey authority. 'We're conducting an investigation into the whereabouts of Jonathon Hayes. We understand he worked part-time for the company. Is there someone we can speak to with regards to his employment?'

Both women stopped what they were doing and looked up. The younger woman was lost for words and didn't respond, apart from giving a confused stare, her eyes darting back and forth between Harper and Gardella. The older woman eventually picked up a phone and dialled a three-digit number. She turned away and murmured under her breath, then returned the handset to its cradle, turned back and said in a smooth voice, ' Mr Howerton will be with you in a moment.'

Almost as soon as the words passed her lips, a door on the far wall opened. A balding man wearing a sloppy, two-piece suit emerged. A desk job and middle-aged spread had given him a rounded paunch that protruded proudly from above his belt. He made a beeline towards Gardella, his hand extended, accompanied by a nervous smile.

'Detectives. To what do I owe this pleasure?'

Gardella shook his hand, grunted his name, and passed him on to Harper.

'Detective Harper, Christchurch CIB.'

'Harper … You're, you look familiar,' Howerton said as he cast a knowing eye. 'You're not Dylan Harper by any chance?'

Harper clenched his jaw. He'd been asked that question one too many times. It was another reason to hate this place. Everyone knew who he was. At least, they thought they did.

'Yes, that's right,' Harper said deadpan, hoping lack of enthusiasm would kill off reminiscence. It didn't work.

'Yes, that's it,' Howerton continued. 'I remember you. You're the same age as my eldest son Jacob. So you're in the police now, a detective no less. You've come a long way. Well done you!'

'Thank you, Mr Howerton,' Harper said coolly, ignoring the subtle reference to his troubled upbringing. 'Jonathon Hayes, he is an employee of yours?'

'Yes, he is. What would you like to know? I hope everything is all right?'

'We understand he uses one of your vehicles. We'd like to see if he has returned it please.'

Howerton furrowed his brow. Without breaking eye contact he called over to the reception counter.

'Gloria, can you tell me if Jon has dropped off his truck?'

The older woman rose from her seat. She moved to a wall where several clipboards were hanging, removed the third one from the left, and began scanning the entries. After a short pause, she looked up at Howerton and then back down at the clipboard. Finally, she looked up again.

'It seems not. He signed it out on Friday at eight minutes past five, but he hasn't signed it back in.'

'Give me a look at that,' Howerton said as he marched over to the counter. Gloria passed him the clipboard. He ran his finger down the page until he found what he was looking for.

'Looks like he took out JN76,' Howerton mumbled. 'I bet he just forgot to sign it back in. Come with me gentlemen. We'll see if it's in the yard.'

Howerton dropped the clipboard on the gilded reception desk and moved towards a corridor that had a sign above that said: "Staff Only." About halfway along the corridor he opened a door that led outside to a gravel-covered yard. A fleet of white trucks, each emblazoned with seemingly random combinations of letters and numbers, were lined up side-by-side. A quick search confirmed JN76 wasn't there.

'Nope, he hasn't returned it,' Howerton said as he trudged around the vehicles one last time.

'Why didn't someone notice it wasn't back in the yard?' Gardella asked.

'That particular truck is not used during the week. It has pretty sensitive equipment in the back. We don't want the guys bouncing it around up at the mine. It just sits here most of the time.'

Harper looked at Gardella. 'It's still out there,' he whispered. 'We need to find it.'

Before they left, Gardella used his phone to snap a picture of one of the other vehicles. Back in the office, Howerton found the licence plate details and Gardella wrote them down. They received a copy of the vehicle log, and Harper handed over his card, instructing Howerton to call if the truck showed up. They thanked him and left.

Jonathon Hayes' primary place of employment was just two blocks north on the main street. The Westport News building occupied the corner of Palmerston and Wakefield Streets and had the type of thick stone walls used by nineteenth-century banks to inspire confidence your money was in safe hands. The main entrance was on Wakefield Street so they moved around the corner and climbed a wooden wheelchair ramp to an automatic door. As the door slid open, a young receptionist appraised them shrewdly.

'Good morning gentlemen. I'm guessing you're the investigators from Christchurch. You're here about Jonathon.' It was spoken not as a question, but a matter of fact.

'That's correct,' Harper said, showing his badge to remove any doubt. 'Who is the best person to speak to?'

'Our chief reporter is in charge today. The owner is away on holiday until the end of the month. If you turn around and go through the door on the right.'

The door to the reporter's room was abnormally wide and heavy and had a large square of frosted glass set into it. Inside, a middle-aged woman sat at a desk, typing at a computer. Her shoulder-length hair was jet black except for a thick shock of white, neatly styled for maximum effect. Her pale skin contrasted starkly against her black hair and clothes.

'Morning officers. I'm Natasha Knight,' she chirped, rising from her seat and extending her hand towards Harper. Gardella quickly skirted past, reached out and shook it before making the introductions on behalf of both of them.

It was a smart move. Talking to a reporter was always a balancing act and Gardella was better suited to it than Harper. To get information, you had to give something in return, some minor detail they could use for their story. Do that, and you could use the media to publish key facts and raise public awareness of your case, and in doing so stir memories and generate leads. It was a subtle dance that required each side to know the moves, and when to make them. A minor misstep, someone gets their toes stood on and the whole arrangement would fall apart. Harper didn't do subtle. He shook hands, and all three took a seat.

'I wish we could be here under better circumstances. We're all a bit worried for Jon and Samara,' Knight said.

'That's understandable,' Gardella replied.

'Well officers, I will do my best to answer your questions, but before we begin, I just need to ask. Are we on the record here?'

'We're strictly off the record,' Gardella said firmly. 'If there's something I think the public needs to know, I'll say so. Until then, you're to keep this conversation out of the public domain.'

'Right O,' Knight said. Gardella produced his notepad, flipped to a new page, and wrote the time and location of the interview before beginning.

'Jonathon Hayes was reported missing by his wife on Monday night. We are trying to piece together his movements on Friday evening and over the weekend. Can you tell us when you last saw or had contact with Mr Hayes?'

'The last time I saw Jon was here at work on Friday afternoon. He left around five, I think. That would have been the last I saw him. I didn't see or hear from him over the weekend.'

'That Friday, can you recall his movements? Was there anything out of the ordinary?'

'Ah, no, not really. Jon seemed fine. It was a fairly normal day. He came into work on time and worked in the office for most of the day. He went out on assignment around lunchtime, came back early afternoon, worked in the office until the end of the day, and then he went home. Nothing extraordinary.'

'Did he mention if he was going anywhere for the weekend, camping, fishing or anything like that?'

'Oh no, not Jon. He isn't an outdoorsman. Likes his home comforts too much. Said he was going to have a quiet weekend in front of the TV, maybe do a few jobs around the house. That was it.'

'Where is his workstation?'

'Just through there,' Knight said, nodding towards an inner door. 'He works in the room next to me.'

'Do you mind if my partner takes a look?' Gardella asked.

Knight leaned back in her chair, brought her hands together, fingertips touching, palms apart, forming a triangle that pointed at her chin. She looked at Harper and then back at Gardella. 'You can have a look, but not unsupervised. I want to be there.'

'That's fine. Once we finish with these questions we'll all go through. Now, do you know where Jon went after he left work? Was he going home? Was he catching up with anyone from work?'

'Yeah, Jon and a couple of others from work met up for a few beers.'

'Who does he usually drink with?'

'Jordon Shriver from advertising and Derek Graham our printer.'

'Do you know if he was, in fact, drinking with Mr Shriver and Mr Graham on Friday?'

'I guess so. I mean, I'm not totally sure, but that's Jon's usual crew.'

'You mentioned he had an assignment or an interview on Friday. What was it about?'

'Oh, it was on the increase in tourism. We're experiencing an upturn in overseas visitors. He went down to the Information Centre to get some stats and find out how the Christchurch earthquake might be affecting things.'

Harper had been listening carefully. So far nothing had stood out as holding any significance for their investigation. A story about tourism seemed unlikely to have anything to do with Jonathon Hayes' disappearance. He wondered when Gardella was going to ask the critical questions.

'Were there any other stories he was involved with which might have caused waves around town, or perhaps, upset some people?'

Harper caught a flash of concern on Knight's face.

'Wait. What are you saying?' she said. 'Are you suggesting that one of Jon's stories might have something to do with his going missing?'

Harper glanced at Gardella. The look on his partner's face hadn't changed but Harper could tell he was silently cursing. Gardella would have to backtrack or else he would have the media snooping around looking for suspects.

'No, that is not what I am saying. In fact, we have reason to believe he is driving a vehicle borrowed from the Solid Energy depot. Oh, and that's on the record. You can print that. I can e-mail you a photo of the truck, and we wouldn't mind if you put it in your story with a line appealing for anyone who has seen the vehicle to call the police.'

'Show me the photo,' Knight said.

Gardella retrieved his cell and showed her the picture. After a couple of seconds she said, 'Yeah, we can do that. But you realise those mine trucks are a dime-a-dozen. You're going to get every man and his dog phoning in sightings.'

'The truck has the letters JN76 on the side. Do you think you could manipulate the image to get that on there?'

'That's possible, I guess. We could Photoshop it. I'll give it to our photographer and see what he can do. However, I bet you'll regret it.'

'Thanks for the warning but we'll take our chances. Now, back to my original question. Did Jon work on any controversial stories in the last few weeks?'

'Half the stories we write upset someone or are controversial. That's journalism. How many names do you guys want? I could give you a list as long as my arm.' Knight spoke as if it was something she was proud of, like the mark of a good reporter was measured by how many people you managed to piss off.

'We're just looking for anything unusual that might explain why Jon would want to disappear without telling anyone,' Harper interjected. This brought a sideways glance from Gardella. Message received. No more questions.

'Well, nothing springs to mind,' Knight said. 'Anyway, I'm sure Jon would have told me about something like that.'

'His wife mentioned an article about a doctor at the hospital. She said that the doctor was suing for defamation. That ring any bells?' Gardella asked.

'Yeah, I know the one. The guy's a loser. Everything we published is backed up by numerous sources. He's had half a dozen complaints laid against him. Jon wasn't worried. The guy was after the paper, not the reporter.'

'We will still need to check it out. Do you remember his name?'

'Anand Sharma. Young guy, late twenties, junior doctor. We get all the juniors here. They come because the government offers cash incentives for those who choose to practise outside the main centres. Problem is, the docs we end up with are normally useless. The good ones stay in Christchurch because that's better for their careers. We get the leftovers. They come for the extra money, and after the incentive period runs out, they piss off back to the big smoke and some new fresh-faced kid with no experience comes in to fill the gap.'

Gardella made a note of the name. 'What about at work? Were there any tensions or problems?'

'No. Jon got on pretty well with everyone. He was well-liked in the office.'

'I understand his hours were cut. Did that create any animosity between him and the owners?'

'Not that I'm aware of, no. I mean, Jon would've preferred to be full-time, but he understood the reasons. I doubt there were any hard feelings.'

Gardella probed with more questions about Hayes' behaviour and state of mind, but Knight couldn't think of anything significant. Gardella made no additional notes. Finally, he asked to see where Hayes worked.

Knight got up and opened a side door into a smaller office which was a quarter the size of hers and the three of them had difficulty fitting in the space. It looked like it had once been a corridor leading to another part of the building. A dividing wall had been installed at one end shutting off the space. Hayes' desk sat wedged in the gap created by a small bay window and overlooked an alley and a concrete courtyard framed by a metal-clad warehouse.

On the bureau was a desktop computer with an old CRT monitor the size of a microwave, and a clunky keyboard, its keys covered in yellow-brown grime that probably dated back to the days when smoking was still allowed in the newsroom. Also on the desk was a phone, phonebook, a glass jar containing several pens and a well-used notepad. Various other sheets of paper lay strewn across the desk, along with a copy of last Friday's Christchurch Press.

'That's funny,' Knight said as she surveyed the desk. 'I don't remember Jon taking his laptop.'

'Does he normally take it with him on the weekends?' Gardella asked.

'Occasionally, if he's working a feature. I can't think why he would have needed it this weekend. Most of the news right now is about the earthquakes which we're getting straight from the Associated Press. I don't know. Maybe he had something in the works.'

'Did you notice his computer on Monday?'

'Um ... I don't recall. Mondays are always busy for me because I'm on my own. I was flat out all day and didn't even come into Jon's office. Yesterday, when Jon didn't show up for work, it was the same. I looked in, but I don't remember seeing the laptop.'

Harper lifted the notepad off the desk and began leafing through its pages. It was mostly notes from the stories Hayes was working on. There was the tourist piece that Knight had mentioned, with various facts and figures scrawled in seemingly random order. Another article was about the downturn in coal prices in the wake of the global financial crisis, and how this was affecting the town. From what he could tell, the mine had cut around three hundred workers. Local businesses were worried about the flow-on-effect on retail spending. It appeared he was doing a separate piece on a new gold mine that had begun production, a sports report on the start of the basketball season and finally, a story about a police operation targeting underage drinking at several local bars. Nothing stood out as potentially significant. A calendar was on the wall behind where Hayes would have sat. Harper studied it but it contained no notes and no dates were circled.

'Okay. We're going to need to talk to the two guys he was drinking with on Friday,' Gardella said.

Knight nodded. She led them back to her office, picked up the phone, and dialled an internal number. A minute later a man with pockmarked skin and a smoker's cough heaved his way through the heavy door and introduced himself as Jordan Shriver. However, it quickly proved to be a bust. Shriver was sick on Friday and didn't drink with Hayes. When Gardella asked to speak to Derek Graham, Knight informed him that Graham was not yet at work. He was part-time and only worked the afternoons when the paper was printed. All Knight could offer was his address.

Gardella tried a few more questions, none of them yielding any useful information, before asking Harper, 'Anything to add?'

Harper made a final scan of Knight's office before shaking his head and saying, 'Nope, I think you covered everything, boss.'

'Alright,' Gardella said to Knight. 'We'll be in touch.'

Standing on the footpath outside the Westport News building, Gardella let his frustrations out.

'I learnt next to nothing from that interview.'

Harper shrugged. 'We managed to get the photo in the paper. That's something. You never know, it might generate a lead.'

Gardella seemed unmoved by the optimism. 'Leave the media to me. The last thing I want is for you to blurt out something that ends up in the paper.'

Harper stuffed his hands in his pockets and scuffed the ground with his foot. Nothing good could come from offering a response. It would only inflame things further. Instead, he looked across the street at the courthouse. Hopefully, they would receive better news over there.

CHAPTER 7

Gardella's mood worsened after seeing the judge. She approved the warrants for the cell phone polling data, as well as the bank records, but denied them access to the contents of Hayes' text messages. Gardella had pushed hard, arguing it would be useful to see if Hayes had received any threatening or abusive texts. However, he could not prove probable cause. Based on the evidence, the judge was not satisfied the doctor qualified as a threat. She justified her decision by saying that it would be a breach of privacy to let them trawl through all of Hayes' text conversations searching for something that might not even be there in the first place.

As they left the courthouse, Gardella lamented their limited choice of judges. 'We get one judge to pick from, and she thinks privacy is more important than finding a missing person. For all we know, this guy could be in imminent danger. What good is privacy when you're dead?'

In the city you could shop around the judiciary, picking whichever judge was most likely to give you what you wanted. If you knew, for example, a particular judge had a soft spot for youth offenders, then you steered clear of them when investigating teenage suspects. If you were after access to phone and text messages, you stayed away from judges who were privacy advocates. Things were obviously different on the West Coast.

Both men were feeling defeated and agreed they needed a caffeine pick-me-up. Harper pointed across the street to a café named The Denniston Dog. As they climbed the ramp, Harper could see The Dog was thick with patrons and the place thrummed with music and energetic conversation. Judging by the patchwork of languages he estimated two-thirds of the clientele were tourists, the balance made up of locals who shrewdly eyeballed the detectives as they entered. It was clear they had picked them as cops. Harper ignored the stares and continued to scan the scene.

Black and white photographs depicting bygone scenes of frontier life were dotted around, and for added impact, a variety of historic tools were firmly secured to the walls. Amongst them was an antique miner's pickaxe, its gnarled wooden handle and meaty iron head looked suitably ancient, and next to that, a rusted, two-man saw, its jagged teeth still looking hungry for work.

Most of the inside tables were occupied so Harper and Gardella sat outside on the covered deck. Five minutes later, a frazzled-looking waiter came to take their order. While they waited for the drinks, Harper recounted the timeline so far. 'We know Hayes leaves work at five and picks up the truck a few minutes later. We're told he goes to the bar and drinks with his buddy Graham, he then phones someone around ten-thirty and leaves the bar shortly after. Then … poof, gone. And that's it. That's all we've got. There's a lot of gaps and a lot of unanswered questions. Where do you think we go from here?'

'We question Derek Graham,' Gardella replied. 'Nail down his movements. Snowden told us Hayes made a phone call before leaving the bar. We need to find out more about that call, see if Graham overheard what was said. That might just give us a lead on where he went after he left the bar. Before we pay him a visit, I think we need to do a bit of background on the guy. We know he has a record, so we look him up on the NIA computer. See what it says.'

The waiter returned with two steaming cups. They sat without speaking for several minutes, savouring the coffee and the autumn sun. The area outside the courthouse was getting busier in preparation for the morning hearings. An eclectic mix of people were milling on the footpath fronting the courthouse entrance. Some were smartly dressed and Harper pegged them for lawyers. Others slouched and scuffed along the path in tatty jeans, smoking cigarettes, looking aggressive.

Harper kept one eye on his coffee while the other studied the assortment of lowlifes across the street. He watched their eyes, seeing if any were taking more than a casual interest in what he and Gardella were doing. The longer Harper looked, the more he relaxed. From this vantage point the thugs appeared far too preoccupied with their immediate plight to notice them.

After ten minutes, Gardella paid the bill and they crossed the road to the police station. Like sharks detecting blood in the water, the crowd recognised them as cops.

'Fucking pigs,' shouted a man with a shaved head and a swastika tattooed on one cheek.

'Listen up friends,' Harper said, pretending to be helpful. 'Just so you know, the judge is in a shit of a mood. She told me the first arsehole she meets is heading straight to the big house for a nice long holiday. So good luck in there today everyone!'

His remark was greeted with a chorus of obscenities and pig noises that Harper dismissed with a wave of his hand as he continued towards the station.

'You love to piss people off, don't you,' Gardella said.

'I like to think of it as a form of entertainment.' Harper smirked.

As they pushed through the glass doors of the station Harper saw an officer at the watch-desk that he recognised.

'Hey Monty, what's up?'

Harper and Monty had been through the academy together. Since then their careers had taken very different paths. Harper had quickly climbed the big city ranks while his friend had languished as a small-town patrol officer. Monty had always wanted to work in the town where he grew up, but opportunities for training and promotion were worse than non-existent. Harper, on the other hand, had broader horizons.

As Harper approached, Monty looked genuinely happy to see his old buddy. His real name was Sean Smith, but everyone called him Monty. It came from a bet several years ago resulting in Sean having to do a "Full Monty" down the main street. To minimise embarrassment he was allowed to do it at the end of a late-night shift when the street was nearly deserted. Nevertheless, two female revellers who were making their way home after a night of drinking did see the full show. One even managed to record it on a cell phone.

DEAD GROUND

Fortunately for Sean, it was dark and the footage was too blurry to make out anything significant.

'Harps. How's it going, man? I heard you were back in town. You on the Hayes case?'

'Yup. Just started working it today.'

'How's it going? You need a hand with anything?'

'Actually yeah. We'd like to use your terminal to access the NIA database. Is that all good?'

'Yeah, sure. Help yourself. The place is dead anyway. We're all in court or on the beat so take as long as you like.'

Monty jumped up and let them through the inner door. He showed them to another small room with a computer that had been crammed in between several battered filing cabinets. Everything was the same miserable shade of battleship grey, except for the computer, which was an equally unappealing beige. Harper sat at the terminal and began to log in while Gardella stood looking over his shoulder. Monty was still hanging around at the door like a puppy waiting for his owner to take him for a walk.

'Thanks, man. That's all we need right now. We'll let you know if there's anything else.'

Monty's shoulders slumped. He turned and drifted off down the hall.

Harper logged in and brought up the search screen which contained a number of fields. He entered Graham's details. It took a couple of seconds before his rap sheet sprang up. The list of offences was shorter than Harper had expected. They were mostly drug-related and relatively minor.

Arrested in 2000 for possession of a class C prohibited substance and let off with a warning. Same charge in 2003, and again a warning. In 2003 he was booked and released on a DUI charge. His blood alcohol was twice the legal limit. He was disqualified from driving for six months. In 2005, arrested again but this time charged and found guilty of cultivation. Sentenced to two hundred hours of community service and fined one thousand dollars. Finally, in 2010, found guilty of possession with intent to supply and sentenced to five hundred hours of community work and a five thousand dollar fine.

Just as Snowden had said, no history of violence, resisting arrest, possession of an offensive weapon, aggravated robbery or anything else that might suggest he would harm Jonathon Hayes. However, Harper noted the escalation of offending and, more significantly, that Derek Graham was not just using drugs but had progressed to dealing. That opened up a whole new can of worms and potentially brought Graham, and by association, Hayes, into contact with other criminals in the supply chain. Harper hit the print command. They needed to get out to Graham's place.

CHAPTER 8

Harper gunned the car along the long coastal highway giving scant regard to the passing canvas of velvet green, nor faint respect to the few signposted speed limits. He never noticed the line of Nikau palms swaying amongst the long grass, their pencil trunks and feather-duster heads nodding with each breath of sea breeze. The curling waves of the Tasman Sea crested and crashed and foamed white against blue as if demanding attention. Still, they never even registered on Harper's radar. To him this landscape was like poison and speed was the only antidote. The longer he was exposed, the more danger he was in. At some point the people he had sent to prison were going to realise he was back in town. How they would react was anyone's guess but he could feel the pressure building.

Signs of stress had started with a twitch above his left eye. He attempted to massage it away with the butt of his hand and a strategic yawn. This didn't work. More ticks followed. He'd experienced these before. The first started after the deaths of his biological mother, then his foster parents, and finally his girlfriend. At one point they got so bad he'd experienced double vision and headaches. The only cure had been to get the hell out of town, away from everything and everyone that reminded him of what he'd lost. Given his current mode of employment, that remedy wasn't really an option. Not unless he wanted to spend the next six months explaining to some police appointed shrink why he had bailed on a case that was only just getting started. Detectives in their thirties didn't suffer from stress. That was only for veterans like Gardella, or at least that's what Harper kept telling himself.

So far his symptoms were subtle and Gardella hadn't noticed. Harper made sure with the application of a pair of Ray-Bans. He kept the sunglasses for driving but hardly ever wore them, never liking the way they made him look like a cliché from a B-grade movie or that they screamed cop to anyone in the vicinity. He didn't want to appear rugged or tough. Those looks attracted too much attention. Attention was the last thing he wanted right now.

Gardella must have been thinking the same thing because he sent Harper a look and said, "What's up with the shades?" Harper shrugged and nodded toward the sun. Gardella's stare suggested he wasn't convinced. Harper got the message. The shades would have to come off before they got to Derek Graham's place. He needed to get the twitch under control. He clenched his teeth, zeroed his focus, and thought only of the case.

The farther north he drove the more the mountains crowded in toward the ocean as if trying to squeeze him off the road. Soon they loomed overhead, frozen in time like a vast green wave about to crash down upon him. In the folds of their upper slopes, ghostly clouds clung to the terrain like fading memories of last night's storm.

Harper slowed the car as he passed a green and white road sign announcing their destination. Granity occupied a sliver of land barely two football fields wide, sandwiched between the mountains and the ocean. Weather-beaten cottages flanked the grey road, their rusting roofs and fading paint the symptom of exposure and neglect. Seagulls whirled high in a sky of scudding clouds and the sea-breeze kicked ocean spray up and over the houses in soft plumes of salty mist. Harper rolled down his window. The thump and hiss of the waves and the fresh aroma of the forest drifted on the spring air sending a chill through his body.

Derek Graham's place was an ordinary weatherboard cottage with a small veranda, the roof of which sagged in the middle as if something heavy had once landed on it. Beneath the veranda were two wicker chairs, several pairs of mud-caked boots and an assortment of scattered beer bottles, their contents already drained. A short path led from the house to a broken front gate, which judging from the few remaining scales of paint, had once been white. Running down the right-hand side was a gravel driveway leading to a single, detached garage, which appeared about ready to fall down. Parked in the driveway was a beaten-up blue Ford. On the neighbouring section stood a tiny, whitewashed chapel, with a steeple roof and soaring spire that seemed far too tall for such a small church.

As Harper climbed out of the car, he examined the front of the house more closely. The main entrance was located dead centre with windows on either side. The left window was shut, the right partly raised. Harper thought he caught movement in the open window. He studied the area for several seconds, but saw nothing and brushed it off.

'You happy for me to take the lead on this one, Joe?' Harper asked.

'Yeah, sorry about before. I should have sorted out our strategy a little better back at the newspaper. I just didn't want any details getting splashed on the front cover of tonight's paper. That's all. You take this one.'

They nudged past the gate and moved along the path before climbing the steps to the porch. Harper rapped his knuckles several times against the door and waited. A heavy wave crashed on the beach, drowning out any noise. As the tide receded and the din subsided, both men heard the sound of a rear door opening. Then the sound of someone running.

'Shit!' they said in unison.

Gardella darted down the steps to the path as Harper hurdled the veranda's balustrade, skidding on the wet lawn as he landed. Gardella disappeared down the left-hand side of the house, so Harper opted to go right.

'Stay where you are!' Harper yelled blindly as he came around the front corner onto the driveway.

He sidestepped past the car, glancing through the windows as he passed. Seeing nothing, he continued towards the rear of the property. He poked his head around the corner and stole a glimpse of the backyard. It was a small grassed area with a clothesline, a garden bench and a gap-toothed picket-fence. Beyond the fence rested the foot of the mountain, sub-tropical forest covering its lower slopes. A figure disappeared into the undergrowth.

Harper reached under his jacket and un-holstered his weapon before yelling, 'I'm a police officer. I'm armed. Stop where you are!'

Gardella emerged from the other side of the house, also brandishing his weapon.

'He's gone up,' Harper said as he pointed to the wall of vegetation. 'I'm going in after him. Stay here in case he doubles back.'

'Watch yourself,' Gardella ordered as Harper vaulted the fence and entered the bush.

Harper broke through the outer-most layer of foliage and found himself in another world. The terrain rose abruptly, almost vertically, disappearing into steam and darkness above. The occasional filament of daylight pierced the forest canopy, just enough illumination to conduct a search. The roar of the ocean seemed softer now like someone had dialled down the volume. Harper scanned left and right but could see no one. He stood still and listened. The sounds of thrashing, breaking branches, above and to his right.

He re-holstered his gun and hauled himself upwards. Everything was dark and damp, the ground a soup of mist and branches and tree roots and fern fronds. His feet slid in the muck, his footwear utterly inappropriate for this terrain. He grabbed at tree trunks, branches, vines or any other fixed object to propel himself forward. Harper looked up, probing left and right. He could see only a short distance ahead, the dense undergrowth like a green fog. A pause. More sounds coming from above. They seemed closer, like he had gained ground. Harper kicked on with extra effort, determined to catch his prey.

As he climbed higher, the undergrowth thinned, not to the extent that it stopped clawing at his body, and not enough that he could sight his target, but at least it made it easier to move. Despite this, fatigue had set in. Harper's legs burned, his brow stippled with sweat. He just hoped his fitness was that little bit better than the other guy.

He reached up again and grabbed another low branch, but this time he failed to notice the tree was dead, its branches dry and brittle. It could not support his weight, snapping clean off in his hand. Harper fell face-first into the mud and began to slide back down the mountain, still clutching the useless limb. It happened so suddenly he had no time to grab anything else. Undergrowth rushed by, raking his body. Another branch flew by. He reached for it but missed. His slide continued. He flailed desperately, to no avail. Something slammed into his knee. He winced as he slid past a rock jutting out from the forest floor. He was now picking up speed and needed to arrest his fall soon or it would be too late. He let go of the dead branch and began clawing at the ground.

Out of the corner of his eye, Harper spotted a moss-covered vine draped across the forest floor. He flung an arm and grabbed the lifeline, but his speed was such that it merely slid through his fingers. The friction burned his hand, the pain made him want to let go. He knew he couldn't. He had to slow his rate of descent. He wrapped his other hand around the trailing plant. With both hands firmly clamped, he slowed. The vine stretched with a worrying creak, rebounded like an old piece of elastic, before finally bringing him to a halt.

For a moment, he clung on, reluctant to let go. Harper's left knee throbbed. He flexed it and was able to bend the leg. Probably a deep bruise, maybe a gash, but otherwise he thought it was okay. He looked up and spotted the dead tree, fifteen metres above. It felt like he had slid further than that. Harper sat up, looked down, and swallowed hard. He was perilously close to the edge of a bluff that plunged twenty metres to a boulder-strewn stream. It was a fall you might barely survive, but if you did, you'd soon wish you hadn't. He sucked a sharp breath through clenched teeth and winced at the thought. Harper listened for any noise but heard nothing except the babble of the stream below, and the distant ocean.

'Fuck!'

Harper hauled himself up and rested his back against a sturdy looking tree. After a minute or so, he started making his way back down, careful to manoeuvre away from the bluff towards more forgiving terrain. His knee was beginning to stiffen and would need ice. It was slow going on the injured limb, but eventually he hobbled out of the bush and back into the late morning sunshine. He'd come out behind the church and had to make his way through its grounds to get back to Graham's house. As he came around the front, he saw Gardella leaning against the veranda.

'The arsehole got away,' Harper said, before noticing another man sitting behind Gardella.

'Dylan Harper, I'd like to introduce, Derek Graham,' Gardella said smugly.

Graham sat hunched, elbows on knees, head between his legs, sucking in air and looking sorry for himself. He looked to be in his late fifties and not in great shape. Years of smoking had stained his fingers yellow and robbed him of his breath. His skin clung to the bone with all the strength of crepe paper and his grey hair was long and dishevelled. His clothes hung off him like a circus tent. He twisted his head and viewed Harper with glazed eyes, but said nothing.

'Seems Mr Graham has had second thoughts and decided it would be best if he turned himself in,' Gardella said, looking at Graham with a satisfied smirk.

'Something like that,' Graham managed, still catching his breath. Gardella eased away from the veranda and sidled over to Harper.

'Nice day for a stroll through the woods?' Gardella asked.

'That fucker nearly got me killed,' Harper replied. 'I just about fell off a cliff. I say we lock him up while we decide what we're going to do with him.'

'Slow down, Detective. Let's just take our time. How about we talk to him first. See what he has to say. If we don't like what we hear, then we take him downtown.'

Gardella made sure his voice was loud enough for Graham to hear. Harper looked at his partner, then at Graham, who now sat upright, nervously listening. Harper stared at Derek Graham like a judge considering his sentence. He looked back at Gardella and was about to say something when Graham interrupted.

'I'll talk man. I'll tell you whatever you want. Just don't lock me up. One more time and the boss said he'd fire my arse.'

'I don't know, Joe,' Harper said with a frown and a shake. 'He was evading police, endangering an officer, attempting to pervert the course of justice. We could charge him with any number of offences. We could shut him away for as long as we like. Hell, the judge won't be back in town for two weeks.'

This was all just posturing. They probably wouldn't even be able to file charges, let alone put him in a cell.

'Come on, Dylan. Let's give the guy a chance. If he dicks us around, we bring him in.'

Harper furrowed his brow like he was having a hard time making a decision. 'Okay, whatever," he finally said.

They walked over to Graham. As they approached, he stood up. He was tall, at least as tall as Harper, and a sick kind of thin. Harper had seen this body type in meth addicts before. The drug destroyed the user's appetite and gradually, the body wasted away to a walking skeleton.

'You have any ice in there?' Harper gestured towards the house.

'No way man. I don't do ice. I don't have nothing of that—'

'Not that kind of ice! The frozen variety. For this,' Harper said, pointing at the hole in the knee of his trousers.

'Oh, shit. Yeah. Sorry. Yeah, I got ice. Come in.' Graham turned and led them inside.

A central hall ran from the front to the rear of the house, with rooms branching off on either side. Harper caught a whiff of marijuana and reasoned it had something to do with Graham's dash up the mountain. At the end of the hall, they came to the kitchen. Graham collected a plastic bag from a cupboard under the sink and made his way across the kitchen to a white fridge-freezer. He grabbed several handfuls of ice and partially filled the bag before handing it to Harper.

'Anything else? You want a drink? I got beer?' Graham said, clearly trying to earn some brownie points.

'No thank you, Mr Graham. We're on duty,' Harper said.

'Oh yeah, sorry, should have guessed. How 'bout a glass of water? I can clean a couple of these up real quick,' Graham said as he moved towards a stack of soiled dishes piled so high they spilt out of the sink and onto the kitchen counter.

'Detective Harper and I are fine,' Gardella said tersely. 'We don't need a drink. We do, however, have some questions that need answers. Please, sit down.'

Graham's eyes flicked from Gardella to Harper and a spark of recognition flashed across his face.

'Harper … You're the Harper kid. Ah, Daniel? No, that's not right. Dylan. Yeah, that's it. Dylan Harper. I knew your mother.'

Harper wasn't about to get dragged into another trip down memory lane, so he steered the conversation in a different direction. 'That's all very nice, but we are not here to talk about my mother. We are here to ask you about Jonathon Hayes. You were last seen with him on Friday night. Is that correct?'

'Fuck! I thought you were here about something else,' Graham said, relief evident in his voice.

'You thought we were here about the drugs. Isn't that right Mr Graham?' Gardella said.

'Um, well …'

'That's fine,' Harper interrupted. 'We might be prepared to overlook that, so long as you answer our questions honestly. Any bullshit and we will find a reason to worry about the drugs and evading police. Are we clear?'

'Clear as mud,' Graham said as he took a seat at the far end of the kitchen table. 'What do ya wanna know?'

Harper eased out a chair and sat at the other end of the table, never taking his eyes off Graham. 'You were drinking with Jonathon Hayes last Friday, correct?'

'Yup. Normally have a few brews on a Friday.'

'What bar were you and Mr Hayes drinking at?'

'Black and White, same as usual.'

'You notice anything odd about Mr Hayes last Friday? Anything out of character?'

'Nope. He seemed his normal self.'

'He tell you about his plans for the weekend?'

The creases on Graham's face deepened as if the strain of locating the memory was somehow painful. Harper kept the pressure on with an unwavering stare. After several seconds, it paid dividends.

'He said something about ... taking it easy at home ... I think. Oh, and he said he was gonna do some testing at the creek and would pop in and see me on his way back. But he never showed so I just assumed he changed his mind.'

'What creek?' Harper asked.

'Granity Creek. Just up the road.'

'Where does he test the water?' Harper asked.

'There's a road up to the mine that sort of follows the creek. He goes a ways up there. I can show you if you like?' Harper looked at Gardella who gave a nod.

'All right, let's go take a look.'

They piled into the Commodore and Harper started the engine. They drove north through the corridor of buildings that constituted the tiny township of Granity. They passed a school, a town hall, a line of shops, a band rotunda, a café, and several homes in varying stages of disrepair.

At the end of the settlement they crossed a short bridge spanning a boulder-strewn creek and continued on for another five hundred metres before Graham told them to make a hard right. The access road doubled back on itself before it climbed steeply, hugging the contours of the mountain. As they forged higher, the surrounding bush crowded ever closer until it arched over the road casting deep, cool shadows. Hazy shafts of light cut the shade, capturing the dance of a thousand tiny insects in their beams.

Graham told them the road was used by the Stockton Coal Mine which operated on the plateau above. The open-cast mine once employed two thousand men, but that number was falling almost as fast as the price of coal. Currently, fewer than four-hundred had kept their jobs and there was talk of further cuts, even the possibility of the mine shutting altogether.

This information seemed to be backed up by the fact they hadn't seen a single car on the access road so far. After another five minutes the forest canopy began to thin and before long they emerged back into daylight. As they came around a sharp left-hand bend, Graham shouted, 'There!'

Harper stabbed the brakes and he and Gardella snapped their heads in the direction Graham was pointing, half expected to see Jonathon Hayes standing on the side of the road, smiling and waving.

'Turn there,' Graham ordered.

'Jesus. Don't do that,' Harper said.

'Sorry, sorry. I forgot where the turn was. I thought you were gonna miss it.'

Harper yanked the car right and they drove along a side road.

'There's a turning bay up by the old bridge,' Graham said. 'There's a track by the bridge that runs down to the creek. It's just up here a bit further.'

As they approached, Harper saw the bridge. A sign saying ROAD CLOSED and a line of carefully arranged boulders, each about the size of a washing machine blocked the way. It would be impossible for anything other than a tank to get past. A dirt and gravel turning bay seemed the only place to park. Harper began to turn in.

'Whoa, whoa,' Gardella yelled. 'Park it on the road.'

Harper stopped on the tar-seal and dragged on the handbrake. All three got out of the car.

'You,' Gardella barked at Graham. 'Stay by the car.'

Harper and Gardella crossed the road, stopping where the seal met gravel. The turning bay was semi-circular and blanketed in loose stones. At its far edge the terrain fell away abruptly, a rim of vegetation marking the drop. The view beyond was of the river valley below with the road twisting its way down, a slice of ocean just visible in the distance.

'Right,' Gardella began. 'Watch your step. I'm searching for tyre marks. Look for a wide track and deep tread pattern. You spot anything, snap a picture with your phone. Also, check for shoe impressions, cigarette butts, food wrappers or any other signs someone stopped here.'

They walked in opposite directions along the edge of the road to the far extremities of the turning area. Carefully, they inched forward and worked their way back together, meeting in the middle. They continued this process until they had canvassed the whole area. Harper looked at Gardella. They shook their heads in unison. Nothing but stones and puddles. Last night's rain had destroyed any discernible impressions. If Jonathon Hayes had been here, the evidence had been washed away.

'Where's the track down to the stream?' Gardella called out to Graham, who was leaning against the car and looking left out.

'Up by the bridge, past the barrier and down to the left,' he said.

Gardella glanced at Harper, who flexed his knee with a well-timed wince.

'Don't worry cowboy,' Gardella said with an easy smile. 'I'll check it out. You rest up.'

'Find anything?' Graham asked as Harper returned to the car.

'Don't worry about it,' Harper said. 'What time did Hayes leave the bar?'

'Like I told the other police, he took off about half-ten. Could've been a bit before, or a bit after. All I know was it was earlier than normal. We usually drink till midnight.'

'Do you know why he left early?'

'I remember he was on the phone. When he got off he said he had to go. He downed his beer and left.'

'Who initiated the call, was it Hayes or did someone ring him?'

'Jon made it. I watched him dial it up.'

'He didn't receive another call between the one you saw him make and leaving the bar?'

'Nah man. Like I said. He got off the phone and was outta there. He wasn't hanging around. It was like he had somewhere better to be.'

'You hear what he said?'

'Hear what?'

'When he was on the phone. Did you hear what he said on the phone?'

Graham strained, the lines on his face deepened once more. 'Well, it was really loud, but I think I heard some.'

'And?'

'I think he said, "Have you got the stash?" or something like that. Whatever the other person said must've been good 'cause Jon got real happy, he had this big smile on his face like he'd won the lottery. Then he said, "Really!" I'm definite on that because he turned and looked right at me when he said it. Then he said, "See you soon." He hung up, grinning like an idiot, and said he had to go.'

Harper scribbled this down and read it back to Graham to double-check he had the wording right.

'What do you think he meant when he said, "Have you got the stash?"?'

'I don't know. Like I said before, it was loud. He could've said something else.'

Harper thought about this for a moment. It sounded drug-related. The trouble was Graham could have misheard. Jonathon Hayes could have said something else altogether. There was no way of telling. He moved on with the questions.

'Okay. So what did you do after Jon left?'

'I stayed for a bit longer. Had a few more brews with another buddy, then got a taxi home at about midnight.'

'This buddy. Were you drinking with him before Hayes left or after?'

'After.'

'You got a name for this guy?'

'Tom Smith.'

Harper immediately pegged it as a fake name. 'Where does this Tom Smith live?'

'Yeah, um. I know the house, but not the number. It's on the corner of Brougham and Peel streets. You can't miss the house. It's got this weird shape, like an octagon.' Harper still was not convinced, but he let it go. He would check it out later.

'Was there anybody else drinking with you and Jon?

'Nah, just us.'

'And when you got home, what did you do then?'

'Um, I just hit the hay,' Graham said, looking away.

'Don't try and feed me shit. I want a straight answer. What did you do when you got home?'

Graham squirmed. 'I had a fucking joint, all right! Big fucking deal! You wanna arrest me? Then hurry up and do it. I don't need this kinda heat, man.'

So Graham had a temper. Combine that with running from police and Harper was thinking Derek Graham might have something to hide.

'You live alone?' Harper asked.

'Yeah. Just me.'

'Can anyone vouch for your whereabouts after midnight?'

Graham straightened up, his posture defensive. 'I don't know what you're suggesting, but whatever it is, you're dead wrong. Last I saw Jon he was all well and good.'

'I'm not suggesting anything. I'm just establishing the facts.'

Harper thought it curious that Derek Graham had jumped to the notion something had happened to Hayes. This was a missing person case. There was nothing to suggest anything more serious. Harper tilted his head down a degree or two and glared at Graham from under raised eyebrows like a school principal who had heard one too many tall tales.

Graham's body seemed to slump under the scrutiny. He sighed and said, 'After the joint, I went to bed, slept till ten. Nobody saw me after the taxi dropped me off.'

Harper turned at the sound of Gardella scrambling back up the track. He left Graham and walked over to his partner. Gardella materialised out of the scrub, shoulders hunched, arms hanging loosely, not the look of a man who had found a case-breaking lead.

'Anything?' Harper asked.

'Nada. No shoe impressions, no drag marks, nothing. My guess, Hayes was never here.'

'Maybe he went to a different spot?'

'It's possible, but it would have to be farther up the road. Find out if there are any other places. I'll keep sniffing around.'

Graham told Harper that from this point on the creek took a different path. The only way to access its upper reaches was to travel up to the mine and skirt the edge of the open-cast pit before coming back down the mountain a few kilometres away. Harper thought Hayes wouldn't have wasted the time and effort, but Gardella insisted they check it out. They jumped in the car and made a U-turn and retraced their path to the access road before continuing on upwards.

The higher they climbed the more the vegetation receded until only tussock sprawled across the terrain. Upon reaching the plateau the road straightened out. It cut through a desert-like landscape bereft of trees or shades of green. It was an environment so foreign it hardly resembled the West Coast of New Zealand.

Before long they came to a security gate made of chain-linked steel. A fence of the same construction stretched off into the distance on either side. The road continued beyond the barrier but changed from tar-seal to dirt. There was no sign of the mine, just acres of quiet desolation disturbed only by the wind which rolled through the tussock like ripples on a pond. The gate appeared to be operated by a swipe card. There was no guard-house, no intercom, no way of getting access beyond this point.

Harper diverted his attention to a row of six vehicles parked in a pothole-riddled lot a short distance away. Various makes and models, private passenger type, parked up as if their owners had driven up and caught another ride. None matched the truck Samara had described. Another dead end.

For a while, they sat and discussed their options. If Jonathon Hayes had made it past this point, he would need to have swiped his card to open the gate. That would leave a record. They would make some enquiries later, but for now, they had come to the end of the line. Harper turned the car around.

With the flat expanse of the plateau behind him, the road pitched down sharply affording a view of the ocean far below. Frothy breakers filed towards the beach in long, orderly lines, like the advancing ranks of an invading army, the sweep of coastline, repelling each attack. It was a picture-postcard scene. But Harper was not looking at the scenery. He had noticed something else. It had been there for a second or two, and then it was gone.

'See that?' he said.

'What?' Gardella replied.

'Down there, about a K, moving fast.' They both leaned forward. Heat haze shimmered off the road as the ocean continued its assault on the shore. The sun reflected off something moving quickly through the trees.

'There!' Harper yelled. 'Hauling arse back down the road.'

A vehicle flashed into a small clearing, moving along the road at breakneck speed, too fast to be a lost tourist or a miner scurrying home from his shift. As quickly as it appeared, it was gone, the glare of the sun and the vehicle's speed meant Harper could only be sure it was light in colour and average in size.

Who was it? Even if it was a mine employee rushing off to the pub after a hard day's work, the access road had only one way up and one way down and no one had passed them going down. That meant the car had to have been on the way up when something made it turn around and speed off in the opposite direction. The answer dawned on Harper. Before he could get it out. Gardella beat him to it.

'We're being followed. Go!'

Harper stamped on the gas. The V8 roared. The bush flashed past in a green blur. At the first bend Harper dropped a gear, dabbed the brakes, and flung the car into a right-hand drift, tyres howling. As the curve straightened out, Harper snapped the steering back. The car righted itself in an instant.

He gripped the wheel and positioned the car for the next test, a tight left-hander. As the turn loomed large in the windscreen Harper kicked the clutch, jerked the handbrake and jockeyed the car into the corner. The rear stepped out, Harper counter-steered right, adding throttle through the apex, coercing loud protests from his rubber.

He used every inch of tarmac, sometimes more. At one point the rear wheels slid off the hard shoulder; he backed off the gas to regain traction. Harper blasted down a short straight, another left-hander approaching. He eased right to open up the angle, only this time, he overdid it. A low-hanging branch clipped the wing-mirror, shattering the glass and destroying the mounting. It remained tethered to the car by an electrical cable, flapping angrily against the body-work until the connection gave way sending it sailing off into the bush. Finally, after one last stomach-churning manoeuvre, they blasted out of the forest towards the T-junction with the main road. Harper slammed the brakes, and the ABS shuddered the car to a halt. Harper looked right while Gardella looked left.

'I've got a silver sedan heading south,' Gardella said.

'Nothing going north,' Harper replied.

Harper swung the car south and pinned the throttle. Gardella flicked on the lights and sirens. Up ahead the silver car was just entering the left turn at the southern end of the township, about a kilometre away. Harper had made up ground, but could still lose it on the open stretches of road ahead.

'Watch it,' Gardella yelled.

Harper eased off a notch, scanning for obstructions. Mowing down an eight-year-old walking home from school would be a career-ender. An SUV eased out onto the main road. Harper slammed the horn and swerved into the other lane. He accelerated hard, making the remnants of the township flash by in a blur. At the turn, he flicked the wheel left, floored it down the short straight, launched over the railway crossing, then wrestled the car right to line up with the road heading south towards Westport.

There it was, a few hundred metres ahead, accelerating down the open road. Harper had them now. There was no way the family sedan could outrun the powerful police cruiser and no innocent bystanders to give him pause. V8 power reduced the gap, lights flashing and sirens wailing, job done.

But as he drew near, the other driver sped up. Harper thrust an arm out his window and signalled to pull over. Gardella did the same. A second later, an indicator came on, then brake lights. Slowly, the car eased to the side. Harper drew in behind. He killed the siren but left the red and blues pulsing.

'You take the driver. I'll deal with the passenger side,' Gardella instructed.

Harper and Gardella opened their doors and exited the cruiser in synchronised formation, sending a message that this was a well-oiled machine and it would pay to be obedient. Harper took his time with the approach, treading cautiously, scanning for threats. The back seat appeared unoccupied, a driver and passenger up front. Harper glanced at the wing mirror; the angle was wrong, he couldn't see a face. There was a sticker on the rear glass. Hertz NZ. He came up behind the driver's door and saw that the window was up, probably why he couldn't catch a face in the wing mirror. Harper tapped on the glass. A second later, it rolled down.

The driver was an Asian male, late twenties. Next to him, an Asian woman, similar age. In the back seat a toddler was strapped into a child seat. Harper's heart rate dropped. He asked for a drivers licence and after a lot of confusion and a short game of charades, Chinese papers were produced. His name was Zhu Ping, thirty-one, from Guangzhou. Harper and Gardella retreated to the hood of their cruiser.

'It's not them,' Gardella said. 'They're tourists,'

'How the fuck did we miss it?'

'Either the car pulled over and we drove past, or it had too much of a head start and was long gone before we got to the main road. My guess is the latter.'

Harper nodded his agreement. When he first spotted the mystery vehicle he had estimated it was a kilometre away. He also knew that up in the mountains, distances could be hard to judge, your sense of perspective distorted. It could have been more. Either way, whoever was following had ample opportunity to run and hide. There was nothing left to do but retrace their steps and see what they could uncover.

'There's a café back in Granity,' Harper said. 'I say we go ask if they saw anything. While we're there, let's grab a bite.'

Gardella nodded. 'Sounds like a plan.'

CHAPTER 9

They deposited Derek Graham at his cottage and drove a short distance north to the strip of shops they had passed a few minutes earlier. Drifters was a small café-come-bar located across the road from the community centre and within a stone's throw of the beach. The place was empty, apart from a teenage waitress loitering behind the counter.

When they questioned her she proved of little use. She had been busy cleaning the coffee machine and didn't get a good look at the car, only catching a fleeting glimpse as it sped past. The car was white with a strip of silver trim, and it looked relatively new. She thought she'd seen a single occupant but couldn't be sure. Approximately a minute later she heard a siren and saw another car speed past.

Harper pressed for more detail but she couldn't even tell if the driver was a man or a woman. More questions yielded increasingly vague answers so Harper called it quits and they ordered lunch. Harper got the Drifters Burger while Gardella opted for a whitebait sandwich. The food arrived a few minutes later.

'What do you think?' Harper asked as he took a healthy chunk out of his burger.

'I don't know, but something's not right. Ever since Bones called us in, I haven't felt comfortable. Now we find we've got a tail. Why? Who?'

'Could be one of the boys in blue,' Harper said. 'You think Snowden's keeping tabs on us?'

'You know him better than I do. What's your gut say?'

Harper took another bite and thought it over. He finished and wiped his face with the napkin. 'My instinct tells me no. Snowden's a tight arse. An officer and a vehicle tied up spying on two out of town detectives would be considered a waste of resources.'

'So what does that leave us with?' Gardella asked.

Harper didn't answer. He was eating again. All the excitement had built an appetite and the burger was hitting the spot nicely. It also gave him pause to think through a few scenarios.

'Well ...' He managed between mouthfuls. 'The way I see it, there are two possibilities.' Harper took a swig of water to clear his throat. 'It could be someone with information. Someone who knows where Jonathon Hayes is, or what happened to him. They're just waiting for the right time to come forward.'

'That sounds like wishful thinking,' Gardella said.

'Perhaps, but I'm just throwing out ideas here. Remember, this is my neck of the woods. I understand how the locals think.'

'What's the second possibility?'

'That whoever was in that car is responsible for the disappearance. They're watching us to see what we're doing and what we know.'

Gardella took a bite from his whitebait sandwich and looked out the window like he knew something was missing. Harper had seen this from his partner before. Gardella had a tendency of refusing to accept theories or evidence. Most of the time this worked in his favour. He had an uncanny knack of sniffing out alternative avenues of inquiry. In his twenty-five years as a detective, he had one of the highest clearance rates of anyone in Christchurch CIB. However, there were times where it worked against him. He could become fixated on one suspect, so convinced of their guilt that he would pursue them relentlessly, often ignoring evidence that pointed in a different direction. It was one of the reasons Harper thought they had been paired together. Gardella needed someone younger, someone prepared to question everything, someone who could not be intimidated.

After ten minutes of watching his partner brood Harper paid the bill and they climbed in the car for the trip back to Westport. The journey was quiet, both men deep in thought.

At the hotel Harper got changed. The damage to his trousers meant they were ruined. His limp was worse, his limbs scratched, his pride dented, but otherwise, he would live. He sat in the conference room icing his knee while Gardella brewed a pot of coffee. As they drank they formulated a plan.

Harper would go to the bank and obtain Hayes' bank records while Gardella would action the warrant for the polling data and set up the cell ping. After that they would pay a visit to the doctor who was suing Hayes for defamation. Finally, they would contact Bones and give him a rundown of today's events and then update the wife. They finished their coffees and headed out.

As they drove Harper kept watch for any indication they had company. He didn't see any, not that he was expecting to. Whoever had been following them had probably been scared off for the time being. Harper dropped Gardella at the phone company before continuing to the bank.

The automatic doors swished open and Harper limped into the bank's spacious lobby. The service desk was staffed by a modestly attractive woman wearing a uniform that was part air hostess, part corporate chic. Harper flashed his badge.

'Detective Harper. I need to see the manager.'

The woman looked him up and down before saying, 'He's currently in a meeting. Can you wait?'

'I'm afraid I can't. Tell him it's urgent. I'm investigating a missing person and I need to see him now.'

'I see,' she said through pursed lips. 'I'll pop my head in and see if I can pry him out. I won't be a minute.'

Clearly put out, she wobbled off in red high heels that made walking look more complicated than it needed to be.

Harper looked around. There were two bank clerks behind the counter and five customers navigating the roped-off maze. Elevator music drifted from an unseen sound system and there was a polite hum of activity. Business as usual. After a wait of less than a minute, the woman came teetering back.

'Mr Sullivan will see you now. If you would follow me please.'

Numerous pairs of eyes followed him as he moved through the lobby. They must have noticed the badge or overheard his conversation. The woman came to a door and punched in a code. It opened with a clack and she led Harper down a plush corridor. They passed a glass-walled meeting room occupied by half-a-dozen professional types, concern on their faces. Harper assumed this was the meeting he had rudely interrupted. The woman escorted him into an office at the end of the corridor. It was occupied by a man in a business suit.

'Mike Sullivan,' the man said as he rose from behind his desk. 'Pleased to meet you.' A false smile suggested the opposite.

Sullivan seemed young to be in a position of such authority and he appraised Harper with a critical eye like he was thinking the same thing of the detective. Sullivan's brown hair was sculpted with a healthy dose of product and his skin was blemish-free and glowing. An ivory-white display handkerchief protruded from his right breast pocket and a double knotted burgundy tie bulged from beneath the crisp collar of his designer shirt as if he had just stepped from the pages of a fashion magazine.

'Detective Harper, Christchurch CIB,' Harper said, shaking Sullivan's hand.

'Have a seat, Detective. How can I help you?'

'I have a missing person,' Harper said as he lowered himself into a chair. 'He's a customer of yours. The name's Jonathon Hayes. I have a warrant to access his bank details and obtain a printout of his transactions for the last two months.'

'Oh, wow. I haven't had one of these before. Um, that shouldn't be a problem. I guess I better take a look at the warrant.'

Harper slid it across the table. Sullivan plucked it up and judged it with the requisite dose of concern but Harper could tell the bank manager wasn't really reading. His expression was one of deliberation, but his eyes were not scanning, not taking in the detail. Harper had seen this before. People served with warrants were often in such a state of nervousness that reading the subtler points of an important legal document was the last thing on their mind. Sullivan passed the warrant back and went to work on his computer.

'So. Jonathon Hayes,' Sullivan said as he tapped away. 'You don't have his account number by any chance?'

'Yes. It's on the warrant.'

'Sorry,' Sullivan muttered through a smile of embarrassment. 'I must have missed it.'

Harper returned the warrant and Sullivan plugged the numbers into his computer. He jockeyed his mouse and stabbed at his keyboard for another thirty seconds before the printer on his desk whirred to life. It spat out five sheets which he shuffled together and presented to Harper.

Harper went straight to the last sheet which chronicled the most recent set of transactions. He studied each entry, looking to see if Jonathon Hayes had accessed his bank account since Friday night. The was nothing over the weekend except for five purchases spaced an hour apart between five-thirty and ten-thirty p.m. These were most probably Hayes buying rounds of drinks at the bar. The amount spent was consistent with buying two beers which stacked up with what Derek Graham had said about no one else being with them that night.

Then, right at the bottom, a line that made his pulse quicken. The final transaction had a different date: 3:27 a.m. on Saturday morning.

A withdrawal of eight hundred dollars, more or less emptying the account, save for a few cents. While this was significant, it was not what had sparked Harper's interest. What grabbed his attention were the letters A.T.M.

'This transaction here,' Harper said. 'Can you identify the terminal where this withdrawal was made?'

Sullivan looked at the long series of numbers printed next to the entry. 'Um, yeah. That's a zero-five-two terminal. That's ours.'

'Can I get a look at the CCTV recording of this?'

'That shouldn't be a problem. I'll need to get our tech guy.'

Sullivan picked up his phone and made a call. After a short conversation, he put the phone down.

'Zac says we can't view it from my computer. We have to go to the dungeon.'

'The dungeon?' Harper said.

'We call it that because the room doesn't have any windows. It's where the NAS is. Follow me.'

Without further explanation, he stood up and led Harper back into the corridor. As he went past the meeting room, Sullivan gave the thumbs up to a bunch of clearly nervous suits.

'What's the NAS?' Harper asked as they walked.

'I think it stands for Network Area Storage, or something like that. It's basically a computer that stores files and data. It's where all the CCTV footage is kept.'

Sullivan turned down another corridor lined with doors, all of which were shut. The door at the end was ajar and the room beyond it, dark.

As Harper drew closer he detected a dull glow and the hum of electronics. Sullivan made a cursory knock before sticking his head in and greeting someone inside. With permission to enter apparently granted, he ushered Harper in.

Harper could see why it was called the dungeon. There were no windows or sources of natural light. The only illumination came from a bank of computer monitors lined up on a desk. There were six screens in total, arranged in two rows of three, one row on top of the other. Four had live images of various parts of the bank. One of the screens displayed a general shot of the bank lobby. Another angle showed the main entrance. The remaining cameras were positioned above and behind the tellers and captured the customers as they conducted their banking. The final two screens didn't display camera footage. Instead, they contained multiple dialogue boxes, each with strings of letters and numbers which made no sense to Harper.

A scruffy looking kid fresh out of high school sat hunched over a keyboard, intently focused on the bank of computer screens as if they contained something of immense importance. He made no effort to acknowledge the visitors and instead was using his mouse to open and close windows in rapid succession.

'Zac. This is Detective Constable Harper from the Criminal Investigation Branch in Christchurch.'

'Hey,' was all Zac managed to muster by way of a reply.

Sullivan waited a beat, and when he got no more response from the kid, he said, 'Detective Harper is conducting an important investigation into a missing person. One of our customers. The detective has a warrant to examine a video recording made by our ATM camera. As I explained to you on the phone, I need you to bring up those images. Do you think you can do that please?'

Harper's warrant was only for Jonathon Hayes' bank records. It didn't extend to CCTV footage but he wasn't about to correct the bank manager. If needs be he could always go back and get the warrant amended retrospectively, depending on what he was about to see.

'Just chill for a sec,' Zac said, continuing to manipulate the dialogue boxes. 'I gotta finish this.'

Zac had around half a dozen windows open. He shuffled between them like he was playing a game of digital solitaire. Occasionally a segment of code would be adjusted, but mostly it was just shuffling. After a minute or so, he had finished.

'Sorry. What does he want?' Zac asked Sullivan as he closed the last dialogue box.

'How about I let Detective Harper explain,' Sullivan said.

'First, can you tell me how the ATM camera system works? Is it motion-activated or does it only record when someone makes a transaction?' Harper asked.

'It's a real basic rig, almost as old as I am. It just runs all the time. Records on the NAS over there,' Zac said, pointing towards two black boxes with intermittently blinking lights, stowed under a table in the corner of the room.

'That must chew up a lot of hard-drive space.'

'Not really. The image is low res. It's not like HD or anything.'

'How many days before it starts to overwrite the old footage?'

'About a week. That's if both banks of the NAS are online. Last week I had to shut one down because of a read/write error. It's still not fixed. So, currently, it's probably doing about three or four days. Then it will start to eat the old stuff.'

Harper began counting back. It was now just after two o'clock on Wednesday afternoon. The withdrawal occurred at three-thirty Saturday morning. That made it four and a half days. They were near, or possibly past, the time when the footage would start getting wiped. It could already be too late.

'Get it offline. NOW.'

'I'm not supposed to do that,' Zac said meekly.

'Just do it,' Harper ordered.

Zac looked at Sullivan and Sullivan gave a nod of approval. Zac returned to his screens and made a few clicks with the mouse.

'Right. It's offline from the LAN. It won't be receiving any more data. Once I shut down the camera feed, I will reconnect so we can see what's on there.'

Shutting the camera down took a lot longer than taking the system offline which Zac blamed on old software. Finally, he reconnected the NAS.

'Cool. I think we're just about ready. All I need are the deets?' Zac said, looking at Harper.

'The deets?'

'You know, the details. I need date and time so I can queue the images.'

'Right, ah, Saturday morning, which was the tenth. Three twenty-seven a.m.'

Zac went back to work. He chose the ATM camera from a drop-down list and began to enter the time before Harper stopped him.

'Make it three o'clock on the dot.'

Zac made the changes and Harper held his breath. The machine began probing its memory. Harper leaned closer as if willing it on. A message snapped back "No Results."

'Looks like the footage has been overwritten,' Zac said. Harper's stomach sank.

'Try three twenty-five,' Harper said.

'K, three twenty-five it is.' Zac adjusted the time and began the search.

After a short wait, a box with a grainy black and white image appeared on the screen. It was hard to tell what he was looking at, but after several seconds Harper could make out the footpath and a section of the curb.

For the first sixty seconds, nothing happened. No foot traffic, no movement, no shadows, not even a scrap of rubbish fluttering on the breeze. If it were not for the ticking timestamp he could be forgiven for thinking the video had frozen.

'Why are we watch—?'

Harper killed Zac's question with a raised palm, his eyes not deviating from the screen.

The time-stamp now read three twenty-six. Thirty seconds later, shadows on the ground.

'Here we go,' Harper said.

Into the camera's field of view stepped a man. The resemblance to Jonathon Hayes was obvious. He wore white sneakers, light coloured shorts and a white t-shirt. Harper leaned in even closer. On the screen, Hayes was fumbling to get his wallet out of his pocket.

'He looks nervous,' Sullivan interrupted. Harper held up another hand. He was trying to take everything in. Absorb every tiny detail.

Zac had not exaggerated when he said it was a basic set-up. The camera recorded continuously, unlike modern systems that only grabbed one frame every two or three seconds. In this instance, it was an advantage because they got an extra insight into Hayes' body language and behaviour. Sullivan was right. Hayes appeared uncomfortable.

By now, Hayes had retrieved his wallet and was pulling out his card. He inserted it into the machine and, out of view, punched in his pin. His head was down, and the camera could not see his face. He swayed a little from side-to-side as if trying to find firm footing. A second later Hayes reached for something, paused, and then pulled a stack of cash from the machine. What happened next took everyone by surprise.

Hayes was holding the banknotes awkwardly as if he was not sure what to do with them. He stood like that for several seconds, the money loosely gripped, as if daring someone to snatch it. Then, out of nowhere, he raised his head and stared straight into the camera. Everyone in the darkened room held their breath, the electric hum the only sound. Jonathon Hayes, the man who had been missing for the last three days, was now staring directly at them. There was something about his face that didn't look right but Harper couldn't put his finger on precisely what it was.

For a second or two he just looked at the camera. Then his mouth began to move. He was saying something. There was no audio to pick up the words but Hayes was definitely speaking to the camera. It was a short sentence. Six, maybe seven words. Directed right down the barrel of the lens. Once he had finished, he turned around and was gone.

Harper made Zac scroll back so he could watch it again. As the kid was getting the video ready to play once more, Harper glanced at the live feeds from the cameras in the bank. He noticed Gardella standing at the service desk speaking to the woman in the heels.

'See that guy there?' Harper said to Sullivan, pointing at the image. 'That's my partner. Can you bring him back here?'

'Sure,' Sullivan replied.

Sullivan left the dim room and strode off down the hall. Soon he appeared on the monitor and approached Gardella who was still waiting at the service desk. Sullivan could be seen introducing himself then pointing and leading Gardella off-camera. A few seconds later they appeared at the door.

Harper briefed his partner on what they had seen so far and they viewed the footage again from start to finish without pausing or going back.

'Have you ever seen anything like that before, Joe?' Harper asked.

'Never. I've never seen someone talk to the camera. Not like that.'

'What do you think he was saying?'

'I'm not sure. Roll it again,' Gardella ordered.

They watched the last few seconds again. What struck Harper was that Hayes was looking right at the camera, like he knew exactly where it was. His gaze wasn't too high or low, not to the left or the right but directly into the lens. It was like he knew someone was going to view this video and he was trying to communicate with them.

'Beats me,' Gardella finally said. 'He might've said "okay," but I can't tell.'

Over the next few minutes, Zac replayed the short exchange several times, but no one in the room could agree on what Hayes was saying. Harper asked Zac to scroll back to see how much footage was still intact before 3:27 a.m. He scrolled back to 3:17 a.m. but could go no further. Ten minutes. That was how close they had come to losing the evidence. Had Harper waited for the bank manager to finish his meeting, he would have lost the video. Zac copied the footage to a USB stick and handed it to Harper. They thanked him for his help and Sullivan escorted the detectives back to his office.

Despite the chill of the air-conditioned room, Sullivan had a thin film of perspiration on his brow. He snatched a tissue from a box on his desk and dabbed his face.

'That was some pretty weird stuff,' Sullivan said as he fanned his face with a manila folder. 'What do you think was going on?'

'At this stage, we don't know,' Harper said. 'We need to piece a few more things together. We have another warrant for Hayes' bank details. Principally, we want to set up an alert. As soon as his account is accessed, we want to be informed. We want to know the date, time and location. Are you able to do that?'

'Yeah, sure. I can do that. Just give me the details. I'll set it up.'

Harper called out the numbers once again. Sullivan began tapping the information into his computer. Harper couldn't see what was happening on Sullivan's monitor but it seemed that setting up a transaction alert was not a simple matter. He worked in a focused silence that was only broken once when he requested the detective's cell phone numbers. Finally, they were good to go.

'How quickly will it alert us when a transaction occurs?' Harper asked.

'It's pretty much real-time. Within a second or so you will get a text, assuming you have cell coverage. You'll get a date, time, retailer's name, city and the dollar amount.'

It was impressive technology, but Harper didn't know what good it would do them. Hayes' account was all but empty. He had withdrawn eight hundred in cash meaning he wouldn't need to use his bank card. He would be untraceable. Harper began to worry that maybe this guy didn't want to be found. They thanked Sullivan and made their own way out.

On the footpath Harper checked the area in and around the cash machine. The asphalt was spotted with gum, some so old it had become part of the pavement. A permanent metal awning extended from the exterior wall of the bank providing shelter from the elements. The ATM was old, the numbers on the keypad worn and the touch screen scratched and cloudy. The position of the camera was not immediately apparent. Harper searched for a minute before he spotted it. The aperture was slightly larger than a match head and higher than he had been expecting, just under the letter A of the bank's name. There was a street lamp farther down the footpath and beyond that was another bar. It was a different bar from the one Hayes had been at and it gave Harper an idea.

'Maybe he left the Black and White and came to this place,' he said, nodding in the direction of the bar.

Gardella shook his head. 'Would've shown up on his bank statement.'

'Not if he was paying in cash.' Harper offered. 'It's worth a look.'

Gardella shrugged like he didn't care either way. As it turned out his ambivalence proved well-founded. None of the staff remembered seeing Jonathon Hayes. They left empty-handed.

Back out on the footpath Harper asked, 'How'd you get on with the phone company?'

'Got the phone records no problem. However, when I checked them, something was missing.'

'What?'

'Derek Graham told us that Hayes made a phone call at around ten-thirty, right?'

'Yeah.'

'Well, there's no record of a call at that time. In fact, the last call was at five oh three that afternoon.'

Harper thought about this for a moment. 'Hayes had a burner.'

'That's what I'm thinking. We know he'd been having an affair. The wife thought it had finished but maybe Hayes was having a hard time saying goodbye. I bet you he had a second phone to keep things alive.'

'You want to go back and talk to the wife again?' Harper asked.

'Not yet. We'll come back to her later. Right now I want to track down Anand Sharma.'

CHAPTER 10

At the hospital, the duty manager told Harper that Anand Sharma was on suspension and hadn't been at work for a week. Initially, the manager was reluctant to tell Harper where Sharma lived, but after some gentle persuasion, he gave up the address.

The house was a red-brick bungalow on a flat grassed section surrounded by a low wall made of the same red brick as the house. Apart from the grass, nothing else grew on the site. There were no trees, shrubs, flowers or garden beds. The low maintenance plot made Harper think the house was probably owned by the hospital and rented to staff from out of town.

Harper rapped the door knocker and waited. The sound of an approaching car diverted his attention. He watched as an old pickup rattled by, black soot belching from the exhaust and a grizzled, grey-haired man driving. The old man paid them no attention and Harper relaxed.

Harper banged on the door again, this time using the butt of his fist. A shuffling sound came from inside. The door was unlatched and then opened with a creak to reveal a young woman who appeared to be of Middle Eastern descent. She was five foot nothing and dressed in pyjamas, her long dark hair was scrunched in a birds nest on one side of her head. She yawned widely.

'Yes?' she managed to say as she rubbed her eyes.

Harper took the lead. 'We are looking for Anand Sharma. Is he here?'

She yawned again. 'No. He left.' Harper looked at Gardella who raised an eyebrow.

'When did he leave?' Harper asked.

'I dunno. Saturday, Sunday?'

She looked Middle Eastern but her accent sounded much closer to home.

'Can we come in and check for ourselves?'

'Why the hell not,' she grumbled. Harper and Gardella moved past her and started searching the house.

'His room's on the left,' she called from the front door. Harper went in first.

The curtains were shut, the room dark. Harper found a light switch and flicked it on. The bed was unmade, sheets in a pile on the mattress. The closet door was open but there were no clothes inside. Several coat hangers lay scattered on the floor. A set of drawers next to the bed were open and empty. A desk in the far corner of the room contained no study notes or textbooks. A reading lamp had fallen off the desk and lay on its side next to the bed. It looked like Sharma had made a hasty exit. Harper made his way out into the hall and met Gardella as he returned from searching the rest of the house.

'Any sign?' Harper asked.

'None,' Gardella grunted.

Harper turned to the young woman who was still standing at the front door. She had finished yawning and was scratching at her tangle of hair, trying to shake off the remnants of sleep.

'Who are you?' Harper asked.

'Tabitha Nadar. Who are you?'

Harper realised they had barged in without showing any ID.

'Sorry. I'm Detective Harper. This is Detective Gardella. We're conducting an investigation and Anand may have information that could help us. We need to speak to him. Do you know where he is?'

Another scratch of the head. 'I dunno. Last time I saw him was on Saturday. I've been pulling extra shifts since Anand was stood down. Just finished a night shift. You woke me up.'

'Sorry about that, but, we need to track him down. You sure you don't know where he went?'

'Nah … oh hang on. Yeah, actually I might. He left a note.'

She moved past them, rubbing her eyes as she went. They followed her down the hall before turning into what appeared to be the living room. Afternoon sun bled through drawn curtains giving the place a tepid gloom. Tabitha picked up a white piece of paper and handed it to Harper.

Tabbi

I've had enough of sitting around home so I'm catching the midday bus to Nelson. Gonna stay with Jordon and Jules till the competency hearing.

Catcha.

'This was written by your roommate, Anand?'

'I haven't got any other roommates so, yes.'

'You have a phone number for Anand?' Harper asked. Tabitha glared up at Harper from under her brow and then shuffled off without reply. Harper assumed she was going to retrieve her cell. He passed the note to Gardella who read it and gave it back.

'Coincidence, or is this guy running?' Harper asked.

Gardella shrugged. 'Don't know yet. Let's hold judgement until we talk to him.'

Tabitha returned with her phone and Harper asked her to try calling Sharma. She did, but it went straight to answer-phone. She left a message asking him to call her back. Harper asked if she had the number for either Jordon or Jules. She did, so Harper made her phone them as well. When she got off, she said that Anand wasn't there and that neither Jordon nor Jules had spoken to him or were expecting him to visit.

'He's in the wind,' Harper said.

Gardella agreed. 'Yep. He's running.'

'You have a photo of him?' Harper asked Tabitha.

Using her phone, Tabitha flipped through several selfies she had taken with Anand. None were usable for ID purposes. Most were at parties and Anand was either wearing costumes, pulling faces or holding bottles of beer in front of his face. It seemed he was a bit of a party animal. Harper wondered if that had anything to do with his disciplinary hearing.

'Are there any other photos of him around the house?'

'Nope. That's it,' she said with a shake of her head. 'Hang on. Wait a minute. His hospital ID, would that work?'

'Yep.'

She took them into the kitchen where Harper spotted a lanyard hanging on a coat hook next to the refrigerator. On it was a picture of a man with dark skin who looked to be in his twenties. Underneath the photo, his name, employee number and barcode were displayed. Harper pulled out his cell and took a picture.

'Do you know anyone else he might crash with in Nelson?' Harper asked.

'Um, no. Just Jules and Jords. We went to med school together. They're the only friends we have in Nelson. The rest of our class ended up in Christchurch or Dunedin. A couple might have gone to Auckland.'

'His note mentioned something about a competency hearing?'

'It's like a disciplinary hearing. He's been suspended from duty until the hearing a week tomorrow. He'll probably lose his job after that.'

Harper looked around the kitchen. 'What do you want to do, Joe?'

'Let's go to the bus depot. We need to see if he made it onto the bus.'

Before they left, Harper asked Tabitha for her number, in case they had any more questions. Tabitha gave her details, and he wrote them down. He also gave her his card and told her that if Anand called back, she was not to let on the police were looking for him. She was simply to ask where he was and call Harper straight away.

The bus depot was a nondescript beige building with a masonry façade that Harper decided would come pancaking down in an earthquake. Since the Christchurch quakes he had often found himself appraising old buildings and estimating how they would perform if the ground chose to shake. What he saw in front of him looked about as sturdy as a pack of playing cards. Hanging from the façade was a wood-framed awning with a corrugated-iron roof. Behind this was the body of the building, clad in brick. Harper spied several cracks in one of the side walls. It did nothing to inspire confidence.

They went in through a sliding door which would only open halfway before it became jammed, and made their way to the ticket counter. It was a quiet afternoon and no one was seated in the waiting area. Gardella got to the counter first and dinged the bell. A stumpy little man stuck his head out of a back office.

'Sorry gents, the last bus left an hour ago.'

'We're not here to buy a ticket,' Harper said, holding out his badge.

This attracted the man's attention. He stood up and scuttled over. Reading glasses dangled from a string around his neck, his grey trousers a size too big so the cuffs crumpled over his shoes and dragged at his heels as he walked.

'Sorry? What can I do for you?'

'We are trying to find a man named Anand Sharma. We believe he may have taken a bus to Nelson. Do you keep records of who travels on your buses?'

'Oh, yes, of course. My apologies. I'm a bit hard of hearing you see. Let me bring up the manifest for, did you say, Nelson?'

'That's right, Nelson,' Harper confirmed.

'Nelson, Nelson,' he muttered as he shuffled the mouse of his computer. 'What was the name again sorry?'

'Anand Sharma.' Harper spelt it out. 'We think he was on the midday bus, but we're not sure which day.'

'That's an easy one because we have only one midday service to Nelson, and that's on a Sunday.'

He slipped on his reading glasses and tapped the information in. A second later he ran a thick finger down the screen.

'Anand Sharma, you say. I don't see any Anand Sharma on the manifest. You sure it was Sunday?'

'No, we're not sure,' Harper replied. 'Can you check Saturday, as well as Monday and Tuesday?'

'Well, we don't do a midday service on those days. Oh, and Monday there is no bus at all, but I will check for you on the other days.'

He went through each days manifest but could not see the name mentioned anywhere.

'What about Christchurch. Do you operate a Christchurch service?'

'Yes. You want me to search that too?'

'Yes please,' Harper replied.

The little man pushed his reading glasses back up his nose and typed in the new information. Once again he ran his fingers down the list. Once again, the name didn't appear. It was the same for the following two days. The only other service was a Westport to Greymouth bus. This too came up blank.

'Maybe he used a different name,' Harper suggested.

'Maybe he didn't take the bus,' Gardella offered. 'Maybe he had other transport. We still don't have the truck. He could've driven that.'

'That's a possibility. Where do you think he went?' Harper asked.

'We know he's not at the friend's place in Nelson. Let's see if he's in Christchurch. Call the roommate. See if she knows where he might be staying in Christchurch.'

'She's gonna be pissed when I wake her up again.'

'What? You afraid of her or something?'

Harper gave a thin smile and made the call. He re-woke Tabitha and found out there were three possible places Anand could be staying. He asked her to ring each one and find out if Sharma was there and call back when finished. When he finished the call, Gardella had the bus depot guy doing another search.

'What's he looking for now?' Harper asked, nodding at the man behind the counter.

'Checking to see if Jonathon Hayes left town on the bus.'

'If Hayes has done a runner, why wouldn't he use the truck? Why take the bus when you have your own set of wheels?'

'Just covering our bases I guess.'

For the next few minutes, they stood and watched the man sift through his records. Before he had finished, Harper's phone rang. He took the call, listened for a moment, then gave Gardella the thumbs up.

'Give me the address,' Harper said. As the information came he relayed it to Gardella who wrote it down. Harper thanked Tabitha and hung up.

'He was at the first place she phoned. She spoke to one of the flatmates. Sharma's in the house as we speak. You want to send a car around and pick him up?'

Gardella thought for a moment. 'No. We do that, and he refuses to come in, we're fucked. We can't even arrest him with what we have. He could just take off and we're back to square one. Did the roommate let on that the cops were looking for him?'

'No. I told her to say she was just trying to see where he was because she hadn't heard from him and was worried.'

'Good. Now, let's just think about this for a moment.' Gardella led Harper over to an empty bench seat and they sat down. 'Sharma is about to lose his job because of Hayes. He left town the day after Hayes went missing, lied about where he was going and how he would get there. Sounds to me like he's hiding something. If he knows we're coming, we could lose him. He'll be in the wind.'

Gardella pulled out his cell. After a couple of minutes of searching and scrolling, he'd found what he wanted. 'There's a flight leaving in half an hour. I need to be on that plane.'

'Need backup?' Harper asked.

'No. I want you to stay here. I need you to work things from this side. See if you can uncover anything else on Sharma.'

The airport was usually a ten-minute drive from town, but with full lights and sirens, Harper got there in less than five. Before Gardella could board, there was a standoff when ground staff discovered he was carrying a firearm. After a phone call with police HQ, Gardella was allowed to take his seat, his weapon safely stowed in the hold. The plane took off twenty minutes late.

As it climbed into a cloudless sky, Harper understood he was now on his own. He knew his partner had made the correct move in playing the percentages. They could cover more ground with two separate lines of inquiry. But it didn't make him feel any better. While Harper didn't want to admit it, Gardella had become his security blanket. Someone to lean on for advice. Someone who could step in if things turned sour.

With those years of experience now jetting off to the other side of the country, Harper would have to rely on his own gut instinct, his street smarts, his local knowledge and his powers of persuasion. There would be no one to remind him of proper procedure and no one to curb his guns-blazing attitude. Worst of all, there would be no back-up if things went wrong.

CHAPTER 11

In the car on the way back into town, Harper had time to think. He figured there was a window of twenty-four to forty-eight hours before Gardella arrested Sharma or returned empty-handed. In that time, he was the sole investigator left at ground zero. If a crime had occurred, he knew the evidence lay here. He needed to set aside everything else and focus on uncovering that evidence. By far their best suspect was Sharma. Harper needed to find out more about the junior doctor.

Before returning to the hotel Harper stopped by the Westport News and grabbed a copy of today's edition. Paperboys and girls were milling around outside, their pushbikes leaning against the building waiting for their stacks so they could begin their deliveries. The large roller-door to the press room was open so Harper walked through it into the cavernous space. There were two women to the right standing at ink-stained counters, bundles of newspapers stacked chest-high. They were inserting what looked like advertising flyers into each paper.

The bitter smell of printer's ink struck him. It came from an enormous printing press which filled a third of the space and stretched the entire length of one wall. At the end of the press room closest to the roller door there were three large reels of newsprint that resembled gigantic toilet rolls. These fed paper into six banks of ink rollers arranged one after the other in a production line. At the far end a conveyor belt carried the finished product off the press.

As Harper stood and marvelled at the scale of the contraption, an ear-splitting buzzer sounded. The machine lurched into action and newsprint began being dragged into the press. Harper noticed someone working behind one of the banks of rollers. After a handful of seconds, the press abruptly stopped. Derek Graham emerged carrying a coiled metal printing plate. He immediately spotted Harper.

'What'd you want now?' Graham said.

'No need to panic. Just a copy of today's paper,' Harper replied.

'Just grab one,' Graham said, pointing to a wooden box containing several dozen editions. The box had a coin slot but no lid. One of the charming quirks of small-town life.

'How much?' Harper asked.

'Just take one. Compliments of the Westport News.'

Harper reached in, pulled out a crisp copy, and unfolded the broadsheet.

An article on the Christchurch earthquake dominated the front page. It focused mostly on the investigation into the collapse of the CTV building where over one hundred people had lost their lives. The only other story was about a new gold mine which had recently started producing. It wasn't until he flicked to page two that he found what he was looking for.

Local Journalist Reported Missing

An investigation has been launched after the disappearance of local man, Jonathon Hayes. Family members became concerned when Mr Hayes failed to return home late on Monday evening and notified police. He was last seen drinking with friends at the Black & White hotel on Palmerston Street on the evening of Friday, March 12, where he left the bar around 10:30 p.m. His disappearance is said to be out of character and relatives are concerned for his safety. Mr Hayes, a long-serving journalist with the Westport News, is 53 years old, with two adult daughters.

Two investigators from the Christchurch CIB have been called in and are assisting Westport Police in the search. No one involved in the investigation was prepared to talk to The News; however, it is understood that Mr Hayes may be driving a white Toyota Hilux similar to the one in the photograph. Police are appealing for any sightings of the vehicle with the distinctive markings JN76 painted in blue and the registration plate BRK618. If members of the public come across this vehicle they should contact Westport Police immediately.

There was a photograph of the truck, and Harper could make out where they had added the new letters to the image. There was also a small head-and-shoulders portrait of Jonathon Hayes. That reminded Harper of something. He approached Derek Graham who was removing another plate from the press.

'Hey, Graham. I have another question.'

'What is it?'

Harper got out his phone and found the picture of Anand Sharma. 'When you were drinking with Jon on Friday night, did you see this man in the bar?'

Graham studied the image for a long time. 'I don't know. There were a lot of people in the bar that night. He could've been there, but I wasn't really looking.'

'Do you know who he is?'

'Yep. He's that punk kid who is suing us for telling the truth. I'd seen him before in the bar. He was usually drunk and shooting his mouth off. He's an arrogant little fuck.'

'Did Jon ever mention anything about this man?'

'Just that he was suing the paper, and that he had sent Jon some texts. That was about it.'

'What kind of texts?'

'Jon didn't say. He kinda brushed it off like it was no big deal. I guess you get used to that sort of thing in his line of work.'

'Were the texts of a threatening nature?'

'Like I said, I don't know. Jon didn't say. He just said the kid was sending him messages. He made it sound like it was nothing. I didn't pry.'

Harper pushed further, but Graham didn't know any more, and couldn't say for sure that the doctor had been at the bar. He phoned Gardella. His partner would still be in the air, but he would be able to leave a message summarising what Graham had just told him and suggest he check the messages on the doctor's phone.

After leaving the message, Harper went back to the hotel, unlocked the conference room, and powered on his laptop. With Gardella chasing up their most promising lead, Harper focussed on the evidence in hand. He inserted the USB stick and scrolled past the first few minutes of empty footpath and found the moment Hayes first appeared. He focused on Jonathon Hayes' body language.

He clicked play just as Hayes was fumbling with his wallet. Hayes looked to be in a hurry, almost as if he was trying not to hold up a queue. But there was no one around, no one to rush him. He was pulling at the wallet in his pocket, but something was caught. His movements looked agitated, even panicked. Not fluid and relaxed. When he eventually extracted the wallet, he flipped it open and plucked out his bank card and jammed it into the machine. Off camera he punched in his pin, using the touch-screen to tell the ATM how much he wanted.

The black and white image was low resolution. Still, it recorded every single second allowing Harper to scrutinise his subject's slightest movements. As Hayes stood and waited for his money, Harper spotted something curious. It was such a minor thing that he hadn't noticed it this morning. Even now he was not sure if he had seen it. He paused the clip and scrolled back. With the video in the correct spot, he focused in on Jonathon Hayes' upper body. Harper hit play. He saw it again! It had definitely happened. A subtle movement of the head. It was a small turn to his right that lasted a split second. Harper paused the clip. What did it mean? Was there a noise? Was there someone else there? Or was it just a nervous twitch? With no audio and a narrow field of view, it was impossible to tell.

He restarted the video and kept watching, trying to glean more information. The time-stamp began ticking, but Hayes wasn't moving at all, just standing with the money and staring straight ahead. Harper couldn't think why he would do this. This lasted several seconds until he looked up, spoke to the camera, and then turned around and exited the frame. What was he saying? Harper scrolled back and watched again, trying to work it out. He repeated the process over and over, but it was too quick. He just couldn't make it out. He gave up on the silent message. He had another idea.

He returned to the start and watched it once more from the beginning. However, this time he was not looking at Hayes, but at the left-hand side of the frame. Harper remembered all the chewing gum stuck to the payment and tried to make out any of these marks in the video. But with the reduced resolution, all he could see was uniform grey pavement stretching from the bottom left corner of the frame up to very near the top. At the top of the frame it was just possible to make out the curb and the gutter. He locked his focus on this left-hand side of the image as the footage kept rolling. It was now back to the part where Hayes was telling the machine how much he wanted to withdraw.

Just before Hayes pulled the cash out of the ATM, Harper saw it. It happened at the same time as the subtle head movement. He went back and watched it again. Had his eyes been tricking him? Had he actually seen what he thought he saw? Yes. There was something there. The pavement was a monotonous shade of grey, except for a few short seconds. Just before Hayes turned his head, a patch of the pavement darkened. It was a subtle change, barely perceptible, but it was there. A shadow. The shadow moved in and hovered for a moment before retreating out of frame. Harper sat back and considered what this meant.

He cast his mind back to the visit to the bank that morning and tried to visualise the environment around the cash machine. He remembered the streetlight a few metres from the ATM and the bar further down the footpath. From the perspective of the ATM camera, the streetlight would be off to the left, the same place where the shadow was. It could only mean one thing. Someone was on the footpath between the streetlight and the ATM.

It could be a witness. Maybe they had left the nearby bar and walked in front of the light as they crossed the road. He scrolled back and re-watched the footage. The shadow crept in like a black cloud, hovered briefly, and then retreated back in the same direction it came. It didn't fit with a passing pedestrian whose shadow would have moved in constant motion from left to right.

What else could it be? Harper could think of only one other plausible scenario. There must have been someone else with Hayes. Someone standing just out of range of the camera's field of view. That would also explain the glance. Someone had said or done something and Hayes started to turn in that direction. After he received the cash, there was that odd pause. Harper now understood what was going on. Hayes was receiving instructions. He was being told what to do. What to say to the camera. The message was not coming from Jonathon Hayes, but the person or people responsible for his disappearance. This changed everything. The message was now of crucial importance and deciphering it would be priority number one. Trouble was Harper had made no progress decoding it. He knew someone else who might have more luck.

James Vantulder was a beat cop who had lost his hearing to a viral infection a few years back. Vantulder had remained on the force but for the last five years he had worked a desk doing mundane admin jobs. In that time, he had taught himself how to lip-read and had become quite proficient. If there was anyone who could make out Hayes' words, it was Vantulder. Harper uploaded the file, added his cell number and a few other pertinent details and hit send. All there was left to do was to wait.

CHAPTER 12

It had been over an hour and there had been no reply from Vantulder. From his table the hotel restaurant Harper sent him a text before finishing off what was left of his steak.

A short drive later and he pulled up outside the house where Samara Hayes was staying. He grabbed the phone and bank records from the passenger seat and carried them with him as he crossed the street. This was an upmarket neighbourhood of old weatherboard villas with well-groomed lawns and enough nineteenth-century charm to make you sick with envy. However, it seemed the house Samara Hayes had taken refuge in hadn't got the memo and was bringing the side down.

At the front of the property a wire mesh fence was straining to hold back an overgrown garden. Ryegrass and ivy and daisy bush burst through every possible gap and sprawled across the footpath like a tangled mane of hair. Beyond the fence the vegetation was so thick the house almost completely disappeared from view. It wasn't until he began walking up the driveway that Harper had a view of a rectangular building that could have passed for an army barracks. The corrugated iron roof was in desperate need of a coat of paint and the metal gutters had rusted through leaving holes along its underside. But what really caught his eye sat parked in the driveway.

A white Toyota Corolla, late '90s. He examined the trim running along the sides of the car. There was a dull, grey plastic guard about halfway up each door, reminding him of the one the waitress described speeding past Drifters Café.

The trouble was the description was so vague. White was the most popular vehicle colour so the fact that this vehicle was also white could just be a coincidence. The waitress couldn't remember the make or model which didn't narrow things down. She also thought the car she saw was relatively new which didn't match with what he was now looking at. However, it couldn't be ruled out so before he knocked on the door, he took a photo with his phone. Harper turned around, Samara stood on the front step of the house looking at him.

'Why were you taking a picture of my car?' she asked.

Harper scrambled to think of any plausible answer that would conceal his real motive. 'Oh, well uh, this is just like the first car I owned. What year is it?'

Samara looked at the car like it was going to tell her the answer. 'It's a ninety-eight, I think.'

'Same as mine. The only difference is, mine was red. The red ones go faster you know.'

Harper immediately regretted his attempt at humour. He felt the hot flush of embarrassment and hoped it was dark enough so she wouldn't notice. He studied Samara closely. She looked much better than the last time he'd seen her, as if she'd had some much-needed sleep. The darkness under her eyes had faded and her hair was neatly styled. She stood on the doorstep and studied him with suspicion but didn't argue the point. After an uncomfortable silence she invited him inside and into a sparsely furnished kitchen.

The elderly couple who had taken Samara Hayes in introduced themselves and Harper shook their hands and immediately forgot their names. The silver-haired wife offered to make coffee but Harper had already consumed his daily quota so the couple left the kitchen and went into the next room to continue doing whatever they were doing before Harper had arrived. The volume on the television in the next room was up the theme song from Family Feud hummed a happy tune.

Samara shut the connecting door muffling the upbeat music which seemed out of place given the current circumstances. Without words, they instinctively sat around the kitchen table. Harper began to explain the latest developments in the investigation.

He chose his words carefully, glossing over the day's inquiries without going into much detail. He left out the white car that had been following them and the CCTV footage from the bank. He was still treating Samara as a potential suspect. During his recounting of events he studied her body language. Most of the time she sat slumped forward, arms folded on the table. She either looked at him or down at her hands, her eyes a cold ember from a dead fire, gazing at everything and nothing all at the same time. It was hard to tell if she heard the words or just let them wash over her like water. It took him less than ten minutes to sum up and when he had finished, he asked if she had any questions.

'It's not looking good, is it?' she finally said in a voice scarcely audible.

'It's early days, and we still hold out hope he will be found,' Harper said.

The words didn't seem to make any difference. Her sadness seemed genuine. She sat quietly offering nothing by way of a reply.

'I have a few more questions if you don't mind?' Harper eventually said.

'Okay.'

'Did you notice Jon's computer anywhere around the house when you came home on Monday?'

'No. I haven't seen it. He normally doesn't bring it home. It should be at the office.'

'If he does bring it home, where would he normally leave it?'

'In the kitchen. Jon usually works at the kitchen table. I'm sure it wasn't there when I got home. The only other place is the study. I didn't see it in there either.'

Cheering erupted from the TV in the other room.

'Okay then. Can I get you to have a look through Jon's phone and bank records and see if you spot anything unusual?'

She nodded. Harper pushed the documents across the table until they were in front of her. The babel from the TV had subsided and all Harper could hear was the whine of the refrigerator in the corner.

Starting with the top sheet she methodically scanned each line, her eyes darting left and right as she read. After a minute, she moved on to the following page and repeated the process. Occasionally, a lock of blonde hair would fall in front of her face, but as naturally as taking a breath, she would bring a hand up and tuck the offending strands behind her ear. Harper gazed at her from across the table. Her sad beauty was captivating. If she was putting on an act, it was a convincing one. As she was going through the last page of bank records, he prepared to broach his next set of questions.

'This last one looks a bit odd,' she said stabbing an unpolished fingernail at the final withdrawal. 'Jon never takes out that much money. Why would he do that?'

'At this stage, I don't know,' Harper lied. 'Now, just before you get to the phone records, there was something else I am curious about. When you went to Karamea on Friday afternoon, did you go straight to your studio or did you go to the shops or the supermarket, or anything like that?'

'No. I bought milk and bread and a few other things from home. When I got to Karamea I did go to the local bar for dinner. I couldn't be bothered cooking for myself after the drive.'

'Did you speak to anyone at the bar?'

'Well, I had to order my meal, so, yes. I spoke to the barman and the waitress,' she said.

'When did you last fill up your car with gas?'

Her eyes narrowed. 'What's that got to do with anything?'

'Just trying to fill in a few blanks.'

Samara glared, her eyes darker than ever. 'Um, I think it was on Thursday. Jon gets paid on Thursday, so I think I filled it up then.'

'Did you keep the receipt?'

'I don't know. Maybe. If I did it will be in the car. Otherwise, I probably threw it out.'

'Do you mind if I take a look?'

'I guess that would be fine,' she said. 'But I don't understand what this is all about.'

'Just routine procedure, that's all. While I'm outside,' Harper said as he rose to his feet, 'can you go through the phone records and circle the numbers you recognise and name them if possible?'

Harper made his way towards the door. Just as he was about to head outside, he asked for the keys.

Samara frowned like she was one step away from changing her mind. 'On the hook by the door. I'm still not sure what my car has to do with this?'

Harper snatched the keys and was out the door before she could say another word.

He'd formed a theory. Samara could have driven to Karamea to provide herself with an alibi, making sure someone saw her so she would have a corroborating witness placing her in the township. This would allow her to drive home in the middle of the night, murder her husband, dispose of the body and return to Karamea for the rest of the weekend. On Monday, she would return to Westport as though nothing had happened and report her husband missing.

At this stage, it was just a theory, with no concrete supporting evidence. But a fuel receipt could help. Karamea was a ninety-minute drive up the coast. Samara said she had filled the car five days ago. Factoring in a three-hour return trip to Karamea, and allowing for a bit of running around town in between, should leave around half a tank of fuel. If, however, she made an extra round trip, six hours of driving, her tank would almost be empty. He needed to find that receipt.

Harper made his way to the driver's door, unlocked the car and carefully lowered himself into the right-hand seat. Almost immediately he was struck by the wet smell of dank carpet. He looked around for the source but it was too dark and the sun had set hours ago. There was nothing to illuminate the inside of the car. He flicked the switch for the overhead light. A feeble yellow glow permeated the black dinge.

He had a torch in the patrol car. He climbed out and started to jog down the driveway until the pain in his knee reminded him to walk. He crossed the road, retrieved the torch from the driver's side door pocket, and brought it back to the Toyota. He climbed back into the driver's seat and flicked it on.

Samara may have been tidy when it came to making beds but this apparently did not extend to her car. The cabin was littered with plastic bags, bits of paper, a takeaway coffee cup, two empty water bottles, candy wrappers and various other scraps of rubbish. There was also a strong whiff of paint or solvents mixed in with the stale cabin air. He guessed the car was often used for transporting her artworks. He put the key in the ignition, turned it to the three-quarter position, and watched the fuel needle.

It stirred a fraction, then rested on the empty symbol. Harper's heart rate kicked up a notch. Then the needle crept up the dial, eventually settling just over half a tank. He studied it for a minute as if expecting it to make another adjustment, but it moved no more. Satisfied the gauge had reached its equilibrium he began to scratch around the assorted debris looking for anything that resembled a fuel receipt.

There were plenty of bits of paper to choose from. They were mostly scattered in the footwell on the passenger side but Harper figured a receipt might get slightly better treatment. He focused his search in the centre console just forward of the gear lever. He reached in and pulled out three scraps of paper.

The first was a Post-It note. It appeared to be a hand-written shopping list with about a dozen items. He read through each entry. Mostly food and household expendables. No bleach or carpet cleaner or rubbish bags or zip-ties or duct-tap or anything else to suggest a crime scene had been sanitized or evidence had been disposed of. The next scrap of paper was a prescription for a medicine that Harper thought he recognised as a common anti-depressant. It had today's date on it. He wondered if she had just started taking the drug or had simply renewed a long-term prescription. He found what he was looking for with the third piece of paper. A fuel docket. The date was five days ago. The Thursday, just as Samara had said.

Harper sat for a moment, hands on the wheel, thinking things over. On the surface, it seemed like Samara was telling the truth. One trip up, one trip back, just under half a tank of fuel used. Perfectly normal fuel consumption for a thirteen-year-old car. It indicated she only made one return trip. Unless ... she filled up again.

Harper was now searching for a second receipt. Three minutes later he had located not one, but two fuel dockets amongst the debris in the passenger footwell. He used his torch to study the dates. They didn't fit. One was dated two weeks before Jonathon Hayes' disappearance, the other, four weeks. Harper considered the possibility that she had thrown out a third receipt to hide the extra top-up. The only way to know for sure was to look at her bank statement.

Before he went back inside, he took the opportunity to look through the back seat and boot. There was more rubbish, along with some painting supplies and a bucket, but nothing that raised suspicion.

He stowed the torch in the pocket of his windbreaker and went back into the house. Inside, he found Samara sitting in the same spot he had left her, hands clasped, hollow stare, barely aware that he had come back into the room. The refrigerator shuddered then died, a soft hush filled the void. It seemed to snap Samara from her trance.

She looked up and said, 'I have done the best I can with these. Most of the phone numbers are either the shop, home, or Jon's friends. I've named the ones I recognise. There are a few random numbers that I don't know,' she said as she slid the stack of papers towards him.

'Thank you, Mrs Hayes. Now, one last thing. I am going to need to see a copy of your bank records.'

All at once her sad demeanour dissolved, replaced with annoyance flecked with anger. It was clear what her answer would be.

'I don't think I'm prepared to give you that.' Her indignation suggestive of Harper asking for something much more private than bank records. 'I think I have provided you with enough personal information. I don't see how my bank details will help find Jon.'

'You understand I could just get a warrant, but that will slow me down and divert my efforts from finding your husband,' Harper said.

'Then forget about the bank records. I don't understand what they have to do with anything. You should be out there trying to find Jon.'

'That's exactly what I'm doing. However, if I'm going to do my job properly, I need to look at all possible scenarios. In cases like this, that means looking at family members, as well as friends and acquaintances.'

'What? Are you saying I've got something to do with this? I'm the one who reported him missing. I have answered every question you have asked me. I've done everything I can to help. Now you are saying I am a suspect?'

She was yelling. The door to the adjoining room opened. A man poked his head in to see what the commotion was all about.

'Everything all right in here Sam?'

'It's fine, Sean. The detective was just leaving.'

As Harper walked down the driveway he did his best to shake off the guilt that burned under his collar. The way he had handled the interview had lacked tact. He had been too abrupt, virtually telling Samara that she was a suspect in her husband's disappearance. Not exactly the best way to build trust and foster cooperation. In frustration he kicked out at a loose stone, missed, and strained his knee again. He gave a muffled curse through gritted teeth and wondered when his luck was going to change.

Harper reached the end of the driveway and checked for traffic before he crossed the road. The temperature had dropped and a veil of fog hung thick from the rooftops like a dull Sunday morning hangover. Harper listened for the sound of an oncoming vehicle but heard only the murmur of the night air amongst the trees.

It was then he spotted something that made his blood run cold. In the distance, barely visible in the mist, stood the silhouette of a man. Harper fumbled for the torch but by the time he had retrieved it, the figure was gone. He swept the beam across the deserted street but couldn't find it again.

Without thinking, Harper dashed across the road and leapt into the car. Headlights on full, he gunned the engine and launched towards the spot where he had last seen the figure. Seconds later, he arrived and pulled to the curb. He abandoned the vehicle and continued on foot.

The beam of his torch cut the mist like an air-raid searchlight catching a billion pinprick diamonds of moisture floating in the black syrup of the night. The fog was like soup and visibility had shortened to just a few metres. To his right a row of public school classrooms fronted by a low fence and a strip of neatly clipped grass. Nowhere to hide there. Across the road there was a residential property with a macrocarpa hedge about as impenetrable as the Berlin Wall if not for the gate size hole cut halfway along its length.

His knee throbbing, Harper jogged across the street and stood at the metal gate. Between the bars he could just make out a Victorian-era villa set well back from the street, its lights off and no signs of life. He reached for the gate and pulled. It rattled, but would not give, a heavy-duty padlock securing it shut. He shone a light through the bars. The fog seemed heavier beyond the gate as if it was being generated by something from within the grounds. He could make out dark forms of trees and the outline of a bench as well as a winding path and several crouching shrubs. If there was someone on the other side, they were out of reach.

Continuing down the street he passed villas and cottages and grand colonials dressed in brick and stone and whitewashed weatherboard and in all these places he found no apparent indicators of recent human activity. As he crept forward a two-storey dwelling made of marbled-white stone loomed large from the fog. It seemed to hover in the mist like an image from a vintage movie projector and it looked old enough to predate the surrounding homes by about one hundred years. Harper stopped and held his breath and just listened. Not a sound. But he sensed someone was near, watching, using the night and the mist for cover.

He did a slow three-sixty. Looking, listening, sniffing at the air. Nothing. Inching forward once more, a parked car began to materialize up ahead. It had two wheels up on the footpath like someone had pulled over in a panic. He approached it, keeping close to a squat brick retaining wall for cover. He directed his beam through the passenger windows illuminating greasy pizza boxes, a pile of newspapers, a takeaway coffee cup, but nothing else.

Without warning a sound as cold and black as his worst nightmare filled the darkness. Laughter. Harper froze. It was close. The laughter grew deeper, rippling through the air like evil tremors. It seemed to be coming from all around as if emanating from the fog itself. Harper whipped the beam of his torch in all directions trying to get a bearing on the source. Before he could get a fix, the noise stopped.

As quickly as the laughter had begun it was gone, drifting off into the night like the fading memory of a dream. Harper stood motionless, heart racing, eyes wide. It was no dream. It was a message and he had received it loud and clear.

CHAPTER 13

Sleep would not come to Harper that night. He stayed awake thinking about who he had seen and readied his defences in case they returned. At times he paced the room, occasionally glancing out the window, but mostly he just sat on the bed, Glock within easy reach, the safety off and a round chambered. At one point he thought he heard footsteps outside and went to investigate but found nothing. Probably just his imagination. Trouble was the events of the previous night were all too real. There was someone out there stalking him. Someone with a grudge. Someone who meant him harm and he had a pretty good idea who it could be.

When Harper pulled the trigger on Bozo that night in his foster parent's house it had rid the world of one bad guy, but it didn't end the matter. The subsequent police investigation exposed the gang who sent Bozo. This resulted in police raids of several properties which uncovered drugs, weapons, and a cache of stolen goods. Five people went to prison for various terms of incarceration.

Fourteen years later and they were all back on the street, angry and seeking vengeance. Harper had become accustomed to looking over his shoulder knowing that one day someone would come after him. Being back in Westport made that threat all the more real. He was on his own, with no backup. But that was something he was used to. He was a fighter. He wasn't going to back down. If they dared to cross him, he would take them down. He was not afraid, but he would need to be on guard.

By 6:00 a.m. he felt confident the danger had passed. Any move against him would be made under cover of darkness and not when hotel guests were emerging for their morning runs or popping out for the paper. His mind turned back to the case.

He phoned Gardella. His partner answered after eight rings.

'What's up?' Gardella said with a yawn.

'Nothing. Thought you might need a wake-up call.'

'Piss off Dylan. What do you really want?'

'How'd you get on with the doc yesterday?' Harper asked. 'You talk to him yet?'

'Not yet,' Gardella managed to say through another yawn. 'At the moment he doesn't know we're on to him. We'll drag his arse downtown and interview him today. I'm just waiting on the warrants for his phone. Once we get those, we'll bring him in and see what he has to say for himself. What about you? What's happening in Hicksville?'

Harper laughed. He liked this new side to Gardella. The humour also helped to ease some of the tension from last night.

'I updated the wife. Asked her the A question. She says the barman at the Karamea Hotel saw her Friday night. After that she was alone in her studio. Gives her a window where she could have driven to Westport, knocked him off, and returned to the studio. The problem is, I found a fuel receipt that says she filled up on Thursday, and her tank is still half full. I don't think she could've made two round trips and only used half a tank.'

'Maybe she did make the two trips but only put in half a tank after because money is tight.'

'That's what I'm thinking,' Harper said. 'Problem is, she wouldn't cough up the bank records. We'll need a warrant.'

'Canvass the local service stations, see if anyone remembers her coming in after Thursday. If we can catch her in a lie it'll help grease the wheels with the judge. I don't want a repeat of what happened with the warrant for the texts. Also, go talk to the neighbours, see if they noticed any activity at the house over the weekend. You got anything else?'

'Yeah. I think there might have been someone else with Hayes at the ATM. There's a shadow on the edge of the frame. It distracted Hayes, he turned towards it.'

'Sounds interesting. Send me a copy. I'll let you know what I think.'

'Also, I've sent a copy to James Vantulder to see if he can work out what Hayes is saying.'

'Vantulder?'

'The constable who lost his hearing after that viral thing. He reads lips.'

Gardella was silent for a moment. 'Nope. Doesn't ring a bell.'

'Anyway, he's got it and I'm expecting an answer today. I'll let you know.'

'Good. Anything else?'

Harper paused. He prodded at his Glock on the bedside table, trying to decide if he should tell Gardella about last night. It didn't take long to make up his mind. 'Nope, that's it.'

'Right, stay in touch.'

'Roger that.'

After breakfast, Harper went back to the conference room. He sat for a moment and thought about his decision not to inform his partner about the unwanted attention he had attracted. It had been a spur of the moment call but he decided it had been the right move.

Gardella would have been duty-bound to pass the info higher up the chain and Harper knew what that would mean: someone would get cold feet and pull him off the case. Even if by some miracle they let him continue, it would likely require backup from Greymouth and Harper didn't fancy being babysat by the boys from down the coast. There were already plenty of people who thought he had received a comfortable ride into a detective seat. Running back to Christchurch or hiding behind an armed guard wasn't going to change that perception. He would need to handle this himself. Time to get to work.

Harper opened his emails and composed a message to Gardella, attaching a copy of the video. He wrote a brief description of what to look out for and then hit send. He grabbed his car keys and headed out.

His cruiser was parked between two other vehicles but as he approached, something about it didn't seem right. The car was sitting low like it was parked in a small hollow. As he got closer he realised what was wrong. All four tyres had been slashed. Harper kicked the flat rubber and swore to himself. There was a service station at the end of the block so he arranged a tow and a new set of wheels. He spoke to the forecourt attendants but none could recall seeing Samara Hayes.

From the service station Harper walked the short distance back to Palmerston Street and a takeaway coffee stand he had noticed the previous day. It was a small building next to the Westport News with a window that opened to the footpath. The rising sun was still beneath the mountains and its spreading glow burned orange and red against the fingers of cloud that stretched across the morning sky. The air was cool and tasted of wet asphalt and this had a rejuvenating effect that helped take the edge off his lack of sleep.

Most of the businesses on Palmerston Street were yet to open. Still, the lights were on in the supermarket across the road and a handful of cars populated the adjoining lot. A vehicle crawled by. Harper watched the driver's face for any tell-tale signs but saw nothing that aroused suspicion.

Satisfied he was not being watched he turned to the coffee stand and ordered one espresso with extra sugar. After two mouthfuls the caffeine hit his bloodstream and he was ready for work.

Flush with energy and minus his car Harper walked down to the Black & White and spoke to the barman who was on duty Friday night. He remembered seeing Jonathon Hayes and Derek Graham drinking together. Harper showed him a picture of Anand Sharma. The barman looked at the photo for a long while before concluding that Sharma was in the bar the same night Hayes went missing. Harper texted

Gardella to relay the new information then trudged back to the garage to collect his freshly shod Holden.

By now the effects of the caffeine were wearing off and a dull headache began to take over. His mood deteriorated further when none of the other service stations remembered seeing Samara Hayes or her white Toyota. He drove to the Hayes residence to ask the neighbours if they had seen or heard anything unusual. The neighbour with the best view had been away all weekend and knew nothing. Harper tried the house on the other side but there was no one home. He had slightly more luck across the street. A woman who lived directly opposite said she was woken before dawn on Saturday morning by a thump and the sound of a vehicle. She assumed it was a rubbish truck and went back to sleep, only realising later that it was the weekend and there was no rubbish service. Unfortunately she never took a look outside or heard anything else. Harper canvased a few more houses but none of the occupants had any significant information to add.

Finally, he drove north up the coast to Granity to see if the waitress recognised the photo he had taken of Samara's white Toyota. She said that it was similar to the car she had seen, but it flew by so fast that she couldn't be sure if it was the same one.

As he left Drifters Café, Harper glanced to the west. Over the ocean, towards the horizon, clouds bubbled up in a long, ominous line. They were black clouds, fat with rain and full of menace. Harper stood at the door of his car and looked at the approaching mass. He had an hour, two at the most, before they arrived. He climbed back into the car and began the return trip to Westport.

Not knowing what else to do he headed back to the police station and completed the paperwork for the continuity report. He had amassed several documents and a video recording that needed to be secured and recorded. If it were later determined that a crime had been committed, then these items would become evidence. If they weren't appropriately handled now the documents could be picked apart by the defence and even ruled inadmissible.

When Harper arrived Monty was once again working the watch-desk and he waved Harper through the open door without even a good morning. As he went past, Monty handed him a wad of notes. Harper carried the slips of paper out into the corridor and collided with Snowden.

'Watch where you're going,' Snowden growled.

Harper turned to let the Senior Sergeant by. 'Would you like a progress report?' he said to Snowden's back.

'No,' Snowden snapped, disappearing into a room farther along the corridor. Harper shook his head, moved into the meeting room and placed the slips on the desk.

He looked at the top note and immediately recognised what it was; a phone-in tip from the public; a sighting of the truck. The story had run in last night's paper and it looked like it had paid dividends. A pang of excitement began to build as he took the stack into the meeting room. He sat at the empty table and started sorting through the tips, but as he flicked through the pile, frustration replaced hope. Natasha Knight had been correct. The public had phoned in every sighting of a white truck, regardless of whether it matched the description.

Harper immediately ruled out seven of the thirteen tips because the callers had either described the truck as being plain white with no writing or had described an entirely different make and model. Of the six remaining sightings, one occurred at the supermarket, two saw a white truck driving down the main street, and the other three happened on the road heading out to the mine. None of the callers could specifically recall seeing JN76 on the side, or the correct licence plate number. Harper doubted that Jonathon Hayes or his truck were making trips to pick up groceries, or driving in plain sight around town. To be absolutely sure, he phoned the six tipsters and spoke to them individually. It took thirty minutes, but after the last call he was able to rule them all out.

The calls had chewed up precious time so he wasted no more completing the receipt records and entering summary notes into the NIA database. Technically he was not required to do this as no crime had yet been identified. But after watching the CCTV footage he had a gut feeling it was just a matter of time.

After another hour and twenty minutes all the paperwork was done. Harper was leaning back in his chair with his arms stretched above his head when his cell started to buzz. He pulled it out, expecting to see Vantulder or Gardella's name, but the number on the caller ID was one that he didn't recognise.

'Harper,' he said as he took the call.

'Good morning detective. It's Mike Sullivan.'

It took Harper a moment to place the name. 'From the bank, right?'

'Yes,' Sullivan said.

Harper left a gap, expecting the bank manager to fill it with the reason for his call. Sullivan didn't bite. 'Do you have something for me, Mr Sullivan?'

More dead air. Harper could make out faint noises in the background but couldn't tell what they were. He was about to say something when Sullivan finally responded. 'I think I might have something.'

'And what might that be?'

'It's probably better you come in and take a look for yourself. I'd rather not discuss it over the phone.'

Harper leant forward and put an elbow on the desk. He ran his fingers through his hair and let out a tired sigh. 'What's so important that you can't tell me over the phone?' More silence. 'Look, Mr Sulliv—'

'I think you'll want to see this ... I think it might help.'

Harper took his hand from his head and placed it flat on the table. The monotony of the last ninety minutes had drained his reserves. He didn't need this. It was probably another time waster, just like the phone-in tips. But he had nothing else on the go. Nothing to lose.

'All right, I'll be there in ten.'

When Harper walked through the bank's automatic doors he was greeted by a young woman with a funeral smile and a monochrome voice.

'Come with me,' she droned.

She escorted him down the same corridor as the previous day. The meeting room was empty this morning and all the chairs were neatly tucked in against the boardroom table. The woman knocked curtly at Sullivan's door but didn't wait for a response before leading Harper into the office. Mike Sullivan sat behind his desk wearing another expensive suit worth several months of Harper's salary. Sullivan made no effort to get up or shake hands. Instead, he sat as rigid as a corpse, inspecting Harper as if sizing him up for a mortgage. Several seconds of awkward silence passed before Sullivan spoke.

'Thank you, Sian. Close the door on your way out,' he said.

Harper took a seat. The door snapped closed. More uncomfortable silence.

A leather-bound document holder lay on the desk. Sullivan had both hands resting heavily on it as if he was afraid someone might snatch it from him. The fingers of one hand began slowly drumming the leather. There seemed to be much to consider because Sullivan just sat there, staring, and drumming, and clenching his jaw like it somehow helped with the decision making process.

'So,' Harper said, glancing at his watch 'What's in the folder?'

The question broke Sullivan's trance. The drumming stopped. He looked down as if reacquainting himself with what lay beneath his hands. When his eyes came back up it was clear a decision had been reached.

'I have something I think you need to see,' Sullivan said, taking his time with each word.

'Well, let's have it then,' Harper said, suppressing a yawn while sounding less than impressed.

Sullivan hesitated. 'The issue is … it's… it's something I probably shouldn't be showing you.'

Harper nodded. 'I understand. Show me what you have and I'll decide if it's relevant. If it is, I'll get the appropriate paperwork to make this all legit. If it's nothing, I'll forget this meeting ever happened.'

Sullivan's eyes remained locked on Harper for a long time before he finally pushed the document holder across the table.

'Nothing leaves this room?' Sullivan asked.

Harper nodded.

'Okay, then' Sullivan continued. 'After you and the other detective left, I did a bit of snooping. I know I shouldn't have, but I was curious, I've never had this sort of thing happen before.'

'And you found something?'

'At first, no. I went through Mr Hayes' cheque account again and it all looked to be pretty standard. I mean the big withdrawal was odd, but you already know about that. Anyway, I was about to give up and just leave it at that when …' Sullivan paused. 'I noticed he had a link on his account.'

Harper raised an eyebrow. 'A link?'

'A link is an indicator that there is another account attached. It normally means the customer has set up a hidden or secret account. We get them from time to time. The husband or the wife comes in and wants to have a secondary account that only they know about. It is typically used when one or the other partner wants to hide assets during a divorce. It doesn't show up in printed statements for obvious reasons. The bank will set up the account and issue a bank card, but we don't send out a statement. The catch is, to have a hidden account, the customer must already have another account with the bank. We say they are linked. So, when I was going through his account, I saw the link. It's like a flag. I clicked on it. It came up with that,' Sullivan said, pointing to the folder.

Harper felt a small jolt of excitement. He opened the leather holder. Inside were two sheets held in place at the corners by elastic. He flipped the elastic back and removed the paper.

At first glance, the information looked similar to the bank records he had obtained the previous day, merely a series of non-descript transactions. But as he looked closer, he picked up on some interesting anomalies. The first was the name of the account, Westside Art and Craft. Harper guessed it was the name of Samara's business.

However, the first page of transactions wasn't what he would have expected from a small art and craft retailer. Instead, they looked more typical of a married man who was having an affair. There were motels, restaurants, jewellers, florists, and then more motels.

After finishing the first sheet, Harper's initial burst of excitement had dissolved. This was old news. Sullivan thought he was helping and wouldn't have known Harper already had this information. He frowned and turned to the next page. More of the same transactions. The same motel, more alcohol, flowers, the odd restaurant meal. Then the spending abruptly stopped. No more motels or lavish gifts. It seemed Hayes had told his wife the truth about the affair being over. But that wasn't what reignited Harper's interest. It was the three transactions that followed.

Three cash deposits, increasing in size over a period of five weeks. The first was eight thousand dollars on February 15. Two weeks later on March 1, another deposit, this time for twelve thousand dollars. The last and largest came ten days ago on March 28, amounting to eighteen thousand dollars. Harper let out a whistle as he read the numbers. This put things into a whole new light.

CHAPTER 14

Harper left the bank just as the clouds opened. Back in the car the rain was so heavy that Harper never heard his phone chirp through the clatter. It was only the vibration that alerted him to the incoming message. It was a text from Vantulder.

Saw the vid. I think he says
"I'm okay but need to leave town for a while."
Hope this helps. Vantulder.

Harper read the words while replaying the video in his head. It fit. He knew it fit. Hayes was leaving a message telling everyone he was okay. What didn't make sense was the use of an ATM camera. Why not use a phone, leave a message, send a text, or even leave a note?

He picked up his phone and dialled Gardella's number but went straight to the answering service. He left a brief message asking for a warrant for Jonathon Hayes' secret bank account. He hung up and started the car.

It seemed the faster he drove, the more the rain obscured the windscreen. Even with the wipers on their highest setting he found it difficult to see the road. Off in the hills he thought he heard the rumble of thunder, but it was hard to tell over the noise of the rain. The drive to Granity took twice as long as usual but he somehow made it without running off the road. Harper pulled up outside Derek Graham's house and sat in the car. The lights were on inside the cottage and he supposed Graham was getting ready for work. For ten minutes he waited for a break in the weather and during this time he fine-tuned his plan of attack.

The colour of the sky soon eased from charcoal-black to leaden-grey and the sheets of rain tapered to a steady shower. Harper used the lull to dash across the road, taking shelter under the veranda. Graham opened the door and groaned and turned and walked away and Harper followed without invitation along the dark hall to the kitchen. Graham made his way across the cracked linoleum floor and leaned against the counter and filled a cracked glass with grey water from the tap.

In the kitchen there was a rhythmic tapping like the ticking of a grandfather clock and Harper noticed a bucket catching water from a leak in the ceiling. A damp funk infected the air and mould blackened the walls and Harper's skin crawled and his fingers twitched. He scowled and shuffled away from the door and any other surface that could possibly infect him with a nasty illness.

'When I spoke to you yesterday,' Harper said. 'You left something out.'

'Yeah, and what might that be?'

'You forgot to tell me what Jonathon Hayes gets up to in his spare time.'

'I'm not sure what you're talking about,' Graham said.

Harper's phone buzzed. He retrieved it from his pocket and killed the call. The tapping of water continued. Outside the weather seemed to be getting worse. Harper stared on and said nothing. He waited for Graham to fill the void. It didn't take long.

'C'mon man, what do I look like, the guy's mother? I haven't a clue how he fills in the days.' Graham shook his head as if trying to convince himself it was true.

Harper kept probing. 'You might not be blood brothers but from what I hear, you two are pretty tight. Some might say, best friends. You work together, share a drink every Friday, he even stops by your house on the weekends. I think you know exactly how he occupies his time.'

'Yeah, we're friends, so what. It doesn't mean I know what the dude has for breakfast.'

Harper clenched his teeth, his jaw muscles flared. Fatigue threatened to erode his cool exterior. He took a measured breath. Calm restored, he tried a different approach.

'Okay then, how about I jog your memory,' Harper began, voice low, posture casual like he was just shooting the breeze. 'Your buddy's hours get cut, his wife's business is in the toilet, and his mortgage is killing him. So he takes a part-time job to help pay the bills. Except, it isn't enough, not when he's entertaining another woman on the side. He needs more cash. It's then Hayes spots an opportunity. He's friends with you, a convicted drug user and small-time dealer. He knows you're connected. He talks you into hooking him up with a supplier. From there Hayes sets up a deal where he brings drugs in from Christchurch or Nelson or wherever the hell the shit is getting made, and on sells to the dealers. But there's a problem. Hayes is an amateur.

He gets greedy. He jacks up the price. The dealers realise they're getting ripped off and decide to cut Hayes out of the equation. Hayes threatens them, tells them he'll go to the cops. But that doesn't scare these guys. They dial up the pressure. They make plans to get rid of him.

'But Jon gets wind of it and gets out of Dodge before the shit goes down. We've got him on an ATM camera withdrawing all his funds and saying he needs to get out of town for a while. Your friend is in a lot of trouble, Mr Graham. You need to start cooperating. I need to know who he was dealing with, and I need to know right now.'

Derek Graham stood, eyes wide in stunned silence. Harper couldn't tell whether he'd hit the nail on the head, or was way off.

Graham began to shake his head. 'I think you're the one on drugs, man. Sure, we share the odd joint. Fuck, maybe Jon's on heavier stuff too, anything's possible I guess. But he's no middleman in some drug supply chain. Not as far's I know.'

It was now Harper's turn to cast a disbelieving eye. 'You know what, I'll be the judge of that. All I want from you is the name of your supplier. You don't want to tell me. That's fine. I'll just haul your arse down to the station and book you for possession. Going by your record, you're about due for a stint behind bars.'

'Settle down man,' Graham said, voice agitated, hands waving away the mere suggestion of prison. 'I don't want any trouble. It just that, well, you're putting me in a real tight spot here. These guys, if they find out I narked, my arse is grass, man.'

'That's a pretty big if. Here's a guarantee. Don't talk and you'll be going to prison. Probably lose your job. You need to weigh up those options, work out which one gives you the best odds.'

Graham glanced out the kitchen window. Outside, the rain had regained strength, javelining down at forty-five degrees, each impact like a hammer blow against the tin roof. The house creaked under the assault. A single light bulb swayed. The dripping intensified. Harper imagined this was what it felt like to be inside the hold of an old wooden sailing ship during a storm.

'Okay man, you win. I'll tell. But you've gotta keep me out of it. You and me, we never had this little talk.'

'What talk?' Harper said with a thin smile. His phone began to buzz. Once again he sent the call to voicemail.

'Okay, well, you know Nine Mile Road?' Graham asked.

'Yeah, I know it.'

'There's this guy who has a farm out there. He's got a bit of land, but that's not his bread and butter if you know what I mean. That's where he operates from. He does house calls so not to draw too much attention. But that's where he lives. It's real quiet, no nosey neighbours, just lots of trees and fields and shit.'

Harper waited, expecting more, but Graham shoved his hands in his pockets like that's all he had.

'You're going to need to be a bit more specific. I can't just go up to the first house with a field, some trees and a few cows, and start asking questions, can I?'

'Hey man, relax. I'm getting there,' Graham said, plucking at his clothing like something was crawling under his skin. 'Go down Nine Mile Road, the first part is sealed, then it changes to gravel. So you keep going, it crosses the railway line and goes on for about another K. Then, the road bends to the right and crosses back over the tracks. His house is just a few hundred feet past that. It's a right turn off Nine Mile Road. There's a pond in the front yard. He lives in there.'

'You got a name for this guy?

'Quentin Jarvis, a.k.a., Dozer.'

Harper wrote the details down. He asked a few more questions just for background. Before Harper left, Derek Graham made him promise again that he would not reveal his identity. Harper made all the right noises and Graham had to take him at his word. He ran back across the road, getting another soaking, and dived into the car.

The story he had just spun was all speculation, a textbook police tactic designed to convince the suspect that the cops knew more than they actually did. Occasionally you got lucky and hit the nail on the head and the suspect would release the game was up and come clean. But more often than not, the person would take issue with the police version of events. They would come out and say, 'That's not what happened,' and provide an alternative theory. By studying their reactions a good investigator could pick up which bits were true and which weren't. Graham had seemed genuinely surprised which made Harper think he didn't know about Hayes and drugs.

As he sat in the car Harper tried to work out how it could be that Graham would not know. Perhaps Hayes never told him. Hayes probably figured telling Graham was too much of a risk; the fewer people who knew the better. Besides, there was definitely someone else at the ATM that night and now he had a name of someone who might know something about that.

Harper was still parked across the road when he noticed Graham coming down the front steps of his house. Graham hurried through the rain to the driver-side door and climbed into his road-weary Ford. Harper watched as it backed out of the flooded driveway and drove off in the direction of town.

He thought about following him, but when he looked at his watch, he saw it was nearly midday. The rain was still torrential. It would take Graham at least half an hour to make it to Westport. He wouldn't have time to do anything other than be late for work.

Harper remembered the two missed calls. He checked his phone. Each call had come from Gardella. Rather than check his messages, he called back. The phone had barely rung once when his partner picked up.

'Where the hell have you been?' Gardella said.

'Nice to talk to you too.'

'Whatever. Look, listen up. This guy Sharma. We got his phone records. You were right. He's been sending texts to Hayes. Get this. There's this one where he threatens to kill him.'

'You're shitting me?'

'No, straight up. Also, he admits to being in the bar that night. That was good work on your part. I told him we had a witness placing him there and he had to come clean. Then I ask him about the note. I say

"How come the note says you're going to Nelson and yet here you are in Christchurch?" After that, he gets all defensive and lawyers up. He's not talking.'

'You thinking Sharma killed Hayes and used the truck to skip town?'

'You got it. I'm picking we find the truck here in Christchurch. Anyway, we've got enough evidence to send an ESR team out. They're driving over as we speak. They should get there by three. I want you to get the roommate out of the house until forensics clear it.'

'She's going to love us, Joe.'

'I couldn't give a shit what she thinks. Just get her out. I don't want her in there screwing up any trace.'

'You watch the video again?' Harper asked. 'What do you think about the shadow?'

'Yeah, I saw it. There's someone there all right. I'll bet you it's Sharma.'

'You think he's capable?'

'He's our best bet so far. Unless you have someone better?'

Harper spent the next five minutes explaining what Vantulder had come up with and discussing what it meant. Gardella said that he thought Sharma could have manipulated Hayes to throw the cops off the scent and divert attention. Harper then walked his partner through the drug connection, the hidden bank account and Quentin Jarvis. Gardella said he thought it was unlikely that someone like Hayes would get involved in that kind of thing.

'So, you never got the warrant for the hidden account?' Harper finally asked.

'No. Didn't know what it was about so never wrote it up. I think we focus on the doctor. Number one priority is securing the house. Let the ESR geeks do their work and see what we get.'

Harper managed to disguise his annoyance as the call wound up. True to his reputation, Gardella had made up his mind and was shutting himself off from other options. Sharma might be strengthening as a suspect but Harper still wasn't convinced. He needed to do more digging.

CHAPTER 15

After a forty-minute drive Harper was back on the main street of Westport. He pulled in at Gibby's Café and ordered a mince and cheese pie with Coke and took his lunch to the car to avoid running into anyone.

Palmerston Street was more subdued than usual. Only those with good reason had ventured out to brave the conditions. At the end of the block an Asian family peered skyward from under a street-side awning searching for a break in the weather only to be rewarded with a face full of rain. They pulled their jacket hoods tighter and sought refuge deeper under the shelter.

A trickle of pedestrians negotiated the footpath making the best use of cover provided by the canopies. At the curb rainwater spewed from the open mouths of downpipes into roadside gutters that were barely coping.

This lack of activity suited Harper just fine. It made it easier to spot anyone who might be watching. Eliminating the pedestrians one by one he turned his attention to the dozen or so vehicles parked within two blocks of his position. He scanned each one carefully. After several minutes he felt confident none of them looked suspicious. He spent another twenty minutes eating his pie and watching vehicles drive along the street, making a mental note of each so that if one came past more than once, he would know. None did. He started the car.

As he pulled out Harper checked for company. Initially, he saw nothing. Palmerston Street was mostly devoid of traffic except for a flatbed truck and a motorbike ahead, while in the rear, a Toyota Hiace pulled into a loading zone to make a delivery. Tension eased he dropped the car into second, then third, before he noticed a silver BMW joins the road behind him. It was half a block back and matching his speed. He continued along Palmerston, eyes flicking from rear-view to windscreen and back again. The Beemer held position. He drove by the ATM where Jonathon Hayes had been caught on camera, then past the clock tower as the bells tolled for the half-hour. Approaching the Lyndhurst Street intersection Harper slowed as if preparing to make the turn, then sped up and continued straight on, watching in his rear-view as the BMW mirrored his speed, keeping the gap steady.

By now another car had pulled into the gap and the driver of the BMW probably thought it was providing a nice little screen. But Harper's radar couldn't be so easily defeated, his attention firmly locked-on target. He continued on past the NBS Theatre and the library, keeping close tabs on his new friend. As he slipped by the petrol station he decided to play a little game. He made the right turn onto Pakington, drove the short block before turning right again onto Russell. In his mirror, he watched as the silver Beemer made the same turns. There were now no cars in the gap. He had a clear view. It was a nondescript late-model three-series, still matching his pace.

He continued along Russell as the road skirted the tree-lined perimeter of Victoria Square and pulled up to the stop sign at the

Brougham Street intersection. There he paused as if waiting for a break in the traffic. A red pickup grumbled by and then the road was clear. Harper kept idling, eyes fixed on his rear-view mirror waiting for the trailing car to come closer. But instead, the vehicle pulled over and nudged up against the curb a half block back by the park.

Harper swivelled in his seat, craning to look out the back. The car was too far away, its windows too rain-soaked to identify the driver. A VW Kombi pulled out of a driveway and drew in behind obscuring his view. Harper checked his side mirrors but couldn't pick out the silver car. The VW gave an impatient honk.

Harper had a decision to make. He could drive on, maybe circle the block to see if the car was still there. But that risked giving them the chance to escape. He couldn't let that happen, not after last night. He yanked on the handbrake and climbed out into the rain.

He walked past the VW, ignoring the profanity coming from the driver's window. The silver BMW was still parked against the curb. As he went to the front of the car he reached under his jacket and placed a hand on his Glock. He grabbed the driver's door handle and wrenched it open with such force he almost tore it off its hinges.

Sitting inside was a man he recognised. A man who had spent five years behind bars because of Harper. Omar Solomon was a low level hired hand who once upon a time collected debts and made house calls for the drug gangs. He had been one of the heavies who had smashed up Harper's place fourteen years ago.

Solomon's face was half pasty white, half tattoo black with a puckered, pink scar running along his left cheek from behind his ear to an inch from his nose. What he lacked in looks he made up for in size. His hulking frame filled the cabin leaving little room for anything else. But Harper was too angry to be impressed.

'Get the fuck out,' Harper roared.

'What's the problem, officer?' Solomon said with an arrogant smirk.

Harper didn't bother to answer. He just glared at Solomon with his hand still resting on his weapon. Eventually, Solomon got the message and casually extracted himself from the vehicle. He stood face-to-face with Harper, eyeballing him with the same stupid smirk.

'Stand over there,' Harper said nodding his head towards a park bench.

'Hey man, what's this all about? I ain't done nothing.'

'I'm searching this car for prohibited substances. Move away from the vehicle. I'm not going to ask again.'

Solomon's smile dissolved as he moved towards the footpath, complaining the whole way. 'This is shit man. Cops think they can do whatever they want. Fucking pigs.'

Harper was on shaky legal ground conducting a search without probable cause but he just needed to find something he could use to lock this useless piece of shit behind bars for a day, maybe two if he got lucky. After that he hoped the message would get through not to fuck with him.

Harper leaned in and began examining the interior. The cabin was a mess of junk food wrappers, takeout containers and it reeked of stale food and body odour. He reached over and opened the glovebox. More rubbish. Harper sifted through the trash with the butt of his torch but couldn't find any weapons or evidence of drugs. The back seats were more of the same. Harper popped the boot.

Compared to the rest of the car, the boot was clean. Too clean, like it had been sanitised. Harper lifted the carpet and found the spare wheel, jack and tool kit. He opened the vinyl tool bag and saw a tyre iron, screwdriver and various spanners of different sizes. He used his torch to scrutinise the implements. No signs of blood, weapons or illegal activity. No signs of a crime. Harper tossed the bag, slammed the boot and returned to the cabin. He looked under the seats, in the seat pockets, beneath the sunshades and in the door pockets. All he found was more rubbish.

Harper glanced at Solomon through the passenger window and caught the beginnings of another smirk. He climbed out of the car and wandered over, stopping close enough to taste Solomon's hot, ripe breath. He sniffed but didn't pick up the whiff of alcohol. For several seconds Harper stood and glared, the muscles in his jaw flexing, his eyes narrow and focused.

'Last night was cute,' Harper said through clenched teeth. 'Nice bit of evening entertainment. As for the tyres, cheers, I needed a new set.' He closed the gap until his face was just inches from Solomon's. 'But I'm done playing games. Stop hiding in the shadows like a pussy. Front up or fuck off. I haven't got time for this bullshit.' Harper turned and headed back to his car.

When Harper arrived at the doctor's house he made two loops around the block, one in either direction, to make sure Solomon hadn't followed him. Satisfied he was alone he parked outside Sharma's house and waited for the forensic team. This gave him time to piece together how the doctor fit with the evidence they had.

It was likely that Sharma would lose his job. Sharma had pinned the blame on Hayes and had made at least one death threat via text message. A witness had placed Sharma in the bar with Hayes on the night he disappeared. There was someone, possibly Sharma, with Hayes at the cash machine. Sharma had skipped town the morning Hayes went missing and was not cooperating with the police. The evidence was circumstantial, but it was mounting. However, other factors seemed to point away from the doctor.

The phone call was one. Hayes had phoned someone he knew, someone he was on good terms with. He was smiling and happy when he went off to meet this person. Next was the four and a half-hour gap between when Hayes left the bar and the moment he was seen on the ATM. Who was he with during this time? Then there were the missing suitcase and clothes. Would the doctor be bold enough to enter Hayes' house in the middle of the night not knowing if the wife would be at home in bed?

The biggest question was the money. Could Hayes have been blackmailing Sharma? Had Hayes offered to drop the story or at least keep Sharma's name out of the paper. But the sums involved were hardly pocket money and Sharma didn't look like he had that kind of cash. Harper couldn't rule out the possibility of wealthy relatives, but if that was the case why had Sharma chosen to work in a rural hospital? He wouldn't need the government grant if there was money in the family. The more he thought it through, the more questions he had.

Harper sat there and stewed on the details and ran all kinds of scenarios trying to find one that answered all his questions. Time dragged on and tick above his eye returned and in the end he drew a blank. Something was missing. Sharma had the motive but it was doubtful he had the means or the opportunity. Eventually, he gave up and turned his thoughts to the forensic team who were due to arrive any time now.

Two cars and a mobile site lab pulled up twenty minutes later. Gardella had arranged for an extra police unit to take charge of the scene management. Bones had probably been happy to green stamp the additional personnel, simply to keep his staff occupied.

After they presented their warrant to Tabitha Nadar, Harper briefed them and left them to it. He was now free to pursue other lines of inquiry.

He pulled up outside the Westport News and made his way up the ramp and through the automatic door and into the reception. The woman behind the desk hardly lifted her eyes before waving him through to Natasha Knight's office.

'Detective Harper. How is the investigation going? Do you have any theories on what has happened to Jon?'

'We're working a few lines of inquiry. That's all I can say.'

'Right O. I'll take that as a no comment. How can I help you?'

'I want to look at a piece Jon wrote a while back. Do you keep copies of previous additions?'

Just as Knight was about to answer, one of the phones on her desk sprang to life. She raised a "hold on" hand and took the call, reclining in her chair like the chairman of the board.

'Knight, Westport News,' she said in well-rehearsed form.

There was a long silence. Knight ran a grooming hand through her hair as she listened.

'Uh-huh,' she eventually said, her gaze returning to Harper. More silence. 'Give me the details.' She leaned forward and dragged a pen and yellow legal pad toward her and began to write. 'Uh-huh … yes. … How many? … Where? … Interesting.' Knight dropped the pen and peeked at her watch. 'Right, I'm onto it. Thanks for the heads up. Cheers. Bye.'

She hung up and returned her attention to Harper.

'What was that about?' Harper asked.

'Just a phone in. Sorry, what was it you wanted to look at?'

'A few of the stories Jon wrote. I want to look through your archives.'

'That's right. How far back are we talking?'

'Two months, maybe three.'

'If you tell me what you're after I can narrow it down for you.'

'The stories Jon wrote about the series of complaints laid against Doctor Sharma.'

Knight nodded. 'Come with me.'

She guided Harper out of the office and through an adjacent door into a darkened room that had the smell of old books. The room had no windows and the walls were layered with shelving. Stacks of newspapers filled each shelf, the oldest were yellowed with age. A desktop computer occupied a space between the stacks.

'Up until the mid-nineties we kept paper copies of every edition. Since then we've been fully digital. We're gradually digitising the older papers as well but we've been in print since 1871 so as you can imagine we've got a bit of work to do. Now, as for the articles you're interested in, the first one was published in February from memory.'

As Harper looked over her shoulder Knight entered "Anand Sharma", "Westport Hospital" and "complaints" into the search fields, then clicked the display tab and selected, "Oldest-newest."

As the computer began its silent mission, Knight headed for the door.

'I've got a deadline looming so I'll leave it to you. If you get stuck, the girls on reception can help,' Knight said as she left.

'Great. Thanks,' Harper called out as she hurried away.

As the door drew shut it sucked away the light, returning the room to gloom. Harper turned toward the cool blue glow of the monitor and began sifting through the search results.

The system had come back with nine matches. Harper scanned each one. Three had nothing to do with Anand Sharma. They had come up because the words Westport Hospital had appeared somewhere in the article.

The remaining six all mentioned complaints about a doctor at Westport Hospital. The first four were dated between February 25 and March 19. Each reported the same basic details including accusations of incompetence, misdiagnosis, inappropriate language, lateness and so on. However, in all of these articles, the doctor's name was not mentioned.

In the fifth article, dated March 22, the doctor was finally named. It revealed that Anand Sharma had been suspended from practising medicine pending a competency hearing in early April. The final story of March 26 largely covered old ground and gave little new information, apart from reporting that Sharma had initiated a lawsuit against the Westport News alleging defamation and seeking unspecified compensation for damaged reputation and lost income.

Harper zeroed in on the dates, specifically the date when Sharma's name was first made public.

Back in the conference room of the Westport Motor Hotel, Harper had the printout of Jonathon Hayes' secret bank account and his notes from the computer search lined up side by side. The conclusion was obvious.

Blackmail or bribery, it didn't matter. Sharma could have made those payments to Hayes to keep his name out of the paper. But Hayes went ahead and published the name regardless. An enraged Sharma then murdered the reporter and skipped town. There was just one problem. The dates didn't work.

Sharma's name went to press on March 22. The last deposit was a cash payment on March 28. Even allowing for two days processing time, this still meant the payment was made after Sharma's name was public. It didn't make sense. What could Sharma hope to gain by making this last payment?

The money was the key. Find out how it got into Hayes' account and he would find Jonathon Hayes. With Sharma looking less likely, his next best prospect was Quentin Jarvis.

CHAPTER 16

Shopping was the last thing Harper anticipated he'd be doing in the middle of a missing person investigation. Yet here he was, standing in Westport's only department store, picking out clothes. Fifteen minutes later he stood in front of the mirror and couldn't help but laugh. A black bucket hat with a red brim, a green and white checked shirt, sky-blue cargo shorts, and a pair of hiking boots. A complete mess, just the look he wanted.

He drove to the airport and parked the police cruiser before going into the terminal and renting the cheapest car from the Avis desk. According to Graham, the Jarvis farm was located in a place called The Nine Mile, a secluded region of farmland to the east of Westport. Nine Mile Road was the only way in and out which made it ideal for providing plenty of advance warning of an unexpected police visit. Harper would have to be careful.

Harper pushed the rented car hard along Nine Mile Road. The storm had flooded several sections, but he ploughed through sending fans of grey water spewing skyward. The tar-seal had run out a kilometre back, giving way to mud, gravel, and a distinct lack of traction. Rounding a bend the car slewed drunkenly, coming close to leaving the road and introducing itself to a fence. Harper wrestled it back under control. It should have made him more cautious. But caution was not in Harper's DNA. Instead, it gave him an idea.

After successfully navigating the next several kilometres, the road turned right and crossed the railway tracks. He estimated Jarvis' farm was less than five hundred metres ahead. It was time.

On the next bend he opened the throttle and felt the car begin to slide. He held the drift until mid-corner, then pinned his foot to the floor. The back end spun around and went off the road, dragging the rest of the car with it. The grass verge was sodden and the wheels dug in and for a second Harper thought he might flip. But his speed hadn't been high enough and the rental rocked from side-to-side before settling into the muck. Just to make sure, Harper gunned the throttle, digging the wheels in even further.

Satisfied with his efforts, he stepped out and admired his handiwork. Confident that whoever came across the scene would think it was a genuine accident, he turned his attention to locating Quentin Jarvis' house.

Through curtains of rain he identified a silver-grey roof behind a stand of trees. He trudged towards the house in no great hurry; after all, he wasn't going to get any wetter. At the gate, there was a cattle guard made from lengths of disused railway iron. Beyond that, an oval-shaped pond completely covered by lily pads. A driveway of crushed limestone skirted the edge of the pond then swept to the right before wrapping around the front of the homestead and disappearing behind the building.

The house looked old but well cared for, its whitewashed stucco bright against the gloom. There were no vehicles in the drive and no signs of activity inside the house, except for a yellow glow that radiated from several windows like a fading fire on a winter's night. The property was hemmed with swaying eucalyptus and knotted bushes with waxy green leaves and a cattle fence fashioned from disintegrating posts strung with rusting barbed wire.

The metal rails of the cattle guard were smooth and slick and Harper gingerly stepped across them before making his way up the drive. Parallel wet tyre tracks were stamped in the loose limestone, their imprint too wide and deep to have been made by a family sedan. Harper didn't have his phone so the best he could do was memorise the tread pattern while trying not to be too obvious about it. If this was a drug house then someone inside would already be watching.

Harper was still some distance from the front door when it swung open. Framed by the light emanating from inside stood the silhouette of a woman. She leaned against the door frame and watched and curled her fluid black hair between her thumb and forefinger without so much as a word.

'Hi there,' Harper said after a handful of seconds. 'My car, it slid off the road. It's stuck pretty good. Is there someone who could give me a tow?'

For a long moment she said nothing and just kept toying with her hair as if it was the only thing she knew how to do. When Harper had almost given up waiting, she spoke. 'What are you doing all the way out here?'

'I was looking for the museum, Coaltown, but I got lost. Must've driven right past it. Then, stupid me, I was going too fast and lost it on the turn, went into the ditch.'

'Where're you from?' she said.

'Auckland. Down here on holiday. Driving around the country and thought I'd do the West Coast. I've heard it's beautiful. Not used to driving on these roads though, especially in the rain.'

'Aucklander. Yeah, that figures. That shirt's a dead giveaway.'

'Yeah. Um, do you think I could come in out of the rain?' The question got her attention. She stopped leaning and playing with her hair and glanced behind like the answer would be found inside. When she turned back, her eyes were not on Harper but on the driveway behind. It made Harper turn and look, but there was no one there. When he looked back her eyes were on him again.

'Sure Aucklander. Come on in, I like the look of ya.'

He approached the front steps and took off his muddy boots before coming inside. He walked past the woman who closed the door and stood between him and the exit. She looked him up and down. A small smile pulled at the corners of her mouth.

He guessed she was ten years older than him but her face had a playful, almost childlike quality that was hard to define. Her skin had a soft gloss of natural blush while her jet black hair glistened like wet paint. A dark blue spaghetti-strapped slip dress flowed from her defined shoulders, softly following the contours of her body, finishing mid-thigh. She was tall but still had to look up to Harper who stood dripping, his clothes stuck to his body like cling film.

He stood in an entrance hall. To his right was an arch which opened into a living room where Harper could see a couch of deep-buttoned black leather and above that a large piece of contemporary art. Farther down on the right was another arch which led to the kitchen. On the left was a corridor which led to the rest of the house.

'What's your name, Aucklander?'

'Glen. And yours?'

She paused like it was somehow a difficult question. 'You can call me anything you want,' she said with a smile.

'And if I don't?'

'Then that's no fun at all,' she said, replacing the smile with a pout. 'I suppose you can call me Erin.'

'Okay, Erin. Thanks for letting me in. What I could really use though is a tow.'

'Hubby won't be home for a while so you're gonna have to wait on that. In the meantime why don't I get you out of those wet clothes?'

The offer caught Harper off guard. 'And into what?'

'Hmm. Well, I've got a bathrobe, but I guess that's up to you,' Erin said, the smile back.

'The bathrobe will be fine.'

She shrugged like it wasn't the answer she wanted and brushed past Harper as she went off to retrieve the garment.

Harper gave a faint smile. He was not un-used to female attention although he never understood why he seemed to attract it. Since Sara's death he'd had several relationships; none lasted more than a year. Harper blamed the job. Detective work wasn't especially conducive to a healthy personal life. Neither was his tendency not to get emotionally attached. His fear of loss had shaped his personality in ways that made it hard to establish close bonds.

'Get your clothes off and give them to me,' Erin demanded as she returned down the corridor holding what looked like a towel. 'I'll put them in the dryer,' she said, tossing a towel and a bathrobe at Harper's feet.

Harper waited for an offer of privacy or for Erin to at least turn around but she looked on as if a man undressing at her front door was an everyday experience. Harper raised an eyebrow and shot a lopsided smirk before using his finger to make a circular motion in the air.

'Shy are we? That's too bad,' she said as she turned her back.

Harper stripped off and dumped his clothes in a wet heap on the floor. He had never been self-conscious about being naked around women before. He was in good physical shape without an ounce of misplaced fat. However, standing there without a stitch of clothing made him feel ill at ease. He grabbed the towel and hurriedly ran it over his wet body, only partially drying himself, before putting on the bathrobe. Even under its thick fabric, he still felt exposed. Erin, sensing he had covered himself, turned around and gave a smouldering look. Harper collected his wet clothes and handed them to her. She held a smokey gaze for a long moment as if considering a piece of art, then she turned away and disappeared down the hall.

'Have a seat in the living room,' she called out from somewhere farther down the hall. Harper walked through an arch into the adjoining room and cast his eye about trying to learn as much as he could.

There was a second couch of the same button-downed design and a coffee table that looked like it had been made from the wood of an old sailing ship. Gaping picture windows gave out to the limestone drive and a lily-pad infested pond. A set of couches by the windows were upholstered in a royal-blue fabric embellished with a repeating gold fleur-de-lis pattern.

In a far corner was another arch that led into the kitchen. He moved towards it and poked his head through the gap. A long granite bench nestled below an equally long bay window that looked out on the rear of the property. The crushed limestone driveway continued around the back and led to an open-fronted barn with several bays.

In the first bay, there was a mud-covered tractor, the next contained a quad bike, and in the third, something was hiding under a red tarpaulin. The fourth and final bay held a Toyota four-by-four truck. Harper's antenna shot up. It was the same colour and model to those at the Solid Energy depot, except that there was no writing on the side.

The writing could have been removed. It would have been an easy job, just requiring a heat gun and a bit of patience. There were no other vehicles or anything else of interest outside. He needed to get a closer look at that truck.

Harper brought his attention back to the kitchen. It was a large space with a tiled floor and a U-shaped bench surrounding a central island of the same rustic design. The cabinets had a chic, distressed timber finish and an assortment of pots and cooking implements hung above the central island. Modern appliances were spread throughout and he got the feeling that this household wasn't short of cash.

Harper heard approaching footsteps. He took a seat on one of the buttoned-down couches, its leather creaking as he eased himself down. Erin appeared at the opening between the living room and the entrance hall and stood there for a moment looking at him. 'Your clothes are in the dryer. They're going to take a while. Can I get you something to drink?'

'Ah, something hot would be good. A coffee?'

'Thought you might want something stronger?'

'Just coffee.'

'Coffee's cool, I guess. I can make coffee.'

She went through into the kitchen. Harper listened to the clinking of spoons and water being poured, accompanied shortly after by the aroma of coffee. A minute or so later she returned with two steaming cups, handing one to him before taking a seat on the adjacent couch. They both sipped quietly until the silence got the better of Harper and he attempted conversation.

'Nice place you have here.'

'It's okay. On days like today it can be a bore. But then you showed up and my day is suddenly a lot more exciting.'

'Well, I'm pleased I could brighten your mood.'

She lifted the cup to her lips but didn't take a drink, her eyes stayed on him, peering over the rim like she was plotting his demise.

'So, Mr Glen. Is there a Mrs Glen?'

'No. There's no Mrs Glen.'

Her eyes narrowed as if trying to coax out more. Harper said nothing.

'You're not much of a talker, are you?' Erin eventually said.

Harper took a sip. 'What would you like to talk about?'

'Anything. Anything at all. I don't get many visitors. Not like you. Ask me something.'

Harper made a show of thinking, doing his best not to come off like he had a string of prepared questions already queued up.

'Well okay, um, how long have you lived here?'

'Coming up two years. We took over the place when my husband's uncle kicked the bucket. We lived down south before that.'

'How big's the farm?'

'We sold most of the land, except this patch here. I wouldn't call it a farm. What you see is what you get.'

'I must admit, when I first saw you I didn't think you look the farming type.'

'What type did you pick me for then?' she said, pretending to be offended.

Harper took a slug of coffee and let the question hang a moment. 'Well, you look more like a city person, I suppose.'

'And I suppose an Aucklander would know.'

Harper grinned. 'Yeah, I suppose.'

Another squall swept through. Rain streaked the window. Wind stirred the pond. Harper nursed his coffee, satisfied his deception was working.

'I like talking to you,' Erin said, a finger curling a loose strand of hair. 'You're sweet. Ask another question, anything you want, don't be shy.'

'Okay. What do you do for a living?'

'Nothing. I mean, I don't have a job if that's what you're talking about. My husband makes enough. I do whatever I please.'

'So, what does your husband do?'

'He's a businessman.'

'He owns a business in town?'

'You could say that. Anyway, enough talking about him,' she said as if the mere mention of her husband was spoiling the atmosphere. 'I want to talk about you. I saw you as you dried off. You're in fine shape. Quite a specimen.' She bit her bottom lip as she finished the sentence.

The look of surprise must have been evident because she answered his question before he could ask it.

'The glass in the front door. Makes a pretty good mirror when it's dark outside. I may have been facing the other way, but I saw everything I wanted to see.' Harper could feel the flush of embarrassment on his face. 'Don't worry, you've got nothing to be ashamed of. I feel bad for spying. That was rude. I'll make it up to you.'

She placed her mug on the coffee table and stood up. One by one she slid the straps of her dress off her shoulders. Harper tried to say "stop", but the word just wouldn't form on his lips. He watched as the shimmering fabric cascaded down her body, coming to rest in a crumpled pool at her feet.

She wore no underwear and Harper couldn't help but run his eyes down her body. Shoulders with barely protruding bones shaped to a narrow waist and perfectly proportioned hips. Her breasts showed little effect of gravity or the passage of time, her flat stomach was trim and toned. Her long legs were gently touching, one knee slightly bent in front of the other so the heel was partially raised.

Her body had a lean strength with a hint of refined bone structure under smooth curves that made her more athletic than thin. If Harper had nothing to be ashamed about, neither did she. Suddenly he felt a burn on his fingers and realised he was spilling coffee from the mug he had forgotten he was still holding. He cursed and put it on the table.

'So, what do you think, Aucklander?'

'I think we're even,' Harper said with a sheepish smile.

'Well, I'm feeling generous. Why don't I make it up to you, and then some?'

Harper didn't answer. He had managed to peel his eyes away from the naked woman just long enough to glance out the window behind. He saw headlights coming up the road and estimated they had just passed the point where his car was stuck in the mud. They would be here in seconds.

Cold fingers of dread slid over his skin. Was this a setup? A distraction to catch him off guard? Was he about to be silenced, murdered even? Or was this just a random piece of bad luck that might turn out to be just as deadly? Whatever the case, one thing was for sure. Help wasn't coming. No one knew where he was, not even Gardella. Why hadn't he told someone, anyone, where he was going? Too late. Nothing he could do about that now. Time to rescue this situation and fast.

He assessed his options and realised he had none, at least none that were any good. No clothes, no car, no easy avenues for escape, and nowhere to go even if he did. But his number one concern was standing naked right in front of him. If there was any chance of walking out the front door he needed to solve that problem first.

With deadpan calm, Harper said, 'Why don't you put your clothes back on. I think your husband is home.'

Erin swung around.

'Fuck!' She reached down to retrieve her dress.

Harper watched as the car continued towards the house. Erin retreated down the hall, presumably to find her underwear. He hoped she would be back in time to explain why there was a man wrapped in a bathrobe sitting in the living room. The car pulled up outside the front door. A rough looking man climbed out.

His head was shaved and his nose bent like it had been broken more than once. Sharp, angry eyes leered out from beneath a rutted brow. He walked with the general air of a man it would pay not to annoy. He came through the front door just as his wife returned down the corridor.

'Hey, guess what? Some fuck head's gone off the road,' the man said.

'Yeah, I know. His name is Glen.'

It took a second for what she'd said to register. When it finally did he pushed past her and into the living room.

'What the—what the fuck is this?'

'Calm down, calm down,' Erin urged. 'He came here looking for someone to tow his car. I told him you'd be home soon and I dried his clothes for him. He was soaking wet.'

'I told you. No one inside the house.'

'I wasn't gonna make him stand out there in the rain till you showed up. Christ, Quent, what was I supposed to do?'

'You tell him to fuck off is what you do.'

'Where's he gonna fuck off too, huh? There's no one around here for miles. Where's he gonna go?'

'Anywhere but my goddamn living room!'

'All I need is a tow. That's it,' Harper said, both hands up in a non-threatening manner.

'YOU,' the man screamed, pointing at Harper. 'You shut the fuck up. I'm not talking to you. I'm talking to her.'

'Look, Quent,' Erin said. 'You can sit there bitching, or you can get the truck and pull his car out. The more you bitch, the longer he stays.'

Jarvis' chest heaved. His glare flicked between his wife and Harper and back again.

'I just need a tow, that's all,' Harper said. 'If you've got a truck or something, you could take me out to my car, I'll hook her up, you pull me out, and I'm gone. It'll take five minutes. You won't even get your feet wet.'

Jarvis scowled daggers. 'Fine. But you don't move from this room,' he said. 'When I pull up out front, you better be ready.'

Harper nodded his agreement while pondering what Jarvis could possibly do if he weren't ready and he toyed with the idea of deliberately being late and finding out. In the end he decided it wasn't the time to start poking the hornet's nest.

Erin went off to fetch Harper's things as Jarvis stormed out a back door. Erin quickly returned and Harper threw on his still-damp clothes and was standing on the front steps when a four-by-four roared around the side of the house.

The truck skidded to a halt Harper peeked at the tyres. The tread pattern was a match for the markings he had seen earlier. He climbed in the passenger side and closed the door expecting Jarvis to set off immediately. When he didn't Harper looked over to see Jarvis eyeballing him from across the cab.

'You touch her?' Jarvis said through clenched teeth.

'Nope. But I did enjoy your wife's lovely coffee,' Harper replied. Jarvis was still glaring so Harper faked a confused smile. It did the trick and Jarvis made a grunt before dropping the truck into gear.

On the short journey Harper took the chance to look around the cab. He angled his head to give the impression he was looking out the windshield while using his eyes to take in the interior. There were no apparent features or markings that indicated this truck had ever belonged to Solid Energy. No ID stickers on the windshield, not even a trace of sticky residue showing were they might have been. The CB radio was also absent. It too could have been removed but Harper could see no evidence of mounting holes or brackets. The cabin had a stale smell like it hadn't been driven or cleaned in a long time and a thin film of clay-coloured dust covered the exposed surfaces. The vinyl on the dash was cracked from sun damage and the gear knob was frayed and worn. By the time they made it out to the rental Harper had concluded this was not Hayes' truck.

Jarvis slammed on the brakes and said the tow strap was in the back. Harper climbed out and went to the rear. The truck's rear bed was mostly empty, except for the yellow tow strap and an old chainsaw whose chain had come off. There was no sign of any water testing equipment or any fresh drag marks indicating something heavy had been removed.

He grabbed the tow line and secured it to the rental as Jarvis backed the truck in. Harper hooked up the other end, climbed into his car, and gave a signal to take up the slack. Instead, Jarvis lurched forward, slamming Harper back in his seat as the rental was catapulted free. Momentarily dazed from the sudden acceleration he took a second to recover. As he regained his bearings Harper saw Jarvis turn around and look at him through the rear window of the truck. A wide grin filled the drug dealer's face.

Harper's blood began to boil. He desperately wanted some payback, something to even the score. The cop in Harper would have casually tossed the tow cable in the nearest muddy field or delivered a few carefully chosen words in a don't-fuck-with-me tone. But right now he wasn't a cop. He was Glen the tourist. Tourists didn't typically niggle with skinheads who had anger management issues. They kept their mouths shut and thanked their lucky stars. Keeping in character Harper fumbled his way out of the rental, unhooked the tow cable, and deposited it in the rear bed of the truck. Jarvis floored it and headed for home.

CHAPTER 17

After returning the rental to the airport Harper headed back into town. He retrieved his cell from the glove box of the Commodore but there were no missed calls or messages from Gardella or anyone else. He took it as a sign Sharma was still stonewalling. Harper had hit a wall as well. His theory on Jarvis hadn't panned out and he didn't have any other strong leads to run down. Despite his wet clothes he called in at the station to see if any new information had come in. Bevan was crewing the watch desk when Harper pushed through the double doors.

Bevan did a double when he saw Harper. 'Haven't you heard of an umbrella?' he said.

Harper didn't attempt a comeback. Bevan shrugged and released the lock and Harper entered and made his way around to the watch office. Bevan sat slouched, coffee in one hand and a sandwich in the other, watching a live stream of a basketball game between the Chicago Bulls and the Utah Jazz.

'Any more call-ins about the truck?' Harper asked.

Bevan's mouth was so full of sandwich and all he could do was wave a dismissive hand at a pile of paper on the far corner of the desk. Harper entered the tight office and scooped up the pile. He carried the slips to the grey room with the filing cabinets. He dumped the stack on the small wooden desk and began sorting through them.

Ten individual tip sheets had been filled out by the officer who had taken each call. Of the tip sheets that had been filled out in full, the same officer's name appeared each time, Sean Smith. Monty had done it by the book.

Five of the ten sightings had occurred today while two sightings occurred earlier but had only been phoned in today. Of those earlier sightings, one was made on Saturday morning while the other occurred on Sunday night. The remaining three had no date or time recorded. It was impossible to tell when those calls had come in or what date the truck had been sighted. All ten sheets had notes scrawled in barely legible handwriting.

As Harper read through each one it became apparent they were all dead ends. Witnesses had seen a white truck at the petrol station. At the post office. At the library. In the movie theatre car park and at several other high profile places around town. None of the tips had specifically identified JN76 on the side of the truck and there were no reports of a man matching Jonathon Hayes' description. Harper concluded the sightings were probably other Solid Energy trucks going about their everyday business.

As a last resort he went back to the watch office on the off chance he had not gathered all the sheets. The basketball game seemed to have finished and Bevan had his feet up on the desk and was sucking back the last of his coffee.

'Was that it for the tips?' Harper asked.

Bevan swilled the coffee in his mouth and took his time coming up with an answer.

'We got an email,' he eventually said, pointing at a two-tiered filing tray on the far wall next to the printer. Harper walked over and grabbed the half dozen documents from the top level of the tray.

'Not those. The bottom shelf.'

There was just one sheet of paper in the lower tray. Harper returned the other sheets and grabbed a single piece of A4 paper from the lower tray.

It was a straight printout of an email received on the police computer. As he read the text his heart rate quickened. This tip was different. This was what he had been looking for. He reread it, just to be sure.

'When did this come in?' Harper demanded.

'What?' Bevan said, seemingly distracted by his own incompetence.

'This tip. When did it come in?'

'How the hell would I know? You think I sit here all day answering calls like I'm your personal assistant? Fuck off.'

'It's not a phone call, it's an email.'

'Then won't it have a timestamp already on it, wise guy?'

Bevan was right. In his excitement, Harper had focused on the content. He scanned the email again and found it had been sent at 11:23 a.m. yesterday morning. It had been sitting under his nose for more than a day.

'Shit,' Harper said.

A smile spread across Bevan's face as if witnessing Harper's annoyance was the best entertainment he'd had all day. Harper wasn't going to let it slide.

'Don't be so cheerful, fat man. When I'm done I'm going file an IPCA complaint. Hindering an investigation and withholding information. Guess whose name will be on the front page?'

An Independent Police Conduct Authority wrap was never going to stick, but it didn't have too. The mere sniff of an investigation was often enough to stall careers and in some cases, end them. It was a threat with just enough teeth that it needed to be taken seriously. Sure enough, the smile fell from Bevan's face.

'Fuck you,' Bevan said.

Harper grinned and left the watch office and made his way back to the grey room. He sat down and reread the email.

I read in the paper that the police were looking for a Solid Energy truck. I think I saw it at Christchurch Airport. It's parked in the long-term car park. You never see them this side of the Alps so I went over and took a closer look. On the side it had the same letters like the one in the paper so I thought I better let someone know.
Gareth Samuels
027 346 7718.

Harper dialled the number. It went straight to the answering service. Harper left a message asking Samuels to call him back, hung up, and immediately phoned Gardella.

'I think I've located the truck,' Harper said the instant the phone was answered.

Gardella sounded tired and unconvinced. 'Yeah? Where is it then?'

'Christchurch Airport, long-stay parking. A guy saw the photo in the paper and spotted it before his flight. He thought it was unusual for a mine vehicle to be in Christchurch. I think it's our truck, Joe.'

Excitement building in his voice Gardella said, 'This guy saw the numbers? You've got confirmation that's what he saw?'

'No. I haven't spoken to him. His cell's not picking up. He might be out of the country.'

There was a weighty pause and Harper sensed his partner chewing over this new information.

'Long-stay parking you reckon?' Gardella said.

'Yep. When you're done with Sharma you should go check it out.'

'We're already done, had to kick him loose. He lawyered up. Shut his mouth tighter than the Hoover Dam.'

'Did he say how he made it to Christchurch?'

'Yeah, before he clammed up he mentioned something about getting a ride with friends. Wouldn't give names or even what day he came over. If you ask me, he's full of shit. He's hiding something, but we just don't have enough to hold him.'

'You think he took the truck,' Harper said, reading his partner's mind.

'I'm certain of it,' Gardella said.

'He would've left prints. You need to get out to the airport and find it.'

'Okay, I'm onto it. What's happening at the house?'

Harper realised it had been three hours since he left the forensic team at Sharma's house. He had given the site officer his number and told him to ring if anything turned up. The lack of correspondence indicated the ESR team hadn't found anything.

'I'm heading there now but I'm not expecting much.'

'Alright, you go to the house. I'll go to the airport. Hopefully, one of us will come up with something. Keep in touch.'

'Will do,' Harper replied and hung up.

On his way out of the station, Harper tracked down Monty, spying him out back working with a dog inside one of the police garages. Harper ducked out a rear door and dashed through the rain and into the garage.

'Hey man, what's up?' Monty asked.

'Just wanted to say good work with the tips. I appreciate the effort, bud. Thought I'd let you know, we might have a lead on the truck.'

'Shit, that's good news. Where is it?'

Before Harper could respond the dog started barking and bearing his teeth. Monty held up his hand while he put the dog into a van.

'I didn't know you were an animal lover, Monty.'

'Neither did I till the senior sergeant told me I was. Stupid mutt can't tell the difference between old socks and crystal meth.' They laughed at the joke. 'So you reckon you got a lead on the truck?' Monty asked.

'We think it might be in Christchurch. Joe's checking it out. Anyway, just wanted to say, nice work. Anything else comes in, let me know.'

'Will do bud.'

Harper left the station and five minutes later was across the road from the cordon at Anand Sharma's house. Police tape was draped like Christmas ribbon and ESR technicians wearing white plastic coveralls scurried to and fro like busy worker ants. An officer wearing a police slicker stood guard by the gate and he gave Harper a "what's up?" look.

Harper approached and showed his badge and asked to speak to the SOCO. The officer turned and told one of the worker ants to pull Bridget out. Harper hadn't worked with many forensic technicians so the name Bridget wasn't ringing any bells.

As he waited Harper noticed a knot of bystanders watching from a neighbouring property. He assumed they were residents of the street and made a mental note to speak with them as soon as he was done.

The Scene of Crime Officer emerged from the house removing her plastic hood as she came down the path. Her sandy blonde hair was pulled back into a ponytail and she looked hot and bothered. Harper introduced himself but noticed the SOCO looking at him strangely. It took him a beat to work out why.

'It's the clothes,' Harper said. 'You're wondering about the clothes, aren't you?'

'Well, I wasn't going to say anything but, yeah, what's up with that?'

'To cut a long story short, I'm trying hard not to look like a cop. What do you think?'

'Convinced me. I thought you were one of the Beach Boys.'

'Perfect, just the look I was going for,' Harper replied in kind. 'How's the search going? Got anything?'

'Well, surfer dude.' Bridget winked. 'We've got a lot of different prints, more than we would normally see. Suggests more than just two people lived here. You aware of any other roommates?'

'No, just two that I know of. However, we think the male occupant liked to party. That could be the reason for all the prints.'

'Yeah, that would make sense,' Bridget said, making a face like she mostly agreed. 'So, apart from all the prints, we've got a few promising stains, but so far the presumptive testing is coming up blank. No blood. There's a team focusing on fibre and we've bagged a bunch of hairs, but unless we have something to match them against, it's not going to tell us much. We did a general search for any items that might link the two men. That came up empty too. I mean at this stage we're flying blind. We don't really know what we're looking for in there. What would help is a secondary scene, or better yet, the body. I guess by now you think this guy is dead?'

'It's starting to look that way. We might have a secondary scene shortly. His truck may have been spotted. I'll keep you posted.'

'Yeah, and while you're at it why don't you duck down to the beach and check the surf. I brought my board.'

Harper smirked. He had only just met this woman and he already liked her. But he couldn't walk away and let her get the last word in. 'Sure, but I doubt you could handle the West Coast swell. It'll chew you up and spit you out.'

'We'll just have to see about that, won't we?'

Harper's smile lasted all the way to the next-door property. The neighbours confirmed that the doctor's house was used for parties and loud music would go on into the small hours. One neighbour had made a noise complaint and after that the parties became less frequent. No one could recall any arguing, shouting or anything suspicious. No one remembered seeing a white Solid Energy truck.

It was getting late and Harper was hungry. He left Sharma's and drove to Tony's, a fish 'n' chip joint on Palmerston Street that specialised in the type of deep-fried stodge that was never going to win any awards. But Harper wasn't after a fine dining experience. He just wanted to reminisce.

Tony's had once been his mother's favourite place to eat. They used to go there together every Wednesday night, ordering the exact same meal: one scoop of chips, three fish, two Cokes. They would take the food to the park, eat and talk, and watch the world rush by. They were some of the happiest memories Harper had of his mother. Just the two of them against the world. Eventually, whenever his mother decided it was time to go he would plead to stay a while longer. He never wanted to go. Occasionally she relented and they would wait a few more minutes.

Except for the last night. The night before she died. They stayed longer that night. How much longer Harper couldn't recall. The only thing that stuck with him was the memory of the stars, too numerous to count, and his mother's arms wrapped tight around him. It was as if she knew it would be the last time.

Tonight, Tony's was without its usual patronage of men leaning against the walls with their heads down and their hands buried in pockets. Harper was the only customer and he placed his mother's order half expecting the person behind the counter to recognize it and say something to him. But she didn't and a short time later the food arrived. He drove to the park, found a picnic bench, opened the packet, and placed the extra bottle of Coke on the table. He sat alone and ate, watching the cars drive by. There were no people or stars out tonight. The weather had likely scared them away.

He could feel a weight in the air and knew that rain was near. He wished it would hold off and allow him more time with his memories but it came all the same and washed them away. When he stood up to leave there was still a small amount of food and the untouched bottle of Coke remaining. He left them there and returned to the car. Before he opened the door, he looked back, hoping to see her there. But there was nothing but darkness.

CHAPTER 18

After leaving the park Harper went back to the hotel and took a shower. It was then that the sadness welled-up from within. He let it out, the streaming water masking his grief. He had always carried the blame for what had happened. He told himself that he should have noticed, he should have done something. If only he had asked for help how different his life could have been. These thoughts spun in his head without finding a place to rest. Eventually, Harper fought to block them out, just like he had done for twenty years. The hot water rolled over his skin numbing his pain like a warm shot of morphine. He got out, dressed in jeans and a T-shirt and checked his phone.

It had been more than an hour since he last spoke to Gardella, plenty of time for his partner get to the airport and locate the truck. Why hadn't he phoned? Harper called but it went straight to the message service. With plenty of hours left in the evening he headed to the hotel's conference room to type up his summary notes of the day's activities.

He walked through the empty lobby and past a group of patrons enjoying a drink in the dimly lit bar arriving at the conference room. He unlocked the door and flicked the lights. A dozen bulbs burst to life. Compared to the mood lighting in the bar it was like looking directly at the sun.

As his eyes worked to recalibrate he gradually became aware that something was wrong. Something was different. Instinctively he took a step back and raised a hand to protect himself, but it was no use. As his vision snapped back into focus he realised what it was. Writing on the whiteboard. A series of numbers written in blue marker. Harper blinked in disbelief, then refocused on the string of digits.

0213729820125.236.207.22103:00

Adrenaline kicked in. His mind struggled to process the information. Nothing made sense. How did it get there? What did it mean? Who wrote it? How did they get in? The only conclusion he could draw was that someone had breached security and gained access to the room.

He backed out of the conference room and scanned the smattering of patrons in the bar. There was a family with three young boys, an elderly couple, and a sports team of high school girls wearing matching tracksuits. Laughter erupted from the girls as they shared a joke. Harper's phone began chirping. He answered the call. Gardella's voice jumped through the speaker.

'We've got the truck. And you're not going to believe what we've found.'

'What?'

'As soon as I laid eyes on it, I knew it was our truck. The numbers matched up. So I backed away, called an ESR team, and told them to get a flatbed so we could move it downtown. Anyway, when they arrived here, they found the keys still inside.'

'Yeah, so what?'

'They had to use the keys to get it into neutral. When they turned the key someone spotted a red light. The guy looked down and saw a black box wired into the power supply. He recognised it from his time as a security consultant for a private firm. It was a GPS.'

Harper's brain was reaching overload. 'Wait a minute. This thing has a GPS?'

'Yep.'

'So why didn't the manager at Solid Energy tell us that? We could've pinpointed its location in fifteen fucking seconds.'

'You don't understand,' Gardella said. 'It's not a tracker. It doesn't broadcast its location. It's an older unit. It only logs the data. You have to plug in and download the information. The mine manager probably didn't mention it because he figured it wasn't going help.'

Harper closed his eyes and took a moment to compose his thoughts. 'So what you're saying is, once we plug it in we'll be able to see where the truck has been driven?'

'You got it. It's on its way downtown as we speak. I'm about to call Jared from computer forensics. If he can take a look at it tonight, we should have the data by tomorrow morning.'

Harper thought about this for a moment. It could be a crucial lead, or it could be nothing at all. If it showed Hayes drove to Sharma's house, or some other location, it would definitely help zero in on a suspect or at least give them another potential crime scene. If, however, the data showed that the truck drove from the Hayes residence straight to the airport, it would confirm little unless they found prints or other evidence. 'Okay, sounds promising. You get anything else from the truck?' Harper asked.

'Not a lot. We did a cursory examination, but it's pretty dark. We couldn't see much. Once we get it back to the garage we'll give it a good going over. There was one interesting thing we spotted though. At the back of the vehicle, where the tailgate comes up to the canopy, there is a rear window. On the inside of the glass, we spotted these two marks, like something had been in there butting up against the rear window. The marks looked like dry dirt. Thing is, there was nothing in the back that we could see that would make those kinds of markings.'

'Didn't the mine guy say there was water testing gear in the back?'

'Yeah, we could see it in there. It's a box, about the size of a microwave, with a coiled hose. These marks were much higher up and on the left-hand side.'

Harper's jolt of adrenaline faded; his head began to throb. 'Could be important, could be nothing. You've got to have something more than that,' he complained.

'All right smart guy. What have you got then?'

Harper spent the next ten minutes summarising his day. He left out the striptease with the drug dealer's wife but covered off everything else. Gardella didn't have anything to say when Harper explained that the ESR crew was coming up empty at Sharma's house. He guessed from Gardella's silence that he was disappointed more evidence had not been found implicating the doctor. Finally, Harper brought up the numbers.

'Hey, Joe. Before you left yesterday did you write anything on the whiteboard in the conference room?'

'No, why?'

'Well, I'm standing here looking at a string of numbers. I've got twenty-five numbers in one long sequence. Some have dots in between some don't. I don't know what they mean except that someone has been in here.' Harper read them out and he and Gardella mulled them over for a while.

'Read out the last four again,' Gardella asked.

'Zero-three-zero-zero. The three and the last two digits are separated by a colon.' As he read it out aloud, separate from the rest of the chain, he immediately understood what it meant.

Before Harper could say anything, Gardella said, 'I reckon that's a time. Zero three-hundred hours. Wasn't that the time Hayes used the ATM?'

'No,' Harper replied, shaking his head. 'Hayes showed up just before three-thirty. I think you're right about the time though. It's got to mean three a.m.'

'Maybe there's something we missed,' Gardella said after a second. 'Did you go back to three o'clock to see if anyone else was hanging around?'

Harper shook his head again. 'Don't you remember? The footage had been wiped until just after three. If there was something there, it's gone.'

They debated a while longer. All they could agree on was that the last four numbers represented three o'clock in the morning. None of the other figures made any sense. Gardella told Harper to make sure nothing else in the room had been tampered with and to check with the front desk that no one else had been given access to the room. Before they rang off, they agreed to make contact first thing next morning.

Beth was behind the desk in the lobby. It looked like she had been through the wringer. Her hair had lost its body and sagged like a deflated balloon. When she spoke there was no "love" or "dear," just the tired voice of a woman who had probably been on her feet all day. Harper asked if the cleaner or anyone else had been into the conference room. She was adamant that no one had and she hadn't noticed anything unusual all day.

He went back and examined the lock for any marks or scrapings that would indicate it had been picked but found nothing.

Back in the conference room, he took one of the seats and positioned it in front of the whiteboard. He sat down and studied the numbers. The last four digits almost certainly signified a time. The colon between the 03 and the 00 was the giveaway. But that footage was lost and there was nothing Harper could do about it.

He turned his attention to the rest of the numbers. A dot followed the opening string of thirteen digits, then three more numbers, another dot, followed again by three numbers and a dot. Harper stood up and retrieved his cell from his pocket. He took a photo of the numbers and zoomed in so they filled the screen. Using a photo editing app, he drew a line between the 03:00 and the rest of the sequence, then counted backwards and drew another line on the screen. He was reasonably sure he had isolated three distinct number patterns.

0213729820/125.236.207.221/03:00

Harper sat and stared at the phone for several seconds. He knew what he was looking at. The 021 was the prefix of one of the major cellular companies and the seven-digit string that followed was the standard format of a cell number. Confident he had cracked the first code, he turned his attention to the next sequence.

The middle pattern looked vaguely familiar. Three numbers and a dot, repeated three more times. For the next ten minutes he tried to figure out where he had come across the pattern, even taking a pause for coffee hoping the caffeine would stimulate his thinking. But the break and the coffee yielded no new ideas. Harper returned to the phone number. Before calling it he wanted to check a hunch.

Earlier that day when he had filed all the evidence at the Westport Police Station, he had made copies for himself. He took these copies out and spread them on the table. He started with the tip sheets. Almost all of them had a contact phone number. Harper compared each of these to the digits on the whiteboard. No matches. He stacked the tip sheets and slid them to one side.

Next he turned to the print outs of Hayes' phone records. The first page contained the most recent calls and he ran his finger down the list but none of these matched either. He moved on to the next page. Starting at the top he scanned down, eliminating each phone number as he went. He was close to the bottom and about to flip to the final sheet when he saw it, third from last. He did a double-take and checked it against the number on the whiteboard. They matched. Hayes had called the number.

Harper felt a jolt of excitement. He went to the final page but didn't see the number again. He went back to the second sheet and looked at the time stamp. The call was made on February 6. He compared the dates with those on Hayes' hidden bank account. The first sum of money was deposited in the account nine days after Hayes had called the number.

Harper sat back and thought things through. The number had been dialled just once in the last two months. This suggested it was not a close friend or acquaintance. Hayes had used his own phone, not the burner they suspected he had which meant he was not trying to hide the call from his wife. Not long after the phone call sums of money started appearing. Now this same phone number had appeared on the whiteboard. Armed with this information Harper grabbed his phone and dialled. The phone rang for what seemed like thirty seconds. He was about to hang up when someone picked up.

'Hello,' a gruff voice said.

'Hello, this is Detective Harper. Who am I speaking to?'

'Frank Mortimer. Sorry, who did you say you were?'

'Detective Harper, Christchurch CIB. I'm investigating the disappearance of Jonathon Hayes. I'd like to ask you a few questions if you don't mind.'

There was a short silence. 'I read about that in the newspaper. What do you want to know?'

Harper hadn't prepared any questions. There was no way to know who would answer. He took a second to think of what to say.

'First of all, what do you do for a living, Mr Mortimer?'

'I'm a farmer.'

'What type of farmer?'

'Dairy farmer.'

'And how do you know Jonathon Hayes?'

'I don't.'

Harper put an elbow on the table and leaned forward and propped his head against his hand. This was not what he had been expecting. The possibility Hayes had simply dialled a wrong number had not been considered. Harper rubbed his brow and glanced at the phone records. If it was a wrong number then Hayes should have hung up and made another call. There were no other phone calls listed for that day.

'Then can you explain why Jonathon Hayes called your cell phone on February six?'

'Because, I called him.'

Harper was now thoroughly confused. He rubbed his brow some more and silently cursed himself for not doing better prep. He could only think of one thing to ask. 'Mr Mortimer. Why would you call a man you didn't know?'

'I called and left a message. I heard he had some equipment. I wanted him to come and take a look at a stream running through my property.'

'Why did you want him to do that?'

'Half a dozen head of cattle died in that area. I thought there might be something wrong with the stream.'

'Where is your farm?'

'Whitecliffs.'

Harper was silent a few seconds while he processed the new information.

'You still there?' the farmer said.

'Yes, sorry. I was just thinking. Um, I would like to come out and take a look at that stream. Would first thing tomorrow be okay?'

'Well, so long as you don't show up at five-thirty while I'm milking, I don't mind when you come.'

Harper assured Frank Mortimer that he definitely wouldn't be there that early. After asking for directions and writing them in his notebook he hung up and returned his attention to the numbers.

With the first and last part of the puzzle solved there was just one piece left. The more he stared at the numbers the more they glared back, mocking his inability to decipher their meaning. It was the feeling of recognising someone's face, their voice, knowing their whole life story, just not their name. He paced the room and racked his brains. The harder he thought the further from the answer he got. He needed to change tack.

Harper moved to the head of the table, opened his laptop and powered it on. When it booted up he opened Google and started typing the numbers from the whiteboard into the search field. He was halfway through entering the sequence when a spark of recognition hit.

The recurring pattern of three numbers separated by decimal points was the standard format of an IP address. Any device connected to a network or the internet had to have an IP address. It could be a computer, a printer, a smartphone or even something as simple as a street lamp. Just like you need to know a person's street address to send them a letter in the mail, the computer needs to know a printer's IP address to send it a print job.

Most of these addresses were private. For Harper to access these he would need to be logged into the same network or be able to hack in through a back door. He was reasonably proficient with technology, at least compared to Gardella, but his skills didn't extend to hacking. His only hope was if the IP address was public.

He keyed in the numbers and hit "Search." A small grey wheel spun silently as the web browser scoured the internet. After ten seconds Harper knew it would come back with no results. Sure enough a message appeared saying there were no matches. He made several more attempts trying different prefixes each time and these efforts yielded nothing. The address was either incorrect, incomplete, or the IP address was secured and needed to be accessed via a third party application.

Harper leaned back in his chair and looked up at the ceiling and found nothing but a flat white expanse spotted with rows of downlights. He closed his eyes and searched for answers. All he could come up with were more questions. Who put those numbers on the whiteboard? Why give him an IP address he can't access? What kind of device could it be?

A web camera was the only thing that sprang to mind. It had to be a webcam. It was the only logical device that would have a public IP address. But even if he managed to log in, what would he see? It wouldn't be like the bank ATM camera that recorded everything to a hard drive. There would be no way of going back in time and watching past footage. He would only be able to see a live image of whatever the camera was pointing at. He could be sitting for hours watching people doing their laundry for all he knew. Getting into the camera was one thing, knowing when to look was a whole other problem.

That's when it clicked. He already knew when to look. The time at the end of the sequence of numbers now made sense. It wasn't referring to the time of the ATM footage. It was the time Harper would need to be logged into the webcam. At three o'clock this morning something was going to happen and the webcam was going to capture it.

Harper checked his watch. It was well past midnight. The hotel guests had all headed off to bed and the bar was empty. A hollow calm permeated the room. Harper longed for sleep. He was exhausted and the bright lights were beginning to give him another headache. He got up and walked over to the light switch and flicked it off. The room fell into a blue gloom, the only light coming from the laptop screen.

Harper started searching for websites that could locate IP addresses. Forty-five minutes and two-dozen websites later, nothing. The closest he got was one webpage which narrowed the IP address down to somewhere in New Zealand. Another check of the watch; 2:03 a.m. One hour to go.

Giving up on the computer he pried his cell from his jeans pocket and began searching the app store for webcam applications. After browsing through the multitude on offer he downloaded four. He opened the first app and plugged in the IP address from the whiteboard. After hitting search he placed the phone on the table and reached for his coffee, taking a deep slug. The search icon spun dutifully for several seconds yielding nothing but a black screen.

Just when he was about to move on to the next app, the screen changed and a rectangular box appeared. Harper held his breath and dared not move a muscle for fear of upsetting the search. His blood pressure climbed as the search icon spun some more. Then something appeared on the screen.

A grainy black and white image filled the box. The low light and poor quality made the grain look like falling snow. He had to squint to make out any recognisable detail. The timestamp in the top left corner said 02:27. Today's date was also visible but there was nothing else identifying the location of the camera. Initially it was difficult to determine what he was looking at but after a while he began to make sense of shapes and lines.

The left third of the image was black, no discernible detail. Harper assumed it was a park or field. To the right were numerous bursts of light puncturing the night like tiny supernovas and giving off just enough illumination to highlight the outline of several low-rise buildings. The webcam appeared to be in a high vantage point, possibly a high-rise building. It looked down on an urban environment. After more study he identified streets arranged in a grid pattern and the motion of a car's headlights sliding silently through the scene. Sandwiched between the empty black ribbon on the left and the urban lights on the right was a dimly lit road that ran from the top-middle down to the bottom left corner of the frame. Harper took a moment to lean back and stretch. He'd been hunched over his laptop for two hours and his body was telling him to take a break.

He leaned in again and focused his attention on each of the murky shapes. Almost all of the buildings were a single storey with the odd taller structure and there was one brightly lit object middle-right of the frame which jutted up above the others. Initially, Harper thought it was some kind of obelisk or monument. The more he looked at it the more it reminded him of something he had seen before. It took another twenty seconds before he finally recognised what it was. The Westport town clock. He was looking at a video image of Westport.

It was only then that the rest of the picture made sense. The dark area to the left was not a park or a field. It was the Buller River. Next to that, what he had thought was a road, was in fact the railway yards and the port. Backing onto that were warehouses and industrial buildings and to the right of those were the shops of the main street. The high vantage point must be from the top of one of the cement silos. It was now two-thirty and Westport was sound asleep. He watched for ten minutes and only noticed one car drive along a distant side street.

Five minutes passed before Harper realised his phone battery wasn't going to last. He fetched the charging cable from his satchel and plugged the phone into his computer. The tiredness of a few minutes ago had been traded for nervous excitement. With thirty minutes left until the deadline it would be safe to duck away and brew another pot of coffee—an added insurance policy against falling asleep.

When he returned nothing had changed. In the few minutes he had been away he had begun to wonder what he could possibly learn from the webcam. Its elevated position combined with the darkness made it impossible to identify a face, a person, or even a licence plate, and if a car pulled into view he would be lucky to tell what make and model it was.

Time ground on. The image on the screen, stubborn, unchanging. The minutes dripped by, Harper's focus drifted, sleep's black abyss beckoned. He fought back with more caffeine but the war was being lost. Then he saw it. Something was coming up the river.

CHAPTER 19

A single speck of light inched closer, growing in intensity as it came up the river from the ocean. Soon it was close enough to identify; a medium-sized ship, a bulk carrier. Harper strained to pick out a name but that kind of detail was impossible to make out. The vessel had two small cranes, a multi-storey crew quarters, and a bridge at the stern. As it neared the dock its bow swept 180 degrees and it began slowly crabbing towards the wharf.

Harper noticed movement in the railway yard. A train crept into view from the bottom of the screen. As soon as the ship was tied up its cranes swung into action, reaching out to the first train carriage, plucking it off the line and hoisting it over the open hold of the bulk carrier. It hovered a few seconds, then swung back, returning the wagon to the train. The train slid forward and the process was repeated.

It appeared as though the bottom of each train wagon had doors that would open allowing whatever was inside to spill out into the hold of the ship. Harper marvelled at the intricate ballet. Not one second was being wasted. Every movement carefully choreographed with military precision.

He glanced to the right of the image, past the line of warehouses, and saw the lights of Westport and the deserted streets. There was no movement or signs of life. The town was blissfully ignorant of what was unfolding.

Twenty minutes later the last carriage was laid back, the ropes cast off, and the forward crane pulled vertical. The ship slipped its moorings and eased off into the night. The train was moving too, heading back down the line from where it came. As it was disappearing, Harper had an idea.

He ran through the empty bar, past the lobby and out across the courtyard to his room. He snatched his car keys and was in the car in under a minute. He drove south along Palmerston Street towards the Buller Bridge. There was no traffic, no one on the footpath, no lights glinting from the buildings that lined the street, no sign of human activity. The road's black asphalt had a sheen like wet coal and Harper's headlights seared across it like twin flares lancing the night sky.

Up ahead, railway lines crossed the road. The retreating train would need to come past this point. There was nowhere else for it to go unless it stayed in the railway yard and he knew it was on the move. As he approached the barrier arms were still up. Harper slowed to a crawl. He was too soon.

He was just about to pull over and wait when the bells clanged into action. The lights began a second later followed by the lowering of the traffic barrier. It was another thirty seconds before the train appeared.

The locomotive emerged from the dark, its diesel heart throbbing as it rumbled past. Its running lights were off making it blend in with the night, except for a pale glow coming from within the driver's cab. Harper could just make out a man at the controls. As the engine came level the train driver looked straight at Harper, his mouth forming an

O of surprise. He was Asian, probably mid-twenties. His hair greasy, his shirt dirty and partially unbuttoned.

The man quickly turned away as if stung by Harper's eyes. He withdrew to the far side of the cab and out of sight. The locomotive was painted a shade of gun-metal that helped it melt into the darkness. Unusually there were no company markings or logos identifying a mining or freight company.

The locomotive slid by pulling behind it the first of the wagons. Harper knew a coal wagon when he saw one. Smooth bulging sides like a full stomach with a single chute at the base for disgorging its load and a coat of black soot thick enough to make you cough. But he knew immediately that these were not coal wagons. They had corrugated sides like a shipping container with multiple sawtooth chutes like a grain wagon and they were cleaner than Harper's kitchen bench.

As the wagons crawled by Harper noticed something else. Heavy metal hinges ran along the upper lip of each wagon and what looked like a pulley system for opening a top door. If he didn't know any better he would have assumed he was looking at bulk grain carriers.

This didn't make any sense. The West Coast of New Zealand was known for many natural wonders but grain production was not one of them. Something else must have been on that train.

The last wagon ground by and the barrier arms swung skyward and the lights were extinguished and the bells quieted. The train dissolved into the night as its low rumble lingered on a while longer. Harper had counted twenty-three wagons and two locomotives.

For a time he sat at the crossing with his engine ticking over. He looked left and right as if expecting something else. But there was nothing. He weighed his options. The train was heading towards the mountains on the main trunk line. There was no way to shadow it because the highway didn't follow the same route. In the dark and without running lights he would never be able to track it. Harper made a U-turn and headed back to the hotel.

Harper's phone woke him early the next morning. He felt like he'd been asleep for five minutes but the time on the phone suggested he'd been out for three hours. The caller ID said it was Gardella.

'I didn't ask for a wakeup call,' Harper croaked as he ran a hand across his face. There was no answer. Harper sat up in bed waiting for a reply. None came. It occurred to him this could be another stunt pulled by Solomon. He double-checked the phone and confirmed it was Gardella. Confused, he rubbed his eyes and shook his head as if this would somehow solve the riddle. More silence.

'Why did you talk to the press?' Gardella said, not sounding happy.

Harper massaged a kink out of his neck. 'What do you mean?'

'The Westport News ran it yesterday. The Christchurch Press picked it up this morning.'

Harper wasn't following. 'The Press did what? I don't—What did the News run?'

'They outed Sharma. Said we were searching his house. They even knew about the threats. It's on the goddamn front page.'

Harper felt like he had just swallowed a brick. He knew what had happened.

'I didn't say anything. I was at the paper asking Knight for the articles about Sharma. While I was there she got a phone call. It must've been someone tipping her off about the ESR team at Sharma's house. She's put two and two together. Derek Graham probably filled in the blanks and told her about the texts. I fucked up, Joe.'

'This is going to screw the case big time. There's no way we're gonna get Sharma to make a statement now.' Gardella was silent for a long while. Harper said nothing. 'Let's just forget about it,' Gardella finally said. 'There's nothing we can do about it now. Besides, I have other news.'

Thankfull for the change of subject Harper quickly replied, 'Yeah? And what's that?'

'We've got blood in the truck.'

'Wait, you've got blood in what?'

'In Hayes' truck. There's blood in the back. We found it on the lining of the rear tray.'

'How much?'

'Significant quantities. Looks like someone's made an effort to clean it up but they didn't do a very good job. When we sprayed it with luminol it lit up like a Christmas tree.'

'Shit.'

'Say that again. I've got a meeting with Bones first thing this morning. He's likely to upgrade this to a homicide investigation. Probably set up a task force. I'm staying here for the time being but my bet is Bones will send some additional help your way in the next twenty-four hours.'

'Okay. What does that mean for me?'

'I want you to keep working the case from your end. You'll be in charge of the team when they show up. I'll come back if needed but at the moment, I'm staying put.'

'What about the wife?' Harper asked. 'You want to inform her about the blood?'

'Not yet. Just give her the standard line that the investigation is ongoing and that we're chasing down leads, you know the drill. Oh, I nearly forgot. Our computer guy called in sick but someone from the office managed to download the waypoints from the GPS. Looks like whoever drove the truck stopped at a self-service car wash in Christchurch. There's an ESR team checking it out but it's been nearly a week. I doubt they'll find anything. I've put the GPS data in your Dropbox. Take a look and see if you can spot anything.'

'Will do. Anything else?'

'That's it. Anything interesting at your end? You figure out what those numbers were all about?'

'Um, no. I couldn't make sense of them,' Harper lied. He wasn't entirely sure why. Maybe it was because he was embarrassed about the mistake at the newspaper, or maybe it was because he still didn't understand how it all fit together. In the end he decided to keep quiet until he knew more.

'Okay,' Gardella said. 'Why don't you get someone from forensics to dust for prints and see if anything comes up? You sure nothing was missing from the room?'

'Yeah. Nothing else was touched. It's all here.'

'Good. I'll call after my meeting with Bones,' Gardella said and clicked off.

Harper lay back on the bed and stared at the stippled plaster ceiling. It was yellowing and cracked and looked about as bad as he felt. He closed his eyes and tried to forget about the newspaper story and how little sleep he'd had. Gardella might have forgiven him but Harper knew certain people in the hierarchy were eager to see him fail. People who were not happy he had risen through the ranks so quickly. People who wanted to put him in his place. He needed to clear this case and he needed to do it quickly.

Time to get back to work.

He called Bridget and requested a fingerprint officer come to the hotel. She said her FO was still asleep but she'd get someone there within the hour. While he waited Harper powered up his laptop and opened the tracking data Gardella had sent. A map of the South Island filled the screen. A thick red line plotted the three hundred and seventy kilometre journey between Westport and Christchurch.

At first glance, nothing seemed out of place. The tracking data showed no unusual deviations or stops along the way, just a straight run from west to east. Harper wondered how Gardella knew the truck had stopped at a car wash. He clicked the plus icon and enlarged the view.

He zoomed in on the western fringe of Christchurch and the airport. Airport traffic coming in from the Lewis Pass would typically take the western bypass and link up with Russley Road. This route avoided most of the earthquake repairs and was by far the most direct path. But instead, the red track chose the roadwork-riddled northern motorway then turned off at Cranford Street, stayed on Cranford all the way through to Bealey Avenue, then made a hard right just before hitting the earthquake cordons of downtown. It then skirted around Hagley Park and lined up with the morning commuters on Fendalton Road and Memorial Avenue and after all this, finally made it to the airport.

Gardella had made a connection between the detour and the blood clean up and concluded the truck had made an unscheduled stop. He would have done a recon of the route and quickly zeroed in on the self-service car wash. Smart detective work.

He scrolled the map west and concentrated on the Westport side of the track. The red line began at Jonathon Hayes' house, followed the main road out of town, and joined the highway to Christchurch. Harper enlarged the map and looked for deviations. He saw none.

Several tabs ran along the top of the map window, each stamped with a date and time recording the various trips made in the weeks and months before Jonathon Hayes' disappearance. Harper clicked on another tab and a new red line appeared. This one was much shorter. It originated at the Solid Energy depot and finished at Hayes' house. The date and time were consistent with Hayes picking up the truck after work on Friday and dropping it home ready for its weekend duties. He checked the earlier dates but they showed no unusual activity, just the regular pattern of Hayes going about his job. Harper's shoulders sank. Apart from the stop at the self-service car wash the GPS data was a bust.

CHAPTER 20

The fingerprint officer showed up thirty minutes later. He checked the pen for prints but found none. There was nothing on the whiteboard either. He offered to dust the table and laptop but Harper knew they would come up blank. The fact that nothing was taken suggested the intruder had broken in with the sole purpose of leaving the message so Harper didn't want to create a mess that he would have to clean up later. He needed to keep moving forward. He needed a break in the case. He needed to get back on the road.

Before leaving the hotel Harper bundled up all the case documents and placed them in his bag with his laptop. He wasn't taking any chances with another intrusion. Once all the files were secure he took them to the car and placed them in the boot before climbing into the driver's seat.

After a short drive he parked outside the Westport News and went up the ramp and waited for the automatic door to slide back. The door didn't budge. He glanced at his watch and saw it was just after seven-thirty. A sign on the door said office hours were 8:00 a.m. to 5:30 p.m. Frustrated, he walked back down the ramp. As he reached the footpath the sound of the automatic door made him stop and turn around. There stood Natasha Knight, hands on hips, looking like Harper's visit had interrupted something important.

'Looking for someone?' she asked.

Harper didn't respond. Instead, he folded his arms and shot back an angry glare. If anyone had the right to be annoyed it was him. Knight received the message loud and clear. She immediately went on the defensive.

'I had to run it,' Knight protested. 'You've got half a dozen officers searching Sharma's house. It was only a matter of time until someone phoned it in. Your partner was asking questions about the libel case and just yesterday you wanted to read all the articles about it. I've been doing this job long enough to work out what was going on. I couldn't sit on it another day. If I did, I risked getting scooped by The Press.'

Harper let Knight's protestations dissolve into the chill morning air as if they carried no more weight than the wisps of steam coming from her mouth. He waited several seconds before responding.

'You screwed me, Knight,' he said in a low voice. 'You just had to ask for a comment.'

'And I would've got a "No comment" and you know it.'

'That's where you're wrong,' Harper snapped, raising his voice as his anger took over. 'I would've told you not to go ahead. I would've told you you're making a mistake. Now it's too late. Now when the truth comes out we're both going to look like amateurs.'

Knight's response came back so quick it sounded rehearsed. 'Then let's get the truth out. Let's fix the mistake.'

Harper stuffed his hands in his pockets and looked over his shoulder at nothing in particular. He understood what was going on. He was being played. Knight was a veteran and knew all the moves. The "let's help each other" act was probably her go to play. Pretend to have your back then gut you while you're not looking. Trouble was, he needed Knight. She had something he wanted. He had to play ball.

Harper looked back, his mouth a slight grimace like he was doing this against his better judgement. Knight took the hint and stood aside. Harper walked up the ramp and through the door.

The reporter was now at her office door. She held it open. Harper didn't take the bait, opting to remain in the foyer. The signal was clear. This meeting would be on his terms. He would control the flow of information.

'Sharma's not involved,' Harper said, kicking things off. 'The forensic team was at his house for six hours last night and found nothing. We've got nothing concrete connecting him. We have other evidence, which I can't get into, that tends to exclude him as a suspect. So what I'm saying is, don't run another story suggesting he is our prime.'

'Well, I can't fill up my column inches with thin air. I have to write something. It's Friday for Christ's sake. If you don't give me something I'll have to fall back on the Sharma angle until something else crops up.'

Harper shook his head. Knight was more concerned about scooping her rivals than the welfare of her own workmate. He wasn't going to be able to placate her with a straight-out denial. He had to give her something.

'Okay, look. What I can confirm is we've recovered the truck. We've also identified some blood. Human blood. A significant quantity. Enough that we'll almost certainly upgrade to a homicide investigation later today. Regarding Sharma, you can say that he is assisting us with our investigations, but nothing more.'

Harper saw the shock on Knight's face. She must have suspected this could be the outcome but uttering the words was like a hammer blow confirming it.

'You can't contact the wife for comment,' Harper continued. 'I'm yet to inform her. You cool with that?'

'Um, sure, yeah,' Knight muttered.

'Now, there is another reason I came. I need another look at the archives. I'm not going to mention what I'm looking for because I don't want to read about it in tonight's paper. If I do then the next time we chat it will be in the courthouse across the street. Catch my drift?'

Knight didn't respond. Her eyes held a distant look of someone who'd just received bad news.

'You hear what I just said?' Harper asked again.

'Yeah, I get it,' Knight finally said.

She ushered him through into the archives room and turned on the light.

'You know what to do,' she said, gesturing towards the computer.

She left and closed the door. The computer was already powered on as if it had been expecting him, the cursor blinking in the search box.

Harper typed the words "Gold Mine" and made the necessary clicks to begin the search. Several hundred results appeared. Harper clicked on the one dated March 17. The front page of Wednesday's edition filled the screen. The article was located in the prime real estate for any newspaper, front page, top left-hand corner. Big news for a small town at a time when most mines were closing down.

Mackley River begins production

After months of delays and setbacks, InterPacific Mining announced this week that they have finally begun production at the much-hyped Mackley gold mine. The Chinese-based consortium had been battling resource consent hurdles which required high-level backing from officials before finally being given the go-ahead to commence mining operations late last year. Media Liaison Officer Amy Fairweather told The News that the mine is expected to produce between 20 and 50 thousand ounces of gold annually and contribute significantly to the Westport economy. "We expect to make extensive use of local businesses, especially engineering and technical support services, not to mention accommodation and hospitality," Fairweather said.

However, others have questioned what benefits the mine will bring considering that InterPacific has sourced their entire workforce from China. Chair of the Westport Business Roundtable Simon Berryman is disappointed there were no jobs for local miners. "We have a proud history of mining on the Coast and could have offered our expertise on the ground rather than just in a supporting role. We've got dozens of families who have lost their primary source of income and not one of those workers will pick up employment at the new mine."

There are also concerns about what environmental impact the mine will have on the natural landscape. When approached for comment InterPacific said the mine was an underground, hard rock operation with a minimal topographical footprint and that all ore would be shipped back to China for processing. The gold-bearing material would be transported by rail using the existing Buller Gorge line meaning no heavy traffic on the state highway. In addition, the train carriages would be covered to prevent dust and other mining spoil from getting into the ecosystem.

Westport Mayor Gerry Babich welcomed any development at a time when most commodity prices were falling. "It's fairly obvious to everyone that things are not great at the moment. We've got coal prices at an all-time low, the Christchurch earthquakes have scared tourists away from the South Island and businesses in town are struggling. If this new operation can help then I'm all for it."

The first shipment of gold-bearing ore is expected later this week and based on geological surveys, the mine is forecast to produce viable quantities of gold for the next ten years.

Harper read through the article one more time but before he had finished he already knew what he had to do. He needed to get up to that mine.

CHAPTER 21

After leaving the Westport News Harper drove down to Samara Hayes' gallery. He pulled up outside only to find she had not yet opened for the day. He sat in the car and waited. It was just before eight-thirty when her white Toyota pulled up at the curb. Harper crossed the street and met her as she opened up and let him in.

The green-grey linoleum floor gleamed under bright studio lights making the room feel more like an operating theatre than an art gallery. Canvases depicting a range of distinctly West Coast scenes populated the sparse gallery. Most of the art hung against stark white walls, except for four larger works arranged on easels in the centre of the room. One was of a stretch of rugged coastline with foaming waves and bush-clad mountains. Another depicted a river cascading over boulders in the midst of thick rainforest. The third showed the towering face of a sheer rock bluff, soaring above the landscape like an enormous sentinel.

The final painting was different from every other piece in the studio and grabbed Harper's attention. It showed a forest that had been cut down leaving only stumps and debris. There was not a single stick of green anywhere but somehow it was more beautiful than all the other works combined.

Harper knew nothing about art but thought the work was a little too expensive to appeal to the average tourist. In any event, he wasn't here to purchase a painting. He had a more sombre duty.

Harper informed Samara Hayes of the blood in the truck and she took the news calmly. There were no tears, no shock or denial, none of the textbook reactions he'd come to expect from a grieving family member. She appeared numb and detached and it made her hard to read.

Not knowing what to make of her lack of emotion Harper asked if she had any questions. There were a few, mainly about potential suspects, which he deflected with non-committal answers and after twenty minutes he was back on the road.

Harper piloted the car towards the southern end of town. The morning traffic picked up as workers filtered into Westport to earn their keep. He counted over two dozen cars and decided this was what qualified as rush hour on the Coast. At the end of Palmerston Street the road curved right, crossed over the Buller Bridge, and headed into the mountains.

The highway hugged the southern bank of the Buller River as it carved a winding gorge through the towering peaks. Harper gunned the engine, pressing the car into each corner, flowing through the turns like the water in the river below. On the far side of the gorge he spotted a coal train grinding along the tracks, its sooty wagons snaking through the bends like a long steel rope. A yellow road sign warned he was approaching Fern Arch, a wall of rock that encroached so much the highway was cut to a single lane. Harper had to wait for a tourist bus coming in the other direction and as it passed its driver waved his thanks and belched a cloud of diesel exhaust as a parting gift. He was moving again and didn't need to slow until he emerged at Whitecliffs ten minutes later.

Whitecliffs took its name from a series of limestone bluffs that cut through the forest canopy like weeping scabs that refused to heal. In places nature was slowly repairing these wounds but for the most part nothing grew on the sheer white walls except for a few exposed roots that crisscrossed the surface like swollen black veins.

As he rounded the next bend the narrow gorge opened to a clearing of billiard flat farmland surrounded on all sides by mountains. Somewhere out there in the vast expanse was Frank Mortimer's farm.

The road skirted the southern edge of the flatland and Harper looked across the plains searching for the Mortimer homestead. The clearing was about two kilometres across at its widest point and three times as long making the building difficult to spot. Patchwork fields in shades of green and gold were dotted with knots of gnarled trees that appeared as old and rugged as the mountains that loomed all around. It took some careful study before he eventually spotted a light blue roof beyond a grove of ageing pines.

Almost as soon as he saw the house he came upon a farm road. He pulled over. A letterbox bearing the name "Mortimer" told him he was in the right place. Turning left, he made his way down the farm track until he pulled into a gravel yard fronting a tumbledown farmhouse. Harper parked and got out of the car.

First impressions suggested the place had been abandoned. The front porch was minus most of its roofing iron while the house seemed to be shedding lengths of siding quicker than anyone could replace them. In the far corner of the yard the rusted shell of a fifty-four Chevy Pickup sat on cinderblocks under a gum tree, its driver-side door frozen open. Harper saw no signs of human activity. Even the air seemed stale and dead.

Through a disintegrating screen door emerged a man with broad shoulders and a scowl that suggested he had better things to do.

'You're late,' the man grumbled.

Harper took a second. 'Are you Frank Mortimer?'

'Last time I checked, yeah.'

Harper approached and extended a hand which the farmer shook with a crushing force. Frank Mortimer's hands were thick, his skin like rawhide, his face grizzled and cracked like a dried-up riverbed. It looked like he had spent the last thirty years outdoors and hadn't appreciated waiting around inside for Harper to show up. But Harper noticed a warmth in Mortimer's eyes that hinted something softer hid beneath the gruff exterior.

'So what do you want to see?' Mortimer asked.

'Can you take me out to the river where you found the dead stock?'

Mortimer nodded once and stepped off the porch and strode around the back of the house. A vehicle rattled to life and seconds later another old Chevy appeared, this one a later model with marginally less rust and a flatbed laden with bales of hay. Mortimer waved for Harper to get in and then they were off.

They drove back down the farm road until Mortimer swung left onto the highway. The Chevy lumbered along at a speed well below the limit because it wouldn't go any faster or because Mortimer wasn't about to be hurried. It took fifteen minutes before they turned left again and onto another farm trail.

After a short distance they came to a wooden bridge which crossed the river. This far inland the Buller River was only half as wide as at the coast but the bridge that spanned it didn't inspire much confidence. The greying wooden span sagged like the spine of an old horse and was held together with iron fixings that had corroded black and looked about as brittle as a used car salesman's smile. Harper started estimating how much the old truck weighed and when the answer came back he immediately wished they had brought his car instead.

Mortimer nosed the Chevy forward and Harper held his breath. The timber complained and the bridged sagged even more. Harper kept perfectly still, convinced his slightest movement would send the whole lot plummeting into the river. He glanced at Mortimer who showed no signs of concern. Harper relaxed a touch figuring the farmer made this trip often enough to know what he was doing. Even so he manoeuvred a hand to the door handle ready to extricate himself should they end up in the water.

Once across the other side the brush got thicker and branches clawed the vehicle's steel skin like fingernails on a blackboard. The road deteriorated reducing their speed to walking pace. Soon the road emerged into a small clearing. The Buller River was off to the left, swollen and dark its waters swirled and bubbled. Ahead and to the right a grassy field gently sloped up to the foot of a bush clad mountain. The mountain soared upwards and disappeared into a low cloud base.

'This is the place,' Mortimer said, stopping the truck and pointing out the window.

Mortimer killed the engine and climbed down from the cab. Harper followed suit and shadowed Mortimer as he lumbered down the grassy slope towards a low area hemmed with flax. As they neared the bottom of the hill the burble of water over rocks suggested they were not far from a stream.

They fought through the line of flax and stepped out onto a river bank of metal-grey stones. Boulders, branches and tree trunks littered the creek bed. Upstream there was an arched iron railway bridge and beyond that the tributary melted into the shadows of the forest. Downstream the stream spooled into the wide expanse of the flooded Buller River.

'I found them there,' Mortimer said, pointing upstream to a calm pool sheltered from the main flow by a car-sized boulder.

Harper eyed the scene from a distance, taking in the placid waters of the pool as well as both banks of the stream and the green bush beyond that. He wasn't sure what he was hoping to find but so far he saw nothing unusual.

Cursory search completed Harper clambered across the marbled rocks toward the pool. He crouched at the water's edge, the loose material shifting under his feet. Resisting the urge to dip his hand into the pool he studied the body of water from a safe distance. Its surface was like glass and its colour like a well-aged bottle of Merlot. The tannin-rich water was so dark Harper could not see the bottom. He picked up a stone and dropped it in. Ripples slid across the surface in ever-expanding rings before dissolving into nothing. He studied the water for several seconds. Nothing about it seemed unusual.

Not seeing anything in the water he stood up and panned up and down the bank. He immediately spotted drag marks leading through a narrow gap in the flax.

'That's where we pulled them out,' Mortimer said, answering Harper's question before he had a chance to ask it. Harper nodded and continued his scan.

A short distance downstream he saw something glinting in a stray beam of sunlight that had somehow penetrated the blanket of cloud above. It huddled amongst the stones near the water's edge. He moved downstream for a closer look. As he edged nearer he realised it wasn't just one object, but several. Dead fish.

'Is this the area where Mr Hayes came to test the water?' Harper asked.

'Yup,' Mortimer said, using a fingernail to pick something out of his teeth.

'Did he ever get back to you with the results?'

'Nope.'

Harper looked skyward. The cloud was growing thicker and he was growing weary of one-word answers. He needed more information or this trip would be another waste of time.

'So what do you think killed the cattle and these fish?'

Frank Mortimer was still for a long while. Then he folded his arms and gazed up at the mountain. Harper traced his eyes to a wall of dense bush that climbed skyward, disappearing into a grey ceiling of cloud that threatened rain.

'Know what's up there?' Mortimer asked.

'No. But I can—'

'That new mine.'

Harper brought up his mental map of the area. This must be the Mackley River from which the mine took its name. But there was absolutely no sign of anything other than pristine West Coast bush. The mine must be somewhere higher up.

'You think the mine is poisoning the water?' Harper asked.

Mortimer gave a casual shrug. 'All I know is I've never seen anything like it. At least not until that mine came along.'

Harper looked down at the fish and then back at Mortimer. 'Where the hell is this mine?'

'I'll show you.'

It was a long uphill walk and Harper was breathing hard by the time the pair had climbed the grassy slope and arrived at the treeline. Mortimer led the way in, expertly picking a path through the thick tangle, Harper doing his best to stay close. In this sort of country it was deceptively easy to get lost.

Five minutes later they came to a tall, chain-link fence topped with razor wire and on the other side there was a clearing and a railway line running parallel to the fence. Past the tracks and atop an expanse of concrete the size of a football field sat several industrial buildings that appeared to have been recently constructed.

The buildings were clad in khaki-green corrugated metal, the colour seemingly chosen to blend into the surroundings. Some looked like site offices while others appeared to be utility buildings. What caught Harper's interest were two large structures positioned at opposite ends of the site. Each had a square base rising several storeys topped off by steeply pitched roofs. Neither tower had any windows apart from two small openings for the elevated conveyor belt that ran between them.

The tower closest to the railway had what looked like a loading boom. The boom had been stowed off to one side but when extended it could be used to load train carriages on the adjacent tracks. The conveyor belt ran back to the second tower which was sited at the foot of the mountain. Feeding into it was a gondola system that climbed the bush-clad face of the mountain before eventually disappearing into the cloud base. The gondola stood motionless, its wedge-shaped buckets hanging idly between the pylons. It was the same shade of green as everything else making it melt into the forest and become nearly invisible. Harper now understood why he could see no evidence of a mining operation when he was down by the river. The owners had gone to great lengths to maintain a low profile.

As Harper crouched amongst the undergrowth he saw not a soul. The site appeared abandoned. There was no one checking equipment, no one making repairs, no security personnel patrolling the perimeter and no lights on or other signs of human activity. The only movement came from a leaking tap and an unsecured door that swayed lazily on the occasional gust.

Harper rose to a half-standing position. The concrete was young. White and smooth like it had been poured recently. It had a wet gloss from a recent wash-down.

Mortimer said, 'I think they're washing the dust off into the river.'

'What dust?'

'The dust that comes off that conveyor belt.'

Harper studied the offending piece of equipment. 'You've seen dust coming off that thing?'

'Yeah,' Mortimer said matter-of-factly. 'Bout a month ago. I came over to check on some fences. It was evening and the sun was low. Must've been the angle of the light but I could see stuff in the air. I assumed it was dust coming off the belt.'

'But this is a gold mine. Wouldn't the dust contain gold? Wouldn't they try and recover it?'

Mortimer paused like he hadn't considered this possibility. Eventually he shrugged and said in an easy drawl, 'Maybe. But maybe there's other bad stuff in there as well.'

Harper nodded. He didn't know much about gold mining but something told him that chemicals were probably used to separate the gold ore from the waste rock.

A distant boom broke his concentration. Thunder rumbled over the mountain and down into the valley. Harper looked up to see the clouds had turned black. Time to go.

On the return trip Mortimer told Harper that the gold mine had a field office about three kilometres along the main road to the east. Once back at the farm Harper thanked him for his help and set off in that direction.

He drove inland along the main highway following Mortimer's directions to an unmarked gravel turn-off. The mine access road was dry and well maintained. Wide enough to accommodate two-way traffic it also had a channel on one side for drainage and was covered in firmly compacted stones. Judging by the shattered remains of skittled trees that lined the roadside Harper concluded the path through the forest had been forged with the blunt end of a bulldozer. So much for having minimum impact on the environment he thought, remembering the quote from the newspaper.

Another five minutes of driving brought him to a clearing surrounded on all sides by centuries-old West Coast forest. The area was several football fields in size, the forest acting as a perimeter fence keeping everything contained. On the far side were three weatherboard buildings that huddled together like they were protecting each other from some unseen threat. The smallest building had a porch and a glass sliding door and seemed to be the site office. Adjacent were two much larger structures that appeared to be workers quarters. Several men in overalls milled around. Most were sitting under the eaves of the two large buildings trying to stay out of the rain which had started to intensify. Off to one side were four buses with the words Westport Coach Lines stencilled on their sides.

Harper pulled up outside the site office and climbed out of the car. A large blue tarpaulin drooped from the end of the site office and a knot of Asian men sheltered beneath it, cigarette smoke trailing from their lips. Sitting in folding chairs on the porch were five more men. They smoked cigars and eyed Harper with a mixture of nonchalance and suspicion.

'Who is in charge here?' Harper asked, pronouncing each word with deliberate care.

The balding man sitting in the middle of the five waved a dismissive hand toward the sliding glass door. He said something in a language Harper didn't understand and the other men erupted into laughter. Harper didn't budge. He stood firm, staring darkly at the man who had made the joke. The laughter petered out but Harper held his glare. The man raised a hand and plucked the cigar from between his thin, grey lips.

'You go in now,' he said.

Harper maintained his stare and an aggressive stance. All of the five were now looking at him slightly nervously.

'Fuck you. Fuck you very much,' Harper said as he climbed the steps and opened the glass door. As the door slid shut he heard more laughter, but he chose to let it go.

The room was small and dreary. Several carpet tiles peeled off the floor revealing the bare wood beneath and the walls were intermittently glossed in a film of black grime. A woman with shoulder-length dark hair sat behind an L-shaped reception desk. She was on the telephone speaking in a language Harper thought might be Chinese. At her desk there was a desktop computer, a printer, two phones and a charging dock for a hand-held radio. Various sheets of paper were spread across the desk. Hanging on the wall were half a dozen miners hardhats and underneath those, six yellow high visibility jackets. The ceiling had been removed exposing a latticework of rough-cut timber beams and a corrugated iron roof that amplified the clattering rain.

The woman looked up and smiled. She held up a finger indicating she would not be long. Her age seemed somewhere in the mid-twenties but her sharp, clear eyes exuded the confidence of someone older. Smooth skin clung tightly to her slight frame and Harper guessed she might weigh fifty kilos dripping wet.

Another thunder crack shook the windows. Harper winced and glanced outside. All but two of the smokers had retreated inside and the rain was now coming in sideways, pounding against the glass like a million and one tiny fists. Amid the din Harper hadn't noticed that the woman had finished her phone conversation.

'How can I help you?' she said.

'Detective Harper,' he said, startled and fumbling for his badge. 'I'm investigating the disappearance of Jonathon Hayes.'

The woman studied the badge like it was a rare piece of jewellery. 'Oh, yes,' she eventually said. 'I read about that in the paper.'

Harper returned his ID pack to his jacket. 'Sorry, I didn't catch your name?'

'Amy Fairweather. I'm in charge of media relations, but in truth, I'm more of a translator-come-receptionist.'

Harper remembered her name from the story he read this morning. He needed to speak to someone more senior.

'Is the mine manager available?' Harper asked.

'I was just speaking to him. Unfortunately he's stuck up the hill. The weather is pretty bad up there, a lot worse than what we're getting here if you can believe it. They're securing the mine portal and will ride it out till it clears.'

'Is it possible to get up to the mine?'

'I'm afraid not. The only way up is via the aerial ropeway but we've shut it down because of the winds and lightning. You're more than welcome to wait it out but there's no telling how long that might be.'

The last thing Harper wanted to do was sit around waiting for the weather. He needed answers now. His frustration must have been evident because the receptionist immediately offered another option.

'I might be able to answer a few questions. I have a fair idea what goes on around here.'

This wasn't what Harper had come for. He needed to talk to the mine manager. He walked to the rain-streaked window and glanced at the heavens hoping to see any sign the weather might be improving. It wasn't. He let out a defeated sigh. When he turned around the receptionist was smiling as though she was keen to help. He might as well cut his losses and find out what he could. He approached the desk, close enough to smell the cool mint of the woman's perfume. 'Okay. What did you say your role here was?'

'My main job is media liaison. As I'm sure you have noticed, most of our team are Chinese. They speak little or no English. I deal with enquiries and ensure there are no misunderstandings.'

Harper nodded. 'I saw your name in the paper. You dealt with Mr Hayes when he was doing the story on the mine?'

'Yes, that's right.'

'Can you tell me when that was?'

Fairweather took a moment to think. 'Last week. Wednesday or Thursday. We talked on the phone. He came out for an interview.'

'Was there anyone else present at that interview?'

'Mr Qian was there as well.'

'And who is he?'

'Sorry. Li Qian, He's our operations manager.'

Harper got out his notebook and the receptionist spelt the name for him. 'Can you tell me what was discussed?'

'It was mostly about the mine opening and what it could mean for the local economy. Mr Hayes asked the questions. I relayed them to Mr Qian and translated his answers back into English.'

'So, Mr Qian cannot speak any English?'

'Actually, he knows some. Enough to have a basic conversation. However, when dealing with the media it's company policy to have a translator.'

'In your meeting, did Mr Hayes mention anything about water pollution?'

Fairweather furrowed her brow. 'No. Nothing like that came up. Why do you ask?'

'A local farmer found dead livestock near a river on his property. The farmer employed Mr Hayes to conduct some water tests in the area about a month ago. I have reason to believe he may have detected pollution in the river.'

'Water tests? Why was he doing water tests? I thought he was a reporter.'

'He had a part-time job. Anyway, that's not important. So you're telling me there was no mention of water quality or environmental concerns?'

'No, none at all. The meeting was very pleasant. In fact I remember at the end Mr Qian shook hands. I remember that distinctly because he normally never shakes hands. I thought it was out of character.'

Harper made a note of this. He thought it curious that Hayes had known about the pollution but had not brought it up during the interview. The article he wrote made almost no mention of environmental concerns regarding the mine. The receptionist seemed genuine in her surprise and denial. Harper thought she probably had been kept out of the loop by management.

'Tell me about how the gold is mined and brought down the hill.'

'Well, the mine is underground. We use explosives to break up the rock so we can get at the gold. This creates lots of loose material and unstable areas that we first need to shore up before we can extract anything. We then load the gold-bearing ore onto a rail system, haul it out, transfer it onto an aerial ropeway and bring it down the mountain to the rail line. From there, we rail it to the port and load it onto a ship. Eventually, it ends up in China where we apply a chemical called sodium-cyanide that leaches out the gold.'

The mention of cyanide immediately raised Harper's antenna. If the mine was using cyanide and it was getting into the water then that would explain the dead cattle. But something else she had just mentioned didn't support this.

'You apply the leeching chemical in China? Why not do it here in New Zealand? Wouldn't that save you the hassle of transporting all that waste material?'

'That was our original plan but we got knocked back at the resource consent hearing. As soon the word cyanide came up the consent authority got a little nervous. So the decision was made to ship it back to China and extract the gold there. At current prices it's still quite profitable.'

'Do you apply any other chemicals or solvents here in New Zealand?'

'No. Our resource consent is very strict. We don't apply any treatments at all. What comes down from the mine is pure, unprocessed rock. I'm not sure what pollution Mr Hayes picked up, but it can't have come from us.'

Harper thought about this for a moment. If Hayes had not been able to detect any pollution why didn't he report this to Mortimer? Why keep a clean result quiet? It didn't make any sense. The only reason to keep things secret would be if he had found something. Something like cyanide. Harper considered the possibility the contamination was coming from somewhere else. But there were no other mines in this area and a natural source was just too much of a coincidence. Harper didn't believe in coincidences. The mine had to be the culprit.

Based on this thinking, Harper surmised the mine was treating at least some of the ore on-site. This was a clear breach of the mine's resource consent and explained all the secrecy around transporting the ore to the port. The dust Mortimer had seen would have been laced with cyanide requiring the workers to wash down the loading zone. That explained why everything had been so clean and why none of the workers wanted to hang around the loading area. Jonathon Hayes had uncovered the pollution when Mortimer had asked him to test the water. Now he was missing. This changed everything.

Harper retrieved a business card from his pocket and flicked it across the desk.

'I need to speak to Mr Qian. Contact me on that number the minute the storm clears.'

The receptionist picked up the card, holding it at its edges as if trying not to smudge the writing. She studied it for several seconds before looking up and saying, 'That won't be a problem, Detective Harper.'

CHAPTER 22

Berlin's Tavern sat just off the highway, smack in the middle of the Buller Gorge, halfway between Whitecliffs and Westport. Its origins could be traced to the gold rush of the 1880s, one of a dozen similar watering holes that once dotted the highway. During the height of the rush Berlin's attracted hordes of weary miners, offering an easy remedy for their thirst and a sympathetic ear for their stories. But once the gold ran out the many taverns faded away. Only Berlin's was left. The last surviving monument to better times.

Harper had stopped at Berlin's not in search of beer, but in need of electricity. He had forgotten to charge his laptop and the battery was dead. He sat at a table by the window so he could keep tabs on the storm and watch traffic kick up spray on the highway. Berlin's was close to the mine office. If there happened to be a break in the weather he could make the short trip back and interrogate the mine manager.

His laptop powered up and he ordered a coffee and a bowl of French fries and surveyed the scene. Two German backpackers lounged on a sofa while a group of farmhands shared a drink and talked shit at the bar. A log burner crackled in the corner while the bartender sat perched on a stool nursing yesterday's newspaper while snatching glances at the female backpacker. A ginger cat dozed peacefully in front of the fire unconcerned by the world's problems, its only worry was how to simultaneously expose all parts of its body to the warm glow. Harper eyed the cat and wished he could trade places.

The laptop completed its start-up procedure and was ready for what Harper had in mind. He selected the file containing the GPS data from Jonathon Hayes' truck and seconds later the mapping information filled his screen. Several tabs lined the top of the screen, each one labelled with a date. By looking at these dates Harper spotted a pattern; they all coincided with the weekend. This made sense. The manager at Solid Energy had said the truck was not part of the general pool and was not used by other staff during the week. Harper was looking for anything that didn't fit that pattern. It didn't take him long to find it.

Harper clicked on the tab with the only date that occurred during the week. This brought up a map of Westport with the familiar red line overlaid. It showed a trip from the Solid Energy depot to an address on the main street and then back to the depot. The timestamp indicated the journey started at 10:51 a.m. and finished at 11:03 a.m. Harper got out his cell and opened the calendar app. He cross-referenced the date and found it was a Wednesday. Harper looked at the map again. The address was on the corner of Palmerston and Rintoul. It took him a second to work out what was there. A service station.

Excluding it he clicked on the other tabs in reverse order and looked for anything unusual. From what Harper could tell, Hayes picked up the truck each Friday afternoon and drove it home. Over the weekend he used the vehicle to visit various rivers before returning home. Late Sunday evening he would take the truck back to the depot where it would sit for the next five days. There was nothing in this data that stood out as suspicious or unusual.

Harper went through each map again but couldn't see any deviations to this pattern. There were no visits to unknown addresses, no joy rides, no diversions to odd destinations, no suspicious activity. But Harper knew there had to be a smoking gun somewhere in the data. His gut told him the key to finding the missing journalist was sitting right here in front of him. He just needed to keep looking.

The bartender approached with a steaming cup of coffee which Harper gratefully accepted. He took a sip before placing it on the table and moving on to his next avenue of inquiry. He opened his notebook and flipped through the pages. The phone call to Frank Mortimer had occurred on the sixth of February. The map of the seventh showed two red tracks. The first was to Granity Creek, the small stream up the road from Derek Graham's house. Hayes had presumably been up there to test the water. It then showed Hayes returning down the hill and heading for home. But Jonathon Hayes didn't return home. Instead, he drove back to Westport and continued straight through town before linking up with State Highway Six through the Buller Gorge until he reached Mackley River.

Harper reached for his coffee. He lifted the cup and took another sip. His earlier optimism had faded. It confirmed Mortimer's story but little else. It would be a useful piece of evidence but it was hardly a case breaker. Harper was no closer to finding out what had happened to Jonathon Hayes.

As he placed the cup back on the table his free hand nudged the mouse. A small dialogue window popped open. Annoyed, Harper went to close the obstruction. But just before he did, he realised what he had found.

He had inadvertently activated a settings menu. Harper studied the drop-down menu. Amongst the list of selections were several options that allowed the user to optimise how the GPS plot was displayed on the screen. One grabbed his attention. It read "Overlay Interval Markers." It was currently set to off. Curious, Harper turned this feature on and closed the menu.

A series of dots now populated the red line. Around town the dots were bunched tightly together while on the open road they were spaced further apart. It seemed the GPS logger laid down a marker every few seconds. The faster Hayes drove the further apart these markers would be.

At Granity Creek the dots were clustered together like a bunch of grapes showing where Hayes had parked. There was a smaller grouping at Derek Graham's house which suggested he had called in on the way home. At the Mackley River location there was another cluster.

Harper didn't know how the GPS worked but assumed Hayes had either left the truck running or the unit continued to drop markers for a short time after the ignition was turned off. Either way it showed the places he had stopped.

Harper leaned back and ran a hand across his thickening crop of stubble. He caught a reflection of himself in the window. The shadow covering his jaw matched the darkness under his eyes. The lack of sleep was catching up with him. He yawned and took another slug of coffee. It didn't work. He still felt terrible.

The bartender wandered over with the French fries and laid them on the table and tried to steal a glance at what was on the screen. Harper sensed a nosey question and prepared a blunt response but the German tourists called the man away. Harper grabbed a French fry and got back to work.

He started with the tracking data from the eighth of February. He scanned the interval markers and found nothing unusual. He kept going, moving through the dates, studying each GPS log. In every case the same pattern repeated. Hayes would stop at a testing site, there would be a small cluster of dots, and then he would return home. Occasionally he would call on his pal Derek Graham, but apart from that there were no other stops. Nothing out of the ordinary. Harper was quickly coming to the conclusion it was another dead end.

He came to the last trip. Unlike the previous maps, it took the computer several seconds to load the much longer track from Westport across the Southern Alps to the car park at Christchurch Airport. As the laptop crunched the data Harper reached for another French fry. The map blipped onto the screen and his hand froze. His gut tightened and his heart rate shot up. Harper's world shrank to the size of the laptop display. There was no doubt what he was looking at. It was close. He had to get there. Now.

CHAPTER 23

Harper raced back through the Buller Gorge, the Commodore's engine howling in protest. On the passenger seat his laptop was propped open and his cell phone sat in its cradle running Google Maps. Every few seconds he checked his position, comparing it against the spot he had identified from the GPS track on his laptop. After the last check he knew he was almost there, just a few more corners. He wondered what he would find when he got there. The more he thought the more he knew there was only one possible answer.

The windscreen wipers flapped frantically but the rain was relentless and Harper only caught glimpses of the road ahead. It took all his skill just to stay on track. The conditions recommended a speed about half what he was currently doing but he wasn't about to slow down.

It was at that moment his phone's GPS quit working. He had just entered the narrowest section of the gorge and the steep walls were blocking line of sight with the satellite. He shook the phone as if this would convince it to try harder for a signal but it did nothing to resolve the problem. He tossed it to the passenger seat and it clattered against the laptop. In any event he was so close now he didn't really need it.

He crested a shallow rise and rounded a bend before slowing the car. This was it. This was where the GPS had indicated Jonathon Hayes had stopped. Harper's laptop showed a straight section of road with a cluster of dots. It meant the truck had been here for several minutes before continuing on to Christchurch.

With each sweep of the wipers he assessed the straight section of highway. At first glance it seemed like an impracticable place to stop. To the left a vertical rock wall, glistening and jagged and ready to dash a vehicle to pieces, and to the right a tangle of native bush that looked equally uninviting. Halfway along the straight a waterfall cascaded down the rock face sending plumes of spray across both lanes. Harper eased as far right as he dared but water still blasted the car like a shotgun load of stones, the force nearly swiping him off the road.

Harper reached the end of the straight but hadn't identified the parking spot. He cursed and drove on until he found a place to execute a U-turn. For a second time he navigated the same section of road. Once again he didn't see anywhere to pull over.

As he crested the rise at the end of the straight he saw a small gravel area. Harper pulled in and glanced at the river. It seemed to be climbing the bank towards him. With renewed urgency he studied the map, zooming in as far as the software would allow. He traced the contours of each bend. It was an exact match for what he had just driven. He was definitely in the right place. The map indicated the truck had stopped roughly halfway down the straight behind him.

Harper plucked his phone off the passenger seat. The GPS was still down and now there was no cell coverage either. Dumping the useless device he returned to the laptop. After staring at it for another minute he convinced himself this was the right area. He must have missed it on his first pass. There was only one way to be sure. He had to get out and walk the route.

Harper made his way along the hard shoulder, fat bullets of rain stinging his face and soaking his clothes. The hard shoulder was less than a metre wide and beyond that the terrain fell sharply towards green swathes of native bush and the flooded river below. There was nowhere wide enough to park a truck without either blocking a lane or risking tipping down the bank. Harper began to second-guess himself. Maybe this wasn't the right place after all. Maybe Hayes' GPS had malfunctioned and this was another dead end. He was about to give up and return to the car when he noticed something. It was still some distance away, but it might just work.

As he approached his suspicions were confirmed. An overgrown trail barely wide enough for a vehicle plunged off the main road at a precarious angle and disappeared down into the bush. It was hidden from view by the hard shoulder and the steeply sloping bank and only someone sitting high in a big-rig or a bus might notice it. Even then it would have been easy to miss. Knee-high grass had almost entirely grown over the wheel tracks but Harper could just detect two faint parallel lines of thinner vegetation heading into the shadowy undergrowth. As he stood at the road's edge a small buzz of excitement began to build.

Harper shuffled off the hard shoulder and down to where the track met a wall of bush. He lingered there a second as if plucking up the courage to dive in. He took a breath and held it as he brushed aside the supple green stems of a Titoki and followed the trail down. Once past this outer wall the path opened out into something resembling a subterranean cavern. The forest canopy blotted out much of the light and reduced the sheets of rain to a rhythmic patter. The black trunks of the beech forest stood like graveyard tombstones watching on from the mist like the ghosts of departed souls. A chill shuddered through Harper and he stopped, checking to make sure he was alone. Over the sound of the drumming rain he heard the rush of the flooded river. It sounded close. If he was going to find anything he needed to do it quickly, before the river washed any evidence away.

As he descended the trail began to flatten out. It was then that he noticed the smell. At first it was faint but it soon grew stronger. Harper scanned left and right trying to pinpoint the source. It was too dark and the forest too thick. He pushed on, following the pungent stench to a dark green object just left of the trail. Ignoring his growing nausea Harper tread closer. It was a wheelie bin identical to the ones used in Westport to collect rubbish. It lay on its side with ferns and branches draped over. If it hadn't been for the smell he would never have found it. The lid had been taped shut but the tape had not held and it had cracked open an inch. A yellow-green liquid oozed out the gap. Harper's stomach churned. He backed away covering his nose, breathing only through his mouth. He swallowed hard and just managed to keep everything down.

Standing a few metres away he surveyed the scene. Off to one side was a flattish area just wide enough for a three-point turn. He studied the ground. While it appeared to have been recently disturbed the rain had destroyed any tread patterns or shoe impressions. Next he did a sweep of the foliage, checking for broken branches or torn clothing fragments or cast-off food wrappers or discarded cigarette butts. He found nothing.

Harper glanced once more at the river. If the rain kept coming it would be only an hour or two before it would wash the evidence away. He desperately wanted to open the wheelie bin but knew that doing so risked contaminating the scene. It was time to bring in the experts.

He ran up to the road and returned to his car. The cell was still out of commission so he drove back towards Berlin's where it finally snared a signal. He dialled the number for the ESR team, catching them as they were wrapping up at the doctor's house. Bridget told him she could be there in ten minutes. Harper hung up and rang Gardella.

'I think I found him.'

'Found who?' Gardella said.

'Jonathon Hayes.'

Gardella was silent for a moment. Then he asked the obvious question. 'Dead or alive?'

'Judging by the smell, I'd say very much dead.'

There was another pause as the ramifications set in. 'Wait a minute. What do you mean, you think you found him?'

Harper explained how he used the GPS waypoints to narrow in on the spot where Hayes' truck had stopped. He described the smell and leaking liquid. All the while Gardella listened quietly without interrupting. When Harper finished, he spoke. 'Are the forensic people on their way?'

'Yep. Told them to drop everything and meet me at the site. They're five minutes out. I need to get back there now. I'll call you when I know more.'

Six minutes later Harper waved down the ESR technicians and instructed them where to park. He briefed Bridget on the crime scene and waited while she and her team donned fresh coveralls and readied their equipment. Once everyone was good to go, Harper led the posse along the roadside to the start of the track. He pointed the way then fell back, staying a few paces behind as they all made their way down. He looked on as a crime scene tech noticed a freshly broken branch and took samples for future comparison while Harper chastised himself for not spotting it himself. Once down at the site the technicians went to work. A photographer and videographer spent several minutes documenting the immediate scene while Bridget and the remaining criminalists conducted a perimeter search.

Unlike the previous day, there was no friendly banter; the knowledge of what lay nearby weighed heavy on everyone's thoughts. Harper watched as the team carried out their tasks with the reverence of a funeral service. Nobody was holding any hope for a happy ending.

With the preliminary work completed a trail of metal footplates was placed around the wheelie bin. At that point everyone took a step back and all eyes turned to Bridget. She took a breath and pulled on her face mask. The others followed suit and Harper immediately felt vulnerable, wishing he'd opted to put on protective gear. He shuffled back a step as if the extra distance would keep him safe.

Using the stepping stone footplates Bridget conducted a slow walk around inspecting every centimetre of the scene like an airline pilot conducting a preflight check. When she reached the lid of the wheelie bin Bridget crouched low and began examining.

When Harper had made his initial discovery he had noticed the lid was sealed with what looked like packaging tape. It had not been strong enough to contain the weight of whatever was inside and had split and peeled in places. Bridget called for a scalpel and used it to lift one edge of the tape. With gloved hands she carefully prized it away, placing it in a series of evidence bags. With the tape removed, she gently opened the bin.

Harper adjusted his position to get a better view but the lighting was poor and he couldn't make out anything obvious. Bridget exchanged her scalpel for a torch and flicked it on. Initially, all Harper saw was a pile of old clothes. But as he looked closer something caught his eye. A hand, its fingers swollen and black.

'Looks like we've got a body, boys,' Bridget called out to the others. She waved towards the two men holding cameras. They swooped in to document the grim details. As they did their work Bridget came over to Harper.

'Thoughts?' Harper asked.

'Human remains, almost certainly male,' Bridget began. 'The body has been dismembered. Based on the level of decomp I'd estimate TOD five to eight days ago, but don't quote me on that. The body is mostly covered with clothes so I can't tell you much more until we get it back to the lab.'

'How can you be sure it's male?'

'Got a good view of the hand. Even with the bloating I can tell it's male. The clothes too. They're men's clothing. I'm picking they belong to our vic. They don't appear to be damaged so I'm guessing he was killed first, stripped, cut up, placed in the bin, and the clothes dumped on top.'

Harper thought about this for a moment. 'Looks like we've found our missing person.'

'Might not be the guy,' Bridget offered.

Harper almost laughed. 'This is small town New Zealand we're talking about. It's not like we're tripping over bodies on a regular basis.'

'Fair call,' Bridget admitted. 'I just think we should wait for confirmation.'

'And how long is that likely to take?'

Bridget mulled the question. 'The best course of action would be to close it back up, wrap the whole thing and preserve any trace. Then we'll either take it over to the coroner in Westport or more preferably, move it to Christchurch and do a more thorough examination. Might need to use dental. If that's the case we'd be looking at a week minimum, possibly longer.'

'What about prints?'

'You talking about the vic's, or the killer's?'

'Both.'

'We can try and get some off the body. There's not that much decomp yet. But we'll need comparisons to make an ID. Unless the guy's prints are already in the system we're never going to know for sure. Regarding whoever dumped the body our best bet is if there are latents under the lid or inside the bin itself. We can preserve these if we wrap it and move it back to the lab. I just need you to tell me how you want to proceed.'

Harper looked away as if searching for a second opinion. He was sure the body belonged to Jonathon Hayes. 'Can't you remove the clothes to see if we can get a look at his face?'

'The risk is we might contaminate some of the evidence. We smudge a print or drop a piece of clothing in the mud and we've got a problem. Even if we did get a look at the guy's face it might be too far gone to make an ID. As it stands we've got a nice little time capsule holding everything we need. I'd much rather move it to a sterile location and take my time than do a rushed job at the scene.'

Harper looked down at the river. It had crept closer. Soon they would be underwater. Bridget was right. They needed to move.

'Okay, wrap it,' Harper finally said. 'We'll transport it back to Christchurch.'

Bridget nodded her agreement and called over to one of the technicians. 'John, grab the plastic wrap from the van. We'll only need one roll.'

Harper followed John up the track and back along the road to the parking area. The technician retrieved the plastic and returned to the scene while Harper climbed into his cruiser. He was about to start the engine when he noticed a weak signal on his cell. He used the solitary bar of reception to phone the Westport Police Station and requested a hearse and two officers to manage the scene.

Once again he reached for the ignition. For a second time, something stopped him. It took a second for the thought to take hold and another for Harper to leap out of the car. When he made it down to the site he was relieved to see the large roll of cling film leaning against a nearby tree.

Catching his breath Harper asked Bridget, 'Are there any identifying marks on the bin like an address, street name, number, anything like that?'

'Ah, no. We've got remnants of some kind of sticker but most of it has peeled off. See here?' she said, pointing to a wedge-shaped shard stuck to the side of the bin just under the lid. 'That's it.'

Harper moved in and examined what was left of the sticker. All that remained was a thin sliver with no printing or other visible markings. His shoulders sagged.

'You think it was removed deliberately?' Harper asked.

'I doubt it. See these scoring marks?' She pointed to two parallel gouge marks under the lip of the wheelie bin. 'That's where the forks of the rubbish truck grab the bin. The sticker was almost certainly torn off long ago. The damage appears to be old.'

Harper stood up and placed his hands on his hips. Bridget followed his lead.

'Anything else? Harper asked hopefully.

'Nope. We're about ready to stand it up and wrap it. You cool with that?'

Harper stared down at the bin looking for anything that could have been overlooked. He saw nothing. He looked at the other crime scene techs then at the river and finally at Bridget. 'Okay, let's do it,' he said reluctantly.

Bridget wasted no time and summoned the other men. With Harper watching they slowly raised the bin to its vertical position, taking care to hold the lid shut. Once upright, Bridget stooped to inspect the flattened area of foliage beneath. The ground under a body often yielded many clues; shoe and tyre impressions, shell casings, cigarette butts, drag marks, receipts, the victim's ID, and other assorted pieces of trace evidence. But Harper wasn't looking at the ground. He had spotted something else.

'What's that?' he called out.

The others followed the line from his hand. A heavy-duty plastic handle stuck out several centimetres from the top of the bin. But that wasn't what Harper was interested in. It was what he saw underneath that had attracted his attention. Partially obscured by mud were a series of letters and numbers that had been stamped into the thick, rubberised plastic. As Harper moved in for a closer inspection he could see the last two characters were obscured.

'Jamie. Grab your camera and get a photo of this,' Bridget ordered.

Jamie took three photos, checking each one on the LCD display. When he decided he had a usable shot he nodded. Another technician held a clear plastic evidence bag as Bridget used a spatula-like tool to remove the dirt. The photographer took another series of shots and nodded once again. Harper moved in for a closer look.

KOO1457

Harper had left his notepad and phone in the car so he read through the sequence several times, committing it to memory.

'We all good to secure this evidence, Detective?' Bridget asked.

Harper read it once more before saying, 'Yep. Wrap it up.'

As he turned to head back up to the road he noticed the red and blues flashing above. The two officers from Westport had arrived and Harper wondered how they had got to the scene so quickly as he'd only phoned it in five minutes ago. This question was soon replaced by the realisation that it wouldn't be long before a passing motorist spotted the commotion and tipped off the media. He needed to get back into town and inform Samara before someone else got to her first.

CHAPTER 24

Instead of going directly to the gallery Harper stopped at the hotel to change clothes and then drove to the council chambers on Brougham Street. The Westport Council Chambers were housed in a nondescript two-storey shoebox of a building that looked like it had been designed by someone who had flunked out of architecture school.

Harper parked outside and made his way up the steps and through the automatic double doors. The waiting area had half a dozen chairs positioned back-to-back. A woman who looked like she could lose twenty kilos and not notice the difference staffed the reception desk at the far end. She sat with her head down reading a book and made no effort to acknowledge Harper. He made it all the way to the counter before she raised her head and gave him a disapproving look.

'Hi,' Harper said, trying to sound friendly. 'I'd like to trace a missing wheelie bin. The number's K-O-O-one-four-five-seven.'

The woman looked at him dimly and her monotone response sounding like a pre-recorded message. 'Orange form on your right. Code B-D-C-eleven.'

Harper thought about flashing his badge in an attempt to bypass the paperwork but decided against it. He found the form and spent the next couple of minutes filling it out. He presented it to the woman and she typed the information into her computer. Another minute went by before her printer hummed into action. She handed Harper the printout.

'Will that be all?' she said, more out of habit than a genuine question.

Harper didn't respond. He just turned and walked out of the building. Back in the car, he phoned Gardella. He picked up after two rings.

'I need a warrant for the Hayes residence,' Harper said before Gardella even had a chance to say hello.

'What? Why?'

'I've just traced the wheelie bin to the house.'

'Shit.' Gardella said, sounding both surprised and impressed.

'We need the forensic people in there pronto.'

'I'm on it,' Gardella fired back. 'You like the wife for this?'

Harper spoke slowly, forming his theory as he went. 'It's possible. Her alibi only holds up for Friday evening when she was seen having dinner at the Karamea Hotel. After that, no one can confirm her whereabouts until Monday. That's a big window.' Harper drummed his fingers against the steering wheel. 'What if she came home that night, knocked him off, packed the suitcase, then drove to Christchurch, dumping the body on the way. But how did she get back to Westport?'

'She could have booked a flight,' Gardella offered.

Harper felt another piece fall into place. 'That's why she held back the bank records. She knew we would see the booking.'

'What about the fuel?' Gardella interrupted. 'If she returned to Karamea to make it look like she was out of town all weekend, how could she make it back to Westport and still have half a tank?'

'She never went back to Karamea, Joe. She stayed in the house.'

Through the silence, Harper could almost hear the penny drop. 'She was cleaning up,' Gardella finally said.

Harper didn't answer, his mind racing, running the scenario through his head, looking for holes.

'What's the problem?' Gardella asked.

'There's just one thing that doesn't fit.'

'What's that?'

'How'd she get the body into the truck? The bin alone would be too heavy for her to lift.'

Gardella mulled this for a second. 'Maybe she had help.'

A bolt of recognition shot through Harper. 'Shit. I almost had him.'

'Almost had who?'

'The night I went to update the wife. Someone else was there. I gave chase, but I lost him.'

'Who was there?' Gardella asked. 'I'm not following.'

'When I came out of the house a man was standing at the end of the block. It was dark and foggy so I couldn't make an ID. At the time I assumed he was one of the scumbags I put away after Sara was killed. I thought he was just trying to put the frighteners on me. Anyway, the next day I spotted someone following me. I put two and two together and thought it was probably the same guy. I caught him and gave him the once-over and told him to back off. I handled it. That's why I never brought it up.'

'You should've called for backup.'

'Yeah, backup,' Harper scoffed. 'Just what I needed. What were they going to do? Follow me around like bodyguards? You know how that would've gone down back at CIB. Those guys already think I'm out of my depth. The last thing I need is a couple of babysitters. I can handle this. I am handling this.'

Gardella let out a long breath and followed this with a protracted silence. 'So,' Gardella eventually said. 'You think the guy you spoke to helped the wife with the body?'

'Not the guy following me in the car, no,' Harper said. 'I can't see Samara Hayes and that arsehole working together. No. The man in the fog was someone else.'

'So who is he?' Gardella asked.

Harper shrugged. 'Whoever he is, he's got balls.'

A man in a cheap two-piece suit strolled down the steps outside the council chambers and Harper eyed him like he was as good a suspect as any. He continued to watch as the suit walked along the footpath and disappeared into the post office at the corner of Palmerston and Brougham. During this time Gardella hadn't said anything so Harper checked back in. 'What's going on with Sharma? You get any more out of him?'

'Nope. Brought him in again but same dice. He wouldn't cooperate. His lawyer is going apeshit about the newspaper thing and threatening all kinds of legal action. The truck's not looking good either. We're getting no prints from it.'

Harper couldn't believe it. 'None?'

'None. Not even partials. Whoever drove it wiped down every surface, and I mean every surface. The inside of that truck is cleaner than a priest on Sunday. The team is still working it but I'm not holding my breath. What's happening with the body? You manage to get it out of town?'

'Shit.' He had forgotten to clear it with the coroner. 'Yeah, it's on the way, but I haven't told the locals yet. I better get my arse over to the hospital and smooth that one over.'

'You do that. I'll work on securing a warrant for the house and one for the bank account. With any luck I'll email them within the next couple of hours. Good work, Dylan.'

Harper wasted no time getting over to the hospital. The coroner was none too happy when he was told that the body was halfway to Christchurch and he threatened to turn the hearse around. Harper eventually convinced him that the remains were in such a condition that it would require the attention of a forensic pathologist and he smoothed things over by promising a copy of the autopsy report complete with photos and video.

When he arrived back in his car he checked his emails on the off-chance Gardella had sent through the warrants. It had only been twenty minutes and his inbox was empty. Harper couldn't wait any longer. He needed to get over to the gallery before the media got to the wife. He started the car and headed in that direction.

When he walked through the door he found Samara sitting on the same stool, almost as if she had been too afraid to move. She looked like a lost child, scared and alone and waiting for someone to tell her what to do. Harper swallowed hard, trying to suppress his sympathy. It was possible this woman had murdered her husband, cut up the body, and dumped it at the side of the road.

He turned away and his eyes fell on one of the paintings, the canvas he had seen that morning. The depiction of the felled forest with jagged stumps protruded like broken teeth from a landscape laid to waste by human hands, the bodies of trees strewn as far as the eye could see. Harper looked at the small white card tucked into the bottom right corner of the wooden frame.

Dead Ground

S Hayes

2010

'You like this one?' Samara said, surprising Harper.

'Oh, you—I didn't realise you were standing there.'

'I noticed you looking at it this morning. It's not a piece that normally attracts much attention. Most people like waterfalls and dreamy sunsets. What do you like about it?'

Harper thought for a long while before an answer sparked. 'I guess because this is what I'm used to. Death and its aftermath. This is what my memories are of this place. I don't see green trees and blue seas. I see pain and suffering.'

Samara gave a small nod. 'You've had a lot of pain in your life, haven't you?'

'I guess I have, yes. This painting is my reality. All these other ones are what people post on their Facebook profiles when they're trying to convince the world that their life is perfect. But that's not reality. This,' Harper said, pointing at the canvas, 'this is reality. For me at least.'

Samara dropped her head. 'For me too,' she said softly.

Harper studied her, trying to spot the mark of a cold-blooded killer. So far he didn't see it. But that didn't mean it wasn't there. The trouble was he could sense his judgement being clouded, her lonely sadness getting the better of him. He needed to get the situation back on track.

'Mrs Hayes,' he began solemnly. 'There have been some developments.' He waited for a reply but she seemed to know what was coming. 'We have discovered a body,' Harper continued. 'At this stage we're not sure if it is Jon but I thought you should be informed before the media get hold of the news.'

For a moment she stood perfectly still, her green eyes wide and empty and staring at nothing in particular. Slowly, she brought a hand up to her mouth.

'No,' she managed, her voice just a whisper.

Harper went and grabbed the stool and brought it over. He found another and sat in front of her.

'Can I see him? I mean, can I see the body?' she said as a single tear rolled down her cheek.

'Not just yet. We've taken the remains to Christchurch for a specialist autopsy. They will attempt to make an identification. After that, we'll know more.'

'Why can't I see him? I want to see if it's Jon.'

Harper squirmed as he searched for a delicate way to deliver the next piece of news.

'Well, that might be difficult. The body has suffered some decomposition. A visual ID might be difficult.'

Harper had deliberately left out several pieces of information. The dismemberment. Where the body had been located, and the wheelie bin. He had to treat her as a suspect. If he didn't tell her these facts the only other way she'd know would be if she was somehow involved. A good investigator using standard questioning techniques could easily coax this guilty knowledge at a later date.

'But how will a stranger know if it's Jon?' Samara asked.

'Medical records, dental most likely. Do you know if Jon had any operations, surgical implants, anything like that?'

'No,' she said, shaking her head like the idea repulsed her. 'He never had any operations.'

'In that case, they'll probably use dental records. If you like, we can make arrangements to transport you to Christchurch.'

'Um, yes, that would … that would be good.'

'Would you like me to call anyone?'

'No. I think I'll close up. I'll ring my friends and get them to pick me up.'

'That's a good idea. I'll be back in touch as soon as we have more information. Where will I be able to find you?'

'The Brougham Street house. The one you came to the other night.'

'Okay. If you have any questions, call me. Do you still have my card?'

'Yes.'

'Good. I'll be back in touch soon.'

Harper left the gallery knowing he would be in touch sooner than she thought.

CHAPTER 25

It was mid-afternoon and Harper realised he was starved. Two doors down from the gallery was an Indian restaurant. With no better options and no sign of the search warrants he made a beeline for it. The place was empty which made him second guess his decision but in the end he risked it, hoping people had simply been scared off by the weather and not the quality of the food. He took a table in the back and was served quickly. When the food arrived he was pleasantly surprised.

The break gave him time to think. The wheelie bin tied the murder to the Hayes house. There was circumstantial evidence suggesting the wife had means, motive, and opportunity. Harper's dealings with her hadn't convinced him of her innocence either. At times she acted like a grieving spouse, but on other occasions she was defensive and uncooperative. What Harper lacked was physical evidence. He had nothing concrete tying Samara to her husband's murder.

As he finished his meal, Harper checked his emails. The warrant had arrived. Gardella had been thorough. It gave wide-sweeping powers to search for blood, hair, fibre and any physical evidence that a crime had been committed at the address. It gave the police the power to seize anything and everything.

He drove to the station and printed a copy before arriving at the Brougham Street house where Samara had taken refuge. She didn't seem surprised to see him again so soon and didn't bat an eye when presented with the warrant. Harper noted this as yet another odd reaction. She gave him her keys but said she didn't want to witness the search.

Back in the car he phoned Bridget but the called failed. Harper assumed she was still at the body dump site and out of cell coverage. He waited fifteen minutes and tried again. Same result. On his third attempt he got through and Bridget informed him that her team had just finished and were on their way back to town. Harper updated her on the latest developments and gave her the address of the Hayes residence. She told him they would be there in twenty.

Harper parked his car at the Hayes residence and climbed out to the sharp tang of steaming tarmac. A shaft of sunlight had pierced the grey and turned the wet footpath into a simmering hotplate. Aside from this the cloying air was heavy and still and the street was deserted but for the occasional vehicle lodged against the curb. During his last visit darkness had masked much of the dreariness. Now, in the early afternoon light, every weather-beaten surface stood out in high definition. White paint flaked from under the eaves like sunburnt skin while the driveway was buckled and broken like a pane of shattered glass. The lawn was a mess of dishevelled grass and the whole section looked as though no one had lived there for months.

As he glanced towards the rear he saw something he wasn't expecting. A wheelie bin, identical to the one he had just found in the gorge. This jogged his memory. He had seen it there before. The night they first came to visit Samara. He remembered it resting in the same position against the corner of the garage.

In the adrenalin rush of finding the body he had forgotten about seeing the bin on that first night. It had been sitting there the whole time. But if the bin in the gorge belonged to the Hayes household, who owned the one he was now staring at? He needed to get a closer look. Protocol stipulated that he wait for the ESR team but it was too much of a temptation. He couldn't wait. Harper returned to the car and retrieved a pair of latex gloves and snapped them on.

The single garage was wedged hard against the fence, its dilapidated state in keeping with the rest of the property. The paint on the tilt door had dissolved away to nothing exposing weeping patches of corroded steel. A thin concrete path wrapped around the garage and continued on to a rotary clothesline in the backyard. The wheelie bin sat on this path, resting against the wall of the garage.

The handle of the bin was against the wall so Harper couldn't see the serial number. He made a cursory search for the white identification sticker. The first two sides showed no signs, but on the third, he saw something unusual.

Much of the plastic was scoured, grubby and scratched from years of hard use. However, just under the top lip there was a small rectangular patch of clean, undamaged surface. An obvious sign that something had been removed recently. A sticker. There were no fragments left behind suggesting it had been carefully peeled off in one piece. With the identification sticker gone, the only way of tracing it would be to look at the stamped serial number located on the rear.

Making as little contact as possible, Harper placed his latex-gloved fingers under the downturned lip of the bin and dragged it a few inches away from the garage. Judging by the weight he estimated it was about half full. After some jostling he managed to manoeuvre it far enough to get a look at the rear. Down on one knee he peered in through the small gap. His heart sank. He blinked twice and looked again.

'Fuck it,' he muttered.

Under the handle, where the serial number should have been, were a series of diagonal gouge marks that obliterated any information that had been stamped into the plastic. It looked like a metal object, possibly a flat head screwdriver, had chiselled away the surface. Harper swore again and stood up. He walked back to the footpath and waited impatiently for the forensic team. While he stood, he mulled over what all this meant.

Samara had apparently stolen a neighbour's bin to hide that hers was missing and scratched off the serial number so it couldn't be traced back to its original owner. But something didn't fit with that explanation.

If she had taken the time to scratch out the serial number on this bin, why hadn't she done the same with the one containing the body? If she were trying to hide her tracks why didn't she remove both numbers? She had been so careful everywhere else, eliminating prints from the truck, taking the clothes from the closet and getting rid of the computer, not to mention using the ATM camera to divert attention. Erasing the serial number on one bin but not the other didn't fit the pattern.

Maybe she thought the dumpsite would never be found. Had it not been for the GPS tracker it almost certainly wouldn't have been. But it was a huge risk that she didn't need to take. Why had she slipped up? Everything else had been so careful and deliberate. Taking the clothes, the withdrawal of the money, the recorded message and the truck at the airport were all engineered to make it look like Jonathon Hayes was still alive. Why would Samara want that? Yes, it would cover up the murder, but no murder meant no insurance money, not to mention losing her primary source of income. There had to be another explanation.

Maybe she didn't care about the money. Maybe she just wanted him dead. Did she find out he was still having an affair and that pushed her over the edge? So she kills her husband and concocts an elaborate scheme to divert attention from herself. But that didn't explain why she would remove one serial number and not the other. Why be so careful and deliberate everywhere else but leave one flashing neon sign that pointed straight back to her?

A growing din signalled the approach of the crime scene techs. The forensic van pulled in first followed by two other cars. Four technicians piled out and began donning crisp white coveralls. Bridget exited last and approached Harper who was standing on the path.

'This the place?' she asked glancing at the house.

'This is it. What's the plan?' he asked, handing her a copy of the warrant. She took her time reading it, occasionally flicking strands of blonde hair from her face as she studied the powers of search and seizure granted by the judge. Finally, she gave an approving nod and looked up at Harper.

'Based on this we could lift the whole house, throw it on a truck and haul it back to Christchurch,' she said handing the warrant back. 'Let's start with a perimeter search, see if we can spot anything obvious. Then we'll make entry and look for any trace inside. We'll pay particular attention to the bathroom, see if that's where he was dismembered. After that we'll do a more generalised search for blood spatter, blood transfer, possible weapons, etcetera, etcetera.'

'Start with the bin,' Harper said, pointing down the driveway. 'Make it a priority.'

Bridget saw the bin and raised an eyebrow. 'Where did that come from?' she asked.

'Don't know. The number's been ground off. Whoever dumped the body must've stolen it to replace the one in the gorge.'

'We'll check it out. Might contain some prints, but based on the weather, it'll be a long shot. Still, it's worth a go. We might get something under the lid. You never know.'

Harper nodded. Bridget went off to don her own coveralls. She returned with an extra one for Harper which he reluctantly put on.

The perimeter search took an hour, most of which they spent on the wheelie bin. Two partials were found and photographed. The lack of any other prints suggested the rain had washed the rest away. What little rubbish was inside seemed to originate from the Hayes residence. They found a receipt for art supplies as well as a small amount of food waste, bottle tops, plastic supermarket bags, an old light bulb, along with other assorted household items, none of which stood out as significant. With all the rubbish removed, an area of dark staining was observed at the bottom where an unknown liquid had pooled. Bridget decided not to conduct a presumptive test for blood, telling Harper there was a high likelihood of a false or indeterminate result due to contamination. Instead, she wrapped the bin and put it into the van for more detailed analysis back at the lab.

Harper used Samara's keys to unlock the front door and the team entered. Warm, stale air enveloped Harper, getting under his coveralls like a stranger invading his personal space. A vase on a display table near the stairs held six dead roses, their petals shed and lying curled on the floor. A sombre hush occupied the rooms as if the house was holding its breath. The eyes of the Hayes family watched on from photographs as they went about their work.

The team moved slowly through the ground floor and Harper soon found himself in the kitchen. Everything was as he remembered it. Nothing had been touched. He noticed the coffee cup that Samara had drunk from. He called in the fingerprint officer and asked him to check it for prints. Another officer was sifting through the cutlery drawer as if looking for the knife that cut up the body. Harper stood at the kitchen table and watched as the team went about its duties. Their movements were methodical, each action well practiced and deliberate.

After an hour Bridget said she was ready to move upstairs. Harper followed as she inched up one step at a time, looking for any trace as she went. At the top of the stairs she headed towards the bathroom. Harper opted for the bedroom.

It looked exactly the same. The bed perfectly made, the closet open, the contents undisturbed. Samara had probably packed her bags and was ready to leave before Harper and Gardella had even arrived on that first night. She had not wanted to stay a minute longer than absolutely necessary.

He walked towards the open closet and looked at the contents. The lone suit hung at one end, two business shirts and a solitary tie for company. But he was more interested in what was on the shelf above the clothes rail.

Several shoe boxes were stacked either side of a suitcase-sized gap of empty space and a plastic container full of compact disks sat at the far end of the shelf. Harper slid the clear plastic container out and placed it carefully on the bed. Removing the lid revealed music CDs stacked vertically, their spines on display. Harper scanned through the names. Mostly '80s and '90s heavy metal bands. He couldn't see any blank CDs but that didn't mean there were none. One by one he began opening each case to check its contents. He was halfway through the box when Bridget came into the bedroom. Before she could ask any questions, Harper got in first. 'Anything of interest in the bathroom?'

'Ah, not at this stage. There are a couple of hairs caught in the bath plug. I've bagged and tagged them. That's about it. No obvious signs of blood but we'll need to do some more testing before we can say for sure. What are you looking at in here?'

'Just catching up on the classics,' Harper said as he opened a Mötley Crüe album and examined the silver disc.

'Don't tell me you listen to that crap,' Bridget said as she scanned the other titles spread out on the bed.

'All the time,' he replied in a droll voice.

She smiled back. 'Okay. In that case, I'll leave you to it. I'm just ducking out to the van to collect some equipment. Don't go into the bathroom or touch anything without a crime scene officer with you.'

'No problem. Oh, and tell your team to keep their eyes out for a laptop. If anyone comes across one, let me know.'

She said she would and left. He didn't expect the ESR team to find the laptop. If it contained what he thought it contained then it would have been destroyed shortly after the murder. His only hope was if Jonathon had made copies.

It didn't take him long to finish going through the CDs. None were recordable disks. He returned them to the closet and pulled down three crumpled shoe boxes. One contained old wedding photos and another held newspaper clippings from stories Hayes had written over the years. The last box was a collection of old pens. He dug through them looking for anything hidden beneath, but found nothing. Harper closed the boxes and placed them back into the closet.

As he did this he looked again at the suit hanging in the corner. Apart from the shirts and tie it was the only piece of clothing left behind. It hung rumpled and forlorn like it hadn't been worn for a long time.

The suit consisted of a dark jacket and matching trousers—Harper couldn't tell if they were black or dark blue—and a silver tie clip on the left breast pocket. The tie clip caught his attention. Something about it seemed odd.

Harper reached in and slid the coat hanger along the rail until the suit was out of the dark recesses. Now he knew what was odd about the tie clip. It was made from unusually thick metal. He coaxed it off the jacket and held it between his thumb and forefinger. He rotated it slowly, each smooth edge glinting in the light. As he turned it end on he saw a narrow rectangular opening.

Slowly the realisation of what he was holding dawned on him. He used his free hand to prod the metal tang. A USB connector popped out of the small opening. This was what he was after. He was sure of it.

Harper was down the stairs and in his car with his laptop on his lap in under a minute. When the home screen flashed up he eased the memory stick into one of the USB ports and waited for the system to pick it up. A message appeared saying the device was ready. He clicked on the file icon and selected the device from the drop-down menu. A list containing three file names was displayed.

InterPacific resource consent hearings
Mining history in the Buller Gorge
XXXX

Harper opened the first file from the list. The resource consent for InterPacific's application ran to twelve pages. Harper read through the details. It stacked up with what the translator had told him. The only thing that struck him as odd was the lack of specific detail. Harper had limited experience with resource consents but it seemed like this one skimmed over a lot of points without really explaining much.

From what Harper could tell here hadn't been any public hearings either. Typically an operation on this scale would affect multiple groups within the community and would require public consultation, feedback, more hearings and several amendments before getting the stamp of approval. It seemed none of that had taken place. The whole application had been processed under the "Minor Effects/No Notification" exemption and had been rushed through in under forty-five days. There was no mention of potential pollution, the need to fell native trees, or how the use of the rail line and port might affect other stakeholders.

Harper flicked to the back page to see which members of the council had approved the plan. The first name was Li Qian. He had signed as managing director of InterPacific. The next few cosigners were all members of the Buller District Council, including the mayor, Gerry Babich. But it was the last name that took all of Harper's attention. George Southon. Harper had heard of him and knew that his signature didn't belong on this document. Southon was the government minister for Foreign Affairs and Trade and was one of the top power brokers in the country. Why the fuck was he signing off on something like this? This was a local matter that should have been dealt with by the local council.

Then Harper remembered something. He stepped out of the car and opened the boot and retrieved the manila folder with the various documents relating to the case. After climbing back into the car he sifted through the stack of papers until he found the newspaper article about the opening of the Mackley River Gold Mine. He read it again. This time he focused on the first paragraph.

> After months of delays and setbacks, InterPacific Mining announced this week that they have finally begun production at the much-hyped Mackley Gold Mine. The Chinese-based consortium had been battling resource consent hurdles which required high-level backing from the government before finally being given the go-ahead to commence mining operations late last year.

Now it made sense. Southon had stepped in to force the consent through. He had made it "No Notification" to avoid a public hearing and the potential problems that would cause. But why would the central government care if the consent was approved? What were they trying to hide? Harper had a feeling the next two files contained the answer.

He opened the next file and began reading. The first few pages chronicled the boom and bust of the coal industry from 1840 to the early 1970s. During this time a string of accidents claimed scores of lives and spelt the end of several underground operations. Today, the surviving mines were mostly open cast and located in the mountains around Westport. Much of the coal was exported to Asia, with Japan consuming the lion's share, and China increasingly becoming an important customer.

The next section covered the gold rush of 1864–1867. During this time the West Coast region became the most populous in the country with towns springing up like mushrooms wherever gold was discovered. But as soon as the gold dried up the miners disappeared as did the boom towns they had created. Today, centres like Crushington were just a road sign by the highway and a few crumbling buildings were all that remained of a once thriving township. The article did note that a recent global financial crisis had led nervous investors back to gold sending the price soaring to unprecedented heights.

None of this was news to Harper. And it hardly felt relevant to the case. Until he scrolled to the next page.

CHAPTER 26

The words Harper read next made him do a double-take.

"Uranium deposits in the Buller Gorge."

'What the fuck?' he mumbled.

Harper had grown up on the Coast and knew all about coal and gold. Most of his friends had a parent or relative whose job was somehow linked to the mines. If it wasn't mining it was forestry or farming. The West Coast was rich with natural resources but this was the first time he had seen anything about uranium. As he read on he learned more.

At the dawn of the nuclear age many countries rushed to exploit the power of the atom. In 1944 the New Zealand Government jumped on this bandwagon by initiating a search for uranium. However, by the mid-1950s they had not found any deposits so they encouraged the public to go prospecting as a weekend hobby, even publishing detailed instructions on how to build a Geiger counter. This had paid off almost immediately.

In 1954, two ageing prospectors, Frankerick Cassin and Charles Jacobsen were driving through the Buller Gorge. They had been drinking at Berlin's Pub and decided to relieve themselves at the side of the road. As soon as they stopped their homemade Geiger counters began ticking wildly, directing them to a section of rock near Hawkes Crag. Subsequent testing revealed they had stumbled upon an area of highly radioactive rock.

More discoveries were made in the following years. In 1959 New Zealand signed a secret deal with the British Government to supply any viable material to their nuclear programme. However, by 1964 it was determined that the uranium concentrations were too low and the project was scrapped.

There was a brief period of renewed prospecting in the early 1980s when it was thought that nuclear power could solve the country's growing electricity crisis. But this became politically unpopular after the Chernobyl disaster and New Zealand's pledge to become a nuclear-free nation.

When significant quantities of natural gas were discovered in the northern part of the country the need for nuclear power vanished. The plans to search for more concentrated deposits were permanently shelved. The article concluded by saying that as of 2005, all uranium deposits were the property of the New Zealand Government. Further prospecting was strictly forbidden.

Harper could scarcely believe what he was reading. He pulled out his cell and typed "Uranium on the West Coast of New Zealand." Several hits came back and Harper skim read each. They all basically agreed with the article on Hayes' USB stick. One website even had a map that highlighted several areas in red where uranium deposits were either identified or suspected. Two of these were in the Buller Gorge. One was in roughly the same area of the Mackley River Goldmine. Harper was now almost certain of what he would find when he opened the final file. He put his phone back in his pocket, closed the second file and opened the one named XXXX.

The first page was a research paper investigating uranium contamination of water aquifers in the United States. It stated that the maximum acceptable contamination level, MCL, was thirty µg/ℓ or thirty Pico Curies per litre. Considerable testing had been conducted around known uranium mines in the US. These tests had found levels of uranium in the water up to 189 times above this MCL. The paper suggested there was a link between this high concentration and increased rates of renal cancer. Residents in towns with similar levels of uranium were dying of chronic kidney and liver failure, well above the natural rate expected from a population chosen at random. Harper read to the bottom of the first page and scrolled down to the next section.

The next page had a screenshot of an Excel spreadsheet. There was a grid of boxes filled with a jumble of seemingly random numbers and incoherent symbols. However, some parts were recognisable. At the top was a date, 02/07/2011, and location, Mackley/Buller River confluence. Frank Mortimer had called Hayes on February sixth and the GPS data from the truck showed that Hayes had driven out to Mortimer's farm on the seventh. It was Hayes' water testing results from that day.

As he trawled through the numbers, he came to one that was highlighted in yellow.

$$\mu g/\ell = 30{,}000$$

Contamination one thousand times above the maximum recommended safe level. What Jonathon Hayes had found on the seventh of February was not pollution from a gold mine, but radioactive contamination in the river.

With this new information a lot of the other pieces began to make sense. The consent had been rushed through because public hearings would have raised too many questions. The public outcry would have killed the project before it even got off the ground so the Minister of Foreign Affairs and Trade had stepped in and hushed it up.

Harper wondered if political pressure had come from the Chinese. He remembered the highly publicised free-trade deal struck between the two countries in 2008. It was big news at the time because it was the first such deal between China and a Western economy. What didn't make sense was that China already had a reliable supply of uranium from Australia. Why do a secret deal with New Zealand? Harper scanned the rest of the document looking for answers. He noticed a notation at the bottom of the page.

$\mu g/\ell$ may be higher as equipment unable to measure above 30,000.

No wonder it was killing all and sundry. It was a massive dose of radiation. So high the machine couldn't even measure it. Fortunately for Westport their drinking water was sourced elsewhere. Also working in the town's favour was the likelihood that the radiation would be significantly diluted when the Mackley River flowed into the much larger Buller.

The mine ownership had probably been counting on this when they set up their loading facility in that location. It was the perfect spot. Isolated and away from roads but still within reach of a rail line that ran directly to the port where it could be shipped offshore in the middle of the night. They would have figured they could hose away the radioactive dust into the nearby stream and no one would be the wiser.

The plan would have worked had it not been for a small-town reporter with a part-time water testing job and a concerned farmer who noticed some dead stock. Hayes would never have tested the water in the Mackley River had it not been for that phone call from Frank Mortimer. Solid Energy contracted Hayes to make sure their coal mining operation was not contaminating any nearby rivers. The Mackley River was not close to any coal mines.

Hayes had stumbled upon the contamination and gone digging. What he ultimately learnt was enough to give him leverage and the mine was paying him to keep quiet. His bank statement showed that a week after visiting the site money started appearing in his account. At the same time he was writing favourable newspaper stories about the mine and shaking hands with the manager, Li Qian.

Harper flicked open his notebook and thumbed through the pages until he found the notes from the first interview with Derek Graham. Graham had overheard some of what Hayes had said during the brief phone conversation in the bar shortly before he went missing. Graham had thought he said "Have you got the stash?" but Harper now realised it was probably "Have you got the cash?" Hayes was meeting up with Qian to receive his latest payment. But something had changed. Qian had decided enough was enough. It was time to remove the problem. Hayes was murdered and the scene staged to divert attention from the perpetrators.

This changed everything. No longer was it a simple case of a wife scorned or a doctor with a grudge. This was big time. George Southon was the third most powerful person in the country. How much farther up the chain it went was anyone's guess. The Chinese factor further complicated things. These people had a lot to lose if the truth came out. Jonathon Hayes had lost his life because of what he had uncovered. Now Harper had that same information. That made him a target. He needed to file the evidence, and he needed to do it now.

CHAPTER 27

Harper climbed out of the car and into a chill southerly that stung like a slap in the face. Collar up and head down he pushed through the cold wind towards the house. He found Bridget in the upstairs bathroom. The window had been blacked out and she was preoccupied with something in the bathtub, spraying a substance Harper assumed was luminol.

'Got something?' Harper asked hopefully.

Bridget was busy and her reply curt. 'Just getting started. I'll let you know.'

'Listen, I've got to get back to the station and file some evidence. You good to hold the fort for an hour or so?'

'No problem,' she replied, still focused on the task at hand.

'Ring my cell if anything crops up,' Harper called out as he made for the stairs.

Harper bounded down the steps two at a time, energised by what he had uncovered and anxious to get it documented into evidence. Once it was on file it would be much harder to cover up.

At the bottom of the stairs he brushed past a crime scene tech who stood at the front door staring at something outside. As Harper emerged into the fading light two police cars jerked to a halt, their lights pulsing red and blue. Three officers piled out, their expressions, poker face. Bevan, Button and Monty. Harper strode down the drive towards them.

'Must be a slow day if all three of you have turned up here. Don't tell me you've left the fate of the good people of Westport in the hands of Lord Snowden,' Harper said.

Monty looked at Bevan and Bevan looked at Button and no one said anything.

Eventually, Button broke the standoff. 'Detective Harper, we are placing you under arrest.'

Harper stopped dead, a crooked frown showing his confusion. He looked at Monty trying to gauge if this was some kind of a joke but his old pal just shook his head.

'On what charge?' Harper said.

'Possession and trafficking of methamphetamine, a Class A prohibited substance,' Button announced coldly.

'You've got to be fucking kidding.'

'No Detective. No joke. You are under arrest. You have the right to—'

'Don't read me my rights,' Harper barked. 'I know my rights. Who put you up to this?'

'Detective Harper, you need to come with us. We can do this nice and easy, or we can do it another way.'

'This is ridiculous. I'm investigating a murder.'

Beavan and Monty stood stony-faced. Button shook his head. 'That's not the information we have.'

'What the fuck is that supposed to mean? What information?'

'You understand better than most that I can't tell you that, Detective,' Button said.

'This is bullshit. I'm calling central. Bones is going to tear strips off you idiots.'

Harper reached for his phone. As he did the three officers went for their weapons. Harper froze. Slowly, he raised his hands in surrender. He looked back over his shoulder. Bridget and two other techs stood on the porch looking on in astonishment. There was nothing more he or anyone else could do. Any false moves and he would end up like Jonathon Hayes. The best thing was to cooperate. He was sure he could sort this mess out with a phone call and be cleared within a few hours. But this bullshit meant he'd have to put the case on hold just when he was zeroing in on his primary suspect.

Monty edged in and gave Harper a pat-down which revealed his Glock and his cell. Once relieved of these items Harper was handcuffed and escorted to one of the waiting cars. The trip back to the station was short. He didn't say anything to Bevan who had been given the task of driving. He'd hoped for Monty but figured the other two knew about their past association and wanted to keep the old friends apart. At the station Harper was deposited straight into one of the cells.

Outside of his induction training this was the only occasion Harper had spent any significant time inside a holding cell. He had forgotten how claustrophobic the environment could be. The room had a small window at one end, its barred and frosted glass gave a meagre dose of light, enough to lift the mood, but not by much. Below the window a tortured steel bench provided dubious levels of comfort. Nevertheless,

Harper chose it over sitting on the floor, which smelled equal parts of vomit and urine.

Harper sat, elbows on his knees and tried to keep his cool. He knew how the system worked. Bevan and Button were letting him stew and making him uncomfortable in the hope he would try and talk his way out of trouble. Harper had used the ploy many times before. He knew he just had to sit tight and wait it out.

There was just one thing that bothered him. Button's claim that he had information on him. Harper knew the meth charge was bullshit, but Button still needed something to back up the arrest. Had the police finally figured out that he killed the man who had shot his entire family? How could they? The only person he had told was Gardella.

Harper was convinced his partner wouldn't rat him out. It had to be someone else. Who else would have knowledge of Harper's past? Theoretically, anyone with access to the NIA database. But even then they would have to know he had a file. Cops never had files. If they did they usually weren't cops anymore. It had to be someone who knew what they were looking for. Someone with inside knowledge.

Three hours passed before a key clinked in the lock. The cell door opened with a groan revealing the rotund form of Officer Bevan.

'Time for your phone call, sweet cheeks,' Bevan said smugly.

Harper rose to his feet and straightened his back. He moved toward the cell door like he was following instructions but as he passed Bevan he stopped. Harper was a foot taller and used it to his advantage.

'Who put you up to this?' Harper asked, leaning in to accentuate the height difference.

Bevan retreated an inch. 'Listen here, cowboy. You better watch what you say or I might change my mind.'

'No, you listen. I want to know who's behind this.'

'Fine. No phone call,' Bevan said as he attempted to block Harper's path.

Harper realised he wasn't going to get anything out of arguing. He could find out later who was behind his false arrest. Right now he needed to sort this mess out. 'Okay, okay,' he said, hands raised in mock surrender. 'Where's the phone?'

Harper followed Bevan down the short corridor and into an alcove that had a phone bolted to the wall.

'You've got ten minutes,' Bevan warned as he waddled away.

Harper dialled Gardella's number. His partner picked up after a few rings. 'Hey, Joe it's me. I need you to listen—'

'Where the fuck have you been? I've been trying to reach you for the last two hours.'

'I'm in lockup in Westport and—'

'What? You're where?'

'I'm in the cells at Westport Police Station. Now shut the fuck up and let me explain.'

Harper ran through as much information as he could within his ten-minute window. He told Gardella about the USB stick, the mine, the levels of uranium in the water and how he believed Hayes had been blackmailing the mine. He explained how they had found the second bin and that the serial number had been filed off. Finally, he ran down the reason why he was in custody and his suspicions about who had ratted him out and why. Gardella was quiet throughout. Harper hoped his partner had been taking notes because his ten minutes were up and he wouldn't be able to go back over old ground. Right on cue, Bevan lumbered around the corner and started tapping his watch.

'You gotta call Bones,' Harper said quickly. 'Get him to pull some strings to get me out of this shithole, pronto.'

'Yep, I'm right on it. Don't worry partner, I'll have you breathing fresh air in no time.'

While he still had a chance, Harper asked, 'What's happening at your end?'

'The body showed up about an hour ago. I managed to get a pathologist to do the examination straight away. Actually, I've just stepped out of the autopsy to talk to you. The body's in a bad state. It looked like it was going to be a difficult process to determine cause of death, but we got lucky. After a visual inspection, the pathologist decided to jump straight to x-rays. Did the head first and bam, struck gold. Found a massive skull fracture. Blunt force trauma to the right parietal lobe. Looks like he was attacked from behind. A semi-circular piece of skull punctured the brain causing massive haemorrhaging, enough to kill him. Based on her experience the pathologist believes the weapon was most likely a claw hammer, tyre iron or small crow ba—'

Bevan had pushed down on the cradle, ending the call. As rage welled up within, Harper clenched a fist. He slowly placed the receiver back as he prepared to unleash his anger. But in those short seconds he had time to think through the repercussions and knew it would work against him. He released the coiled tension in his muscles and stepped away from the phone.

Bevan gave a self-satisfied smirk. 'That's a good boy. Now it's time for your nap.'

'What about a meal? Anyone in custody overnight is entitled to something to eat.'

'Hungry are we? Unfortunately, we're all out of food right now.'

'I bet you are,' Harper said looking at Bevan's gut. 'I can see where it all ended up.'

'Fuck you, arsehole.'

CHAPTER 28

Sleep was never going to be easy. Harper was too tall for the bench and had to fold his body into the narrow space so that his head butted up against one wall and his feet against the other. His mind raced trying to figure a way out of this situation. He hoped Gardella could convince Bones to grease the wheels and get him released tonight, but as the hours ticked by and the lights in the station flicked off, his optimism faded. Surely by tomorrow morning he would get the all-clear.

The station was quiet now. Harper could no longer detect muffled conversations or ringing phones or the hollow echo of footsteps in the corridor. It dawned on him that he had been left alone. In small jurisdictions like Westport it was common for the station to be unmanned at night. But with a prisoner in the cells it was police policy for a watch-officer to stay in case of fire or other incident. Then again, it wouldn't surprise Harper if they had all gone home. Excluding Monty, the others probably didn't care if the station burned down with Harper locked inside.

Gradually a heavy exhaustion overwhelmed him and he slipped into a shallow sleep. As his conscious thoughts dissolved into nothing they made space for the curling tendrils of dreams.

He was in a field, sun streaming, a soft breeze stroking the long grass, clouds drifting like sailing ships, their white sails billowing. Across the field he saw children playing amongst the grass. He looked at them for the longest time, waiting for one to turn and glance in his direction. But it never came. The children continued with their games, only the sound of their cheerful cries made it back to where he stood.

All at once he became aware of something else. A shadow on the horizon, watching from afar, unmoving. The children went on with their games, safe in the bubble of their innocence. The warm sun kept on, the air, breathless.

A creeping dread filled his chest. His vision honed on the shadow like a telephoto lens. It had no face, just a blackness deeper than night. He sensed trouble. He needed to go back and warn the children.

Before he could react, an arm reached out from the shadow, stretching grotesquely, twisting closer. He tried to yell but nothing came out. He started to run but he was barely moving. The warm air turned cold and a bitter wind pressed against him like a force hell-bent on holding him back. Heavy metal thunder beckoned the approaching storm. There was a voice. What was it saying? His name? It was calling his name. A sudden shock ripped through his body jolting him awake.

'Detective Harper. Wake up.'

Harper sat up, his vision obliterated by an orange light flooding through the open cell door. He extended an arm to shield his eyes and ward off whoever was there.

'What a sorry sight,' someone said.

The voice was familiar but in his confused state, halfway between awake and asleep, he could not place it. As his scrambled senses fell back into place and his eyes adjusted to the stabbing light, he lowered his arm. Standing in the doorway was Senior Sergeant Snowden.

'What time is it?' Harper said.

Snowden checked his watch. 'Just after one.'

He had been asleep for two hours but it felt more like two minutes. Snowden was not in uniform. He wore white canvas sneakers with jeans that rode high on his hips and a red and white checked shirt unfashionably tucked at the waist.

'What the fuck do you want?' Harper said.

'To talk.'

'About what?' Harper leaned back against the cold concrete, his eyes fixed on the senior sergeant.

Snowden didn't respond. His stooped posture made his arms hang at his sides. In a voice that was barely above a whisper, he said, 'Is there room on that bench for me?'

Harper yawned and rubbed his eyes and slid across the bench until he was pressed up against the cold concrete at one end. Snowden sat down but he looked nervous. He was wringing his hands and staring at the floor. After a minute, he spoke. 'You're in some pretty serious trouble, Dylan. I—I don't know if you'll be able to work your way out of this mess.'

'What mess? What are you talking about? I'm conducting a homicide investigation.'

'That's not how it looks. The evidence we have is damning. In the morning two officers will be arriving to transport you back to Christchurch to face additional charges. They are going to oppose bail. It doesn't look good.'

'What evidence? What the fuck is going on here?'

Snowden glanced up from the floor, his eyes distant and dead, looking, but not seeing. 'We received an anonymous tip that you were carrying illegal substances. I didn't believe it but the others had a hard-on for you since day one. They followed you to the drug house.'

'What? What drug hou—' Then Harper remembered. The Quentin Jarvis drug house. 'That was part of my investigation. I—'

'We've been conducting surveillance on that house for the last four weeks. We suspected the property was being used to manufacture meth. Our information suggested it was a new operation relocated from Christchurch because of the earthquakes. They were making it here and shipping it back through the pass. But the surveillance was turning up nothing. The occupants had been smart. They hadn't given anything away. No unusual activities, no one coming or going apart from the owners, nothing to give us probable cause. We were beginning to think they were on to us. We didn't have enough to get a warrant. All we could do was watch. Then we get this tip about you. So the boys followed you. They photographed you going into the house, said you spent half an hour inside. When you left, they snapped you in the same vehicle as the suspect.'

'That's it? That's all you got? That theory has got about as much substance as a cup of warm piss. A judge would throw that out in under a minute.'

'It doesn't end there, Dylan. There's more. When you came back to the station later that day you spoke to Sean, correct?'

Harper thought for a moment. He remembered dropping the rental at the airport and driving back to the station to check the tip sheets.

Monty had done most of the work on the sheets and Harper had gone out to thank him for his efforts.

'Yeah, I spoke to him, so what?'

'Sean was training a drug dog. He said it indicated on you.'

'What do you mean?'

'The dog gave an indication that you were carrying drugs.'

'What! I wasn't carrying any drugs. I was in the middle of an investigation. I was chasing down a fucking lead, not scoring meth. I mean, for all I know it might well be a meth house but I never actually saw any because that wasn't the reason I was there. All I know is that shit sticks to everything. The guys on the drug squad told me that the fumes go right through a house. They say you can get high from just walking through the front door. If it was a meth lab it could have gotten on me in any number of ways.'

Harper remembered his wet clothes.

'Come to think of it, I know exactly how it could. I was soaking wet. The woman who lives there took my clothes and put them in the dryer. There were probably traces in the dryer.'

Snowden turned away and was looking at the floor again. His eyes now had a lonely sadness to them.

'It gave them what they needed. It gave them probable cause to enter the house. This morning a squad from Greymouth came up. We raided the house just before dawn. We found what we thought we would find. It was in a back room. Sophisticated set-up. They were cooking and packaging it on site. We seized several kilos of product. Some crystal, the rest in pill form. We transferred the occupants down the coast to Greymouth where the courts will deal with them on Monday.'

'So what? That simply confirms what I just said. The shit got on me when I was in the house.'

'Dylan. We searched your hotel room,' Snowden's words were spoken like a disappointed parent. An uneasy feeling began to swirl in Harper's stomach. Snowden went on. 'We found pills. Lots of pills. Enough to rule out personal use.'

The walls of the cell seemed to close in on him. Harper suddenly found it difficult to breathe. This was more than just a setup. He was too close to the truth. He was being neutralised. They wouldn't let him solve the case because that would uncover more than just a murder. They, whoever they were, needed to get rid of him. Killing him would be too risky. It would generate a new investigation. More cops. That was the last thing these people would want. They were trying to discredit him. A drug conviction would serve that purpose. He and all the evidence would be tainted. No one, least of all a court of law, would believe a word he said. Not even Gardella would be able to come to his rescue. Everything his partner knew about the uranium had come from Harper. It would be hearsay and inadmissible. He was on his own and fighting for his life with no help from anyone else. His eyes darted left and right, looking for a way out.

The cell door. It was still open. For a split second, he considered making a run for it. He could easily get there before Snowden, maybe even make it out to fresh air. But he would be caught eventually. The attempted escape would be another nail in his coffin. His only chance was to stay and try to convince Snowden this was all a big mistake.

'This is bullshit. Whoever phoned in the tip had it in for me. Those drugs were obviously planted. There's no way—I mean, think about it. Why would I be dealing in the middle of a murder investigation? It just doesn't make sense. It's ridiculous.'

'Don't you think I know that?' Snowden replied, taking his time with each word as if they all carried equal significance.

Harper looked at Snowden. 'It was you. You planted the drugs. They put you up to it, didn't they?

'I think you have misunderstood. I—'

'I know exactly what you mean. They've gotten to you, haven't they? They don't want this case cleared because it will expose them. They've got too much on the line. Probably millions in kickbacks at stake, not to mention the political shit storm if this gets out. So they pay you a few thousand and get you to plant the drugs. Problem solved. But I'm not going quietly. I'll spill the beans on you and the incompetence of your officers. It'll be the end of your career.'

Snowden sat statue-still as if Harper's words meant nothing to him.

'You won't have to do that,' Snowden finally said.

'Yeah? And why wouldn't I?'

'Because it wasn't me who planted those pills.'

'That's easy for you to say. What if I don't believe you?'

Snowden held Harper's stare like it was a lifeline he couldn't let go. Then, he slowly bent forward and placed his elbows on his knees and brought his arms and palms together as if he was about to start praying.

Harper eyed him suspiciously, not sure what to say or do. As the seconds ticked by all he could do was watch and wait. The light from the hall slashed through the darkness like a torch beam creating a rectangular pool of orange on the mottled concrete floor. Finally, Snowden lifted his head.

'I think, maybe, when I am finished, you will believe me. I just hope … you can also forgive me.'

CHAPTER 29

Harper folded his arms and Snowden drew a long breath. Finally, he began his explanation.

'It wasn't supposed to end like this. I mean, I never expected it to play out this way. It was supposed to be different. You were supposed to break the case, expose what was going on and get those motherfuckers off my back. But I underestimated the lengths they would go to protect themselves and their interests. I guess I should have known better.'

'What the fuck does that mean?'

'It means, I knew something was wrong up there at Mackley River. I didn't have the full picture, but I knew enough that alarm bells were ringing. Let's put it that way.'

'You knew and you sent us out there blind. Well, that's just fucking fantastic. You better have a damn good reason for withholding that vital piece of intel or you'll end up locked in here with me.'

'You might be correct in that assumption, Detective,' Snowden replied. 'However, if you hear me out, we might just both be able to avoid doing time.'

'I'm all ears,' Harper said.

'I knew something was up was last January. I received a phone call summoning me to a meeting in the capital. Now, I've been a police officer for thirty years and in that time HQ has not once shown an interest in what we do down here. They might make a big song and dance about how they're putting more police on the beat, pumping more money into the force, but none of that seems to trickle down to us. In fact, at times I think they forget we even exist.'

Ironic that Snowden picks this moment to trot out the woe-is-me routine, Harper thought. He had a hard time feeling any sympathy given his present predicament.

'Anyway, I get up to the capital and waiting for me at the airport is a government limo. The car was full of stiffs in suits who wouldn't tell me jack shit. These pricks looked like government security because they all had earpieces in so I didn't bother asking questions and just sat tight. Pretty soon I noticed we weren't heading downtown. Instead, we were going in the other direction, out of the city. About an hour later we pulled up to this place with automatic gates that swung open like they knew we were coming. The suits escorted me up the steps into the house and deposited me in the dining room before leaving. After a few minutes this guy came in. I recognised him. It was George Southon.'

Harper sat up a little straighter.

'To begin with Southon was all smiles and handshakes, you know, the usual smarmy politician act. He tried to pretend he was interested in what was happening in our jurisdiction but I could see he was just buttering me up. After half an hour of bullshit he realised I wasn't under his spell so he dropped the "let's be friends" piece and got serious. He told me about the new gold mine and how important it would be for the region and the country. He spun some line about how the Chinese don't like attention and that it would be essential to keep the public away for their own safety. He told me in no uncertain terms to stay away from Mackley River. I was not to send any officers into the area and I was to arrest anyone who tried to gain access to the site.'

'You knew,' Harper said. 'You knew right from the start.'

'I had my suspicions,' Snowden said. 'But nothing more than that. I never had the full picture and I knew better than to stick my nose in where it didn't belong. So I did as I was told. No access and no questions. That was ... until things started going wrong.'

Snowden's voice trailed off and that vacant look was back. He took a breath and carried on. 'In November one of the miners was killed in a rockfall. Usually that would initiate a Worksafe case which would involve police and investigators going up to the mine and finding out what happened. But none of that happened. The body was whisked away by private jet back to China and no further inquires were made. That told me two things. One, they would go to any lengths to stop people going up there and two, they weren't mining gold.

'Then about a month ago I heard Frank Mortimer had found some dead stock near Mackley River. That was another red flag because I knew the mine was right in that area. Then the reporter goes missing. Initially, I didn't make the connection. I thought Hayes had opted out of the marriage, you know, done a runner. Everyone knew he was having an affair. But when I spoke to Derek Graham he told me that Jonathon Hayes was supposed to stop by his place after doing his water quality checks. That's when I learnt about his part-time job. I put two and two together and immediately backed away. I knew I couldn't investigate so I called in outside help. That's when you arrived.'

Harper sat stony-faced while he processed this new information. It confirmed a lot of the things he had already suspected. Hayes had either been murdered by the mine operators or possibly by the government because he had become a liability. What Harper hadn't factored was Snowden's involvement. Now a few other things began to make sense.

'It was you following us. You knew about the mine and tipped me off with the numbers on the whiteboard.'

Snowden nodded. 'I saw you were getting nowhere. I needed to get you back on track.'

'Why? What's in it for you? You've kept this to yourself for a year. Why wait till a guy gets murdered to start dropping tips?'

'Because I knew if I told anyone about the mine they'd trace it back to me. I needed someone else to stumble in and uncover the truth. I needed an outside agency. The Hayes sideshow was my opening. I mean, it wasn't like I was waiting for someone to get murdered or anything. That's just how it happened. Anyway, it was my chance to bring in other investigators. I made it look like the wife had requested CIB involvement but in reality it was me. That would leave me free to stand on the sidelines. I wanted it to seem like I was pissed at having outside help because you just never know who else is listening. Should've worked perfectly. You break the case, I keep my nose clean, the mine shuts down, and my little secret dies in the process.'

Harper stroked the stubble on his chin as he thought all this through. He remembered back to the first night where he and Gardella had sat down with Snowden and how the senior sergeant had been less than helpful. In fact, most of what Snowden had said seemed designed to mislead. He had revealed the affair and that Hayes was being sued. This had muddied the waters and cost them valuable time investigating dead ends. Harper also remembered how Snowden had walked out halfway through the meeting. It had seemed like he was deliberately trying to steer them in the wrong direction.

'You fed us a pile of shit when we first got here. How do I know you're not doing the same thing right now?' Harper asked.

'Because they knew you would be meeting with me. I couldn't afford for you to zero in on the mine straight away. Think about how that would look. They would know I tipped you off. I needed you to go down other avenues first. Now I am trying to get you out of this mess. Now I am telling you the truth.'

'Why tell the truth now? Why do you want to help me? It's got to be more than just wanting these people off your back. So long as I'm locked up, your position remains safe. Seems to me it would be easier for you to just walk away.'

Snowden was quiet for a long time. He remained hunched forward, hands knotted in a twisted ball of tension. The station was still and desolate. By now Harper was sure they were the only ones there. Snowden would never have revealed this much if there was even a suggestion of the presence of another person. It was clear he was hiding something and the longer it took for the words to come, the bigger that something would be. Harper waited. He gave Snowden the time he obviously needed. After a long two minutes, it began to pour out.

'I can't walk away this time. Not this time. I need to come clean and clear my conscience.' Snowden sat up straight. He turned and faced Harper. 'That night Bozo shot up your family. I was the one who tipped him off.'

The revelation hit Harper like a left hook to the side of the head. He was stunned. Words wouldn't form. He just stared back blankly. Snowden pressed on.

'The gang paid me for the tip. They said they were just going to scare you. I didn't realise your father had a gun. He never had it registered or licensed so it wasn't on the system,' Snowden said, shaking his head. 'Not for one moment did I think it would lead to three people being shot. It—it just—ah fuck. It wasn't supposed to go down like that.'

The rage Harper expected never came. Instead, he felt numb. He had always assumed someone had leaked information to the gang but Snowden was the last person he would have suspected. Harper opened his mouth to speak but he couldn't get anything to come out.

'Ever since that night, I have been haunted by what happened. I wished I could undo what was done and fix everything. But you can't undo death. Instead, I decided to fix the only thing I had left. The living. You. You remember? I took your statement that night. I couldn't get over how calm you were. At the time I thought you were in shock. But soon it became apparent that your version of events didn't stack up. It was the rifle. The rifle gave you away. It was too long. The silencer made it impossible for him to have his finger on the trigger at the same time the muzzle was under his chin. There was no way that it could have gone down like you described.'

Snowden shook his head as if trying to ward off an unwanted memory. Over the years, Harper had tried to do the same, but without success. It was something he would carry with him until the end of his days. Now he understood that Snowden shared the burden with him.

'I realised it must have been you,' Snowden went on. 'You fired the gun. But I understood it wasn't only you. I had effectively placed your finger on the trigger. I had set this awful chain of events in motion. So I did the only thing left for me to do. By the time I'd worked all this out the house was full of cops and medical personnel and god knows who else but as yet the photographer and fingerprint officer hadn't been through. In the confusion I managed to remove the silencer from the barrel. A couple of people thought they had seen a silencer but when it wasn't recovered they decided their eyes had been playing tricks on them. The lack of incriminating evidence and the general sympathy from everyone on the case eventually cleared you of any wrongdoing.'

Harper sat with his eyes closed and head resting back against the cold concrete. He searched for the anger he had buried within him but all he found was a hollowness that wouldn't go away. He wanted to hate Snowden, but he couldn't summon the emotion. He felt nothing at all.

CHAPTER 30

It took Harper a few minutes to absorb it all. When he finally gathered his thoughts and opened his eyes he became aware of the steady drum of rain on the roof. He wondered how long it had been raining and why he hadn't noticed it until now. Snowden was still focused on him, waiting for some sort of reaction. As their eyes met Harper understood what was about to happen.

'You're going to set me loose. That's why you're here,' Harper said flatly. Snowden gave a faint nod.

'But that's not enough, is it,' Harper continued. 'I can't just walk out of here like nothing happened. There's too much evidence stacked against me. The only way I'm going to get out of this shit storm is if I clear this case and find the people who set me up. Until then, nothing else matters.'

Snowden gave another nod. 'I might be able to help with that. Come with me.'

Snowden rose and led the way down a short corridor. He reached the rear door of the station, opened it, and disappeared out into the night. Harper hesitated, worried this could be some kind of trap. He looked out onto an empty parking area. A security light blazed and silver pencils of rain-streaked the darkness. He searched for anyone hiding in the shadows but saw nothing. Satisfied no one was lying in wait, he ventured out.

There were three garages on the far side of the compound. Snowden jammed a key into the third door, turned the handle and pulled upwards. The door gave a rasping screech as it swung open. Snowden disappeared inside. After several seconds the lights blinked on, making Harper squint until his eyes adjusted.

Each garage was a part of the same building, and while there were three separate doors there were no internal dividing walls so Harper could look down the length of the long garage. Two police vehicles occupied the other two bays. The area in which he stood was mostly empty. A dartboard affixed to the back wall had three of its projectiles sticking out at haphazard angles and a light bar from the roof of one of the police cruisers rested in the corner awaiting repair. Next to that there was an old wooden table with thick battered legs and spread on top of the table was an assortment of tools.

But what really caught Harper's eye was something he had seen before. Pushed up against the wall was a green wheelie bin. A bank of portable lights pointed directly at the bin, the kind of lights used to illuminate crime scenes at night. A long extension cord ran from the lights and snaked off beyond the cars to a power point somewhere else in the garage.

Without explanation, Snowden strode up to the light array and flicked the switch at its base. At first, the industrial-sized bulbs produced a weak yellow glow. Snowden beckoned Harper in closer. In the time he took to walk the short distance the light had intensified and heat reflected off the bin back into Harper's face. He looked quizzically at Snowden, then at the bin, then back at Snowden.

'Watch and wait,' Snowden said.

Harper studied the bin. The intense light against the dark plastic made every scuff and scratch stand out in sharp relief. The gouge marks made by the rubbish truck and the damage at the base where it had been dragged across the ground were clear. However, there was an oval area just below the handle that had been cleaned and polished and it gleamed under the lights. He immediately realised it was the spot where the serial number had been.

'I filed back the gouge marks just enough to get a flat surface,' Snowden said matter-of-factly. 'You need a flat surface to make this work. Keep watching and you'll see why.'

Harper crouched and studied the spot. Even though he was behind the lights he could still feel the heat. As the seconds ticked a film of sweat began to form against his brow and his legs started to ache. He was about to stand when he detected a subtle change. At first it was almost imperceptible. He rocked forward onto his knees to get a closer look. Sure enough, ever so slowly, he began to see something. It seemed that the heat was making the rubberised plastic relax ever so slightly. It took another few seconds before it appeared. A serial number. Only just visible. Not all the digits were immediately evident. Harper had to tilt his head and adjust his position to see each one. Ten seconds later, he had identified all the characters.

DHT7782

'When the manufacturer stamps a serial number, the imprint is made deep into the material. Even if you remove the top few layers a memory remains below. It just takes a little persuading to bring it out.'

Harper stood up and looked at Snowden in amazement, his respect for the man at least partially restored.

'I'm guessing you've run the numbers. Did you get a hit?'

'Yep.'

Harper felt his energy returning. Snowden had an address and another potential crime scene. It was a glimmer of hope. But with police on their way to pick him up he needed to act now or it would be too late. Rules were about to be bent.

'You have a warrant?' Harper asked, already knowing the answer.

'Nope,' Snowden confirmed with a hint of a grin.

Harper responded with his own smirk. 'So you're gonna justify the search on the grounds that waiting may result in the loss of evidence?'

'Yep.'

'What about me? You can't go into this address accompanied by an individual in police custody. Any twenty dollar lawyer would get the search ruled inadmissible. Even if we found the victim's internal organs on ice in the freezer we couldn't use them as evidence.'

Snowden nodded like it was a question he had been expecting. He answered with a question of his own. 'When you were arrested, did those idiots read you your rights?'

'No. I waived my rights.'

'Did they ask you to waive?'

'Well, no. I said I knew my rights and told them not to read them.'

'It doesn't matter if you say you know your rights. Lots of people think they know their rights. By law those rights must be read, regardless of whether you are a supreme court justice or a low life thief. You should know that, Detective. Also, when you were brought in, did they book and process you?'

Harper shook his head. 'No.'

'Then, I'm left with no other option but to release you without charge. Let's get to work.'

Back inside the station, Snowden retrieved Harper's Glock and spare clips from the lock-up as well as his cell phone and his badge. From there they went into the boardroom and began prepping for the raid. The address Snowden had was for a property registered to InterPacific Mining. The council records didn't list the names of the residents, only saying that the building was purchased ten months ago to accommodate mine management.

Using the station's computer Snowden opened Google Earth and typed in the address. A birdseye image of houses and streets appeared with a red pin marking the target. Snowden switched to street-view and swung the camera angle until an impressive two-storey weatherboard house filled the screen. The house sat on a corner section and was surrounded by a tall fence. The only access to the grounds was through a driveway on the eastern side of the property that led to a detached double garage. The only observable entrance was a small door off the driveway. Harper and Snowden spent the next few minutes formulating a plan.

They would approach the house from the south and park a short distance away then move up the driveway and announce their intentions at the side door. If there was no response they would force entry and secure the scene, arresting anyone inside. At first light, they would call in the ESR team to search for evidence. It wasn't the most robust strategy but it would have to do.

They strode out into the wet night and Harper immediately noticed his Commodore parked in the rear compound, the keys hanging from the ignition. He glanced at Snowden.

'You drive,' Snowden said with a dry smile. Harper frowned and checked his watch; 3:07 a.m.

The atmosphere on the short drive was tense. Neither man spoke. This could turn ugly in a hurry. Harper's stomach tightened. Maybe it would be best to just back away. But the more he thought, the more he convinced himself to continue on.

It was likely that Li Qian had been informed of Harper's inquiries at the mine the previous day. This had prompted the drug plant to stall the investigation and divert police resources. Harper would be picked up, taken back to Christchurch, booked and charged. The ESR team would be re-tasked with examining his hotel room. Those responsible for the murder of Jonathon Hayes would have more time to remove any remaining evidence. The evidence Harper was sure still lay inside this house.

Harper made the left turn onto Romilly Street. The target address was at the end of the block but Harper could already make out its roofline above the other houses. As he drew closer he slowed and began to make his observations.

There were no lights on in the windows, no cars on the street, no signs of life. Harper scanned the surrounding properties but they were similarly dormant. Drawing his attention back to the house he saw the driveway was clear and the garage door down. There was no light at the side door and no sign anyone was at home.

At the intersection Harper used the stop sign to his advantage and drew to a complete halt. He was now on the road directly in front of the house. A tall fence obscured the lower floor. Above the fence, the upper-floor windows were visible, the curtains pulled.

'Looks like someone's home,' Harper said, pointing at the curtains.

'Maybe,' Snowden said.

After remaining stationary for as long as he dared, Harper made the left turn onto Brougham. After driving the short block he turned left again onto Peel and circled the rest of the block, eventually ending up back on Romilly. He parked three houses down and killed the engine.

For a moment they waited in the velvet darkness that fell between the streetlights, readying themselves for what they were about to do. These people had killed before and the likelihood that government officials were involved added another layer of complexity. They could take no chances. Harper checked his weapon, grabbed his torch, and climbed out of the vehicle. Snowden followed as Harper skirted the fence line of a neighbouring property using the sagging-wet shrubs for cover. He paused at the mouth of the driveway and listened. Dead silence. The night air was heavy and still and made his shirt stick to his back. It felt like being in the eye of a storm, the calm before all hell broke loose. Harper squeezed his gun tight and peered up the driveway.

The curtains on the ground floor were open and the windows black and lifeless. He turned to Snowden. A nod and they advanced up the drive with their weapons drawn. Snowden drew a deep breath before banging on the door and announcing,

'Police! Open the door!'

Nothing. Snowden gave the all-clear. Harper focused the weight of his six-foot-plus frame through his leg and into the wooden door. It gave a painful crack but did not fail. Harper reloaded and went again. The door shuddered but stubbornly held. On the third kick it yielded sending splintered pieces scattering.

Harper slipped in through the door and scanned the dark interior. Too dark. He plucked his torch from his jacket pocket and flicked the switch. Dead. He shook it and tried again. Still no light. Returning it to his pocket he shuffled to the right, Snowden on the left. Harper swept the room with his weapon, eyes struggling to take in enough light. It seemed they were standing in some sort of anteroom, wide and long with another passage at the end on the right.

Harper stood on something. He looked down and saw the faint outline of shoes. They looked small enough to be children's sneakers. What the hell were children's shoes doing here? Something wasn't right. His stomach tightened.

Harper crept through the anteroom towards the short passage and poked his head around the corner. All clear. He moved forward. To his right was an open door. A bedroom, two beds, neatly made, curtains open, cold and empty. His attention redirected out, he scanned a cavernous stair-hall directly ahead. A broad stairway lined with turned timber balustrades ascended the walls in a series of ninety-degree turns, the top steps hidden from view by the landing. Across the stair-hall on the far wall was a grand old panelled door surrounded by stained glass that seemed to lead outside.

Harper moved into the open space with Snowden close behind. He noticed a door immediately to his left. He slid along the wall and used his free hand to turn the handle. The latch clicked free. He waited a beat, then swung the door open, leading into the room weapon first.

The room had towering ceilings that receded into darkness and walls that yawned wide and patterned carpet that probably went out of fashion before Harper was even born. There was a flat-screen TV in one corner, an L-shaped sofa wedged into the opposite corner, and a grand fireplace that had long ago burnt out. A side table nestled against a wall and French doors gazed out upon a sunken garden of stargazer lilies. Harper eased forward. The floorboards creaked.

A 1970s archway connected the living room with a small bar. In the bar two leather-bound smoking chairs and an occasional table sat waiting for the next round of drinks. Harper swept across the floor, his smooth sideways steps barely raising a whisper. A frosted glass door separated the bar from the next room. The door was open.

He crept through into what looked like a dining room. A rectangular dining table stood in an alcove created by a bay window. To the right, a Formica topped central island filled most of the remaining space, several chairs arranged neatly around. A small kitchenette in the far corner had no dishes in the sink and all the surfaces appeared clean.

Harper skirted the near-side of the kitchen island while Snowden took the long way around. They met on the far side by another sliding door. It too was open and led back into the stair-hall. They had made a loop of one wing of the house and now stood by the stained glass main entrance. Looking up, Harper could just make out the landing but the darkness beyond that too thick to see any farther.

With sight failing him, Harper switched to other senses. At first he heard nothing. He held his breath and tried again. Still nothing. Then he picked it up. Faint, but growing louder. It was coming from outside. A car. It grew nearer and its headlights slashed through the stained glass sending ribbons of colour sweeping across the walls. Harper used the light show to his advantage.

'Police! We're coming up,' he yelled, advancing up the stairs.

By the time the car had receded off into the night Harper had reached the top. The landing was about three metres deep and twice as wide but was home to nothing but darkness. There were no pictures on the walls, no family heirlooms on display, and no other signs of human habitation. Except for the sense of something familiar. Harper couldn't put his finger on what, but something registered. The uneasy feeling began to build once more.

There was a closed door directly to his right and another straight ahead on the far wall. To the left of that there was a corridor and moving further left, another door, this one open. Harper stood frozen, his mind frantically searching for the missing piece that would complete the puzzle. It felt like déjà vu, but not quite. He couldn't work it out. He was sure he had never been here before, but at the same time, there was something ringing alarm bells.

Snowden pushed past as if not sensing the danger and went to the first door to the right. Harper shook off his daze and inched toward the open doorway to the left. He hugged the bannister that ran the breadth of the landing until he reached the door. At the opening he stopped and looked back at Snowden. They held each other's stare, an unspoken message of caution. As if reading each other's thoughts, they burst into their respective rooms simultaneously.

Arms extended, finger on the trigger, Harper swept the room with his weapon. A crack in the curtain bled just enough streetlight for visuals. A floor-to-ceiling closet with its sliding door pulled shut, a small desk with a computer, a single bed against the far wall, and opposite that, a set of bunks. The room was unoccupied.

Harper began to back out. As he did, the familiar feeling returned. What was it? The memory was so close he could almost taste it. Then, like a clearing mist on a winter's morning, his memory drew into sharp focus.

CHAPTER 31

As Harper turned he heard a pair of metallic pops. He looked across the landing towards the door directly opposite and saw a shadow moving towards him. Time slowed to a crawl, his body set in concrete. All he could do was stand and stare at the dark shape staggering towards him like a punch-drunk boxer.

The figure momentarily filled the doorframe, blocking the view into the other room. Harper recognised the profile. Snowden. For a second he swayed and then his body seemed to relax. The tension in his muscles went slack and his legs buckled. Snowden dropped to his knees and Harper thought he heard a final breath drain from the senior sergeant's body.

Harper spotted another shape, this one deeper inside the room. With a rush of adrenaline he pitched sideways towards the corridor. He never heard the sickening thump of Snowden hitting the floor or the neat double pang of the gun. But he saw the flash of the barrel and felt the searing impact in his chest. He fell in a crumpled heap into the corridor.

The first bullet had struck just right of his sternum, a little below the collarbone. The second slammed into his right shoulder, rendering his arm useless and sending his Glock clattering off into the shadows. He placed his left hand over the chest wound and warm blood seeped from beneath his fingers.

Lying on the floor he assessed his injuries. The shots were not immediately fatal. His sudden lunge had saved him from that fate. But without medical attention it wouldn't be long before he bled out. Digging his heels into the thick carpet he pushed his body up into a sitting position, his back against the corridor wall. He was having difficulty breathing. One of the bullets had likely punctured a lung. Fortunately, he had fallen just far enough to be out of the line of fire. He had bought himself some time.

Harper glanced to where his Glock had fallen. It was just out of reach. His only hope was to retrieve the weapon. No one knew he was here. No one would be coming to help. No backup was on the way and the shooter would be coming to finish the job. He summoned all his remaining strength and went for it.

But when his mind said move his body flatly refused, the lack of oxygen rendering his limbs numb. Even the effort to hold a hand over his seeping chest was too much. He strained and tried again but his body would not budge. His head rocked back against the wall in frustration. His breathing had become shallow as his lungs filled with blood. It wouldn't be long until he lost consciousness. As his world closed in around him he heard soft footsteps moving across the landing. He knew he was done. In his final moments he tried one last roll of the dice.

'Backup is coming. You should go.' His voice breathless, the words meek. There was nothing more that he could do. He had come to the end.

As life ebbed from his body, Harper's head fell forward, his eyes open and fixed on the spot where his weapon lay. A pair of naked feet came into view. Now the shoes made sense. They weren't children's sneakers. They were women's shoes. One foot casually slid the gun out of reach. With the last strands of his being Harper managed to lift his gaze.

A familiar face hovered above. It was the face Harper had been expecting. He had worked it out from the smell. It had been faint, almost undetectable. A cool, minty scent of perfume that lingered at the top of the stairs just long enough to spark his memory. Looking down on him was the receptionist from the Mackley River Mine.

Harper's hand slipped from his chest and fell at his side, the front of his shirt soaked in blood. A chill washed over his body. Amy Fairweather stood in a cotton nightgown with a gun at her side and an expression somewhere between amusement and contempt. Slowly, as if for dramatic effect, she raised the weapon. Harper closed his eyes and waited for the blinding flash that would signal his demise.

A deafening blast came first, but it was not accompanied by the flash he had expected. Nor did he feel pain. He was beyond that now. He could no longer feel anything at all. He sensed only a thud as though something had fallen at his feet. He opened his eyes. Fairweather was still looking at him only she was now lying on the floor, her mouth open and her eyes wide with surprise.

Harper heard someone coming up the stairs. Just before he blacked out he caught sight of Gardella.

'Hang in there partner. You're not dying tonight.'

CHAPTER 32

Harper didn't know how long he had been unconscious or even if he was alive or dead, just that he was not where he last remembered. He was somewhere else. A bright light made opening his eyes too painful. His throat felt like he had swallowed a box of razor blades. There were sounds nearby.

'Mr Harper? Can you hear me? Nod your head if you can hear me.'

Harper nodded.

'I'm Nurse Morgan. You're in Christchurch Hospital. Are you able to speak?' Harper shook his head. 'In that case, just shake or nod your head. Are you in any pain?' Harper shook his head again. 'That's good. Like I said, you're in Christchurch Hospital. We've had you under heavy sedation. The drugs will take a while to work their way out of your system. You're going to feel very tired. The best thing is to just rest. Next to your left hand is a button. Press it if you experience any discomfort. Okay?'

Harper nodded. He had many questions but neither the voice nor the energy to ask them. Even a simple nod had drained his feeble reserves. He fell back into a deep sleep.

When he woke again it was dark. It seemed as though it might be night but Harper had lost all track of time. In the distance he heard clattering and voices engaged in subdued conversation. He opened his eyes and saw he was in a hospital room. The bed had been raised so his upper body was elevated. The door to the room was open. A hospital orderly shunted an empty bed down the hall. The stench of antiseptic and steamed food filled his nose and brought him fully awake. It was then he sensed he was not alone.

'Welcome back, partner.'

Harper looked over to see Gardella sitting in a chair beside the bed. He was casually dressed and wore a friendly smile that didn't suit him.

'We thought we might have lost you there for a while. Doc said if we got to you five minutes later you would've gone off for the big sleep.'

'What happened?' Harper managed to say.

Gardella handed him a plastic cup. Harper took a sip and the chilled water soothed his burning throat.

'What happened,' Gardella began, 'is I had to fill out a shit-load of paperwork to account for why I shot a woman who doesn't exist.'

Harper stared back blankly. He didn't remember anything or understand why he was in the hospital. Gardella lowered his voice and began to explain.

'Look, I'm not supposed to be here. Brass wants a statement from you before you speak to me or anyone else. They've got your room guarded around the clock. But I know a guy who knows another guy who knows the officer on the door. He got me in. You've been in an induced coma for a week and on a respirator most of that time. Doc says you're one lucky son of a bitch. Says you would've lost a lung if it wasn't for the good folk at Westport Hospital. You remember that young doctor who lived with Sharma? You know, the one we kicked out so we could turn her place upside down? Well, she was the one who treated you. She saved your life.'

'How did you find me?' Harper said, the memory of that night slowly coming back.

'After you phoned from the cells I decided to get my arse over to Westport. I got in the car and broke every speed limit there was. Made the trip in under three hours. Anyway, I show up at the station and all the lights were on and the door was unlocked and the place was empty. So, I look around trying to work out where everyone was when I noticed the computer. You must have left minutes earlier because the screen saver hadn't kicked in. I saw the Google image of the house. I had nothing else to go on so figured it had something to do with the case. I got the address and plugged it into my phone and off I went. So I'm driving and checking my phone and trying to zero in when I drove right past the place. I circled around the block and came back.'

Images were reforming. Harper recalled the headlights, the stained glass, the kaleidoscope of colour sweeping across the walls.

'I parked by the school,' Gardella continued. 'When I got out I spotted your car just down the road. That's when I knew I was in the right place. I made my way up the drive to find the front door kicked in. I heard something upstairs. I got halfway up, just high enough to see over the landing, and there you were, sitting on the floor, covered in blood. I'm looking at you right between her legs. Before I can say a thing, I see her raise the gun. So I took her down with a single shot. I called emergency services. The rest is history.'

Harper closed his eyes. It had been that close. One missed traffic light and Gardella wouldn't have made it. Finding the computer screen with the image of the house was another stroke of luck.

'Who was she?' Harper asked.

'That's the sixty-four thousand dollar question? According to the documents we recovered, her name was Amy Louise Fairweather, twenty-nine, from Wellington. But when we ran the name, we got shit. We tried NIA, vehicle licensing, cellular providers, even the tax department, but nothing came back. We got nothing on dental. Her prints yielded no hits either. She was a ghost.'

Harper was now fully awake, his eyes wide, his brain working overtime. So Amy Fairweather was not a receptionist or a translator. She probably worked for either the Security Intelligence Service or the Government Communication Security Bureau, New Zealand's version of the CIA. Someone with the right security clearance had placed Fairweather at that mine to keep an eye on things, report on progress, and control any problems. Jonathon Hayes had become a problem. Before Harper could ask the question, Gardella answered it.

'We believe she was involved in the murder of Jonathon Hayes. After we got you off to the hospital we called the crime scene techs. They picked up some trace amounts of blood at the foot of the stairs. I think it was a few specks of spatter between the bannisters. We didn't see it ourselves until it was sprayed with luminol. So we did some more digging. We pulled up the carpet and found a suspicious stain on the underlay. It tested positive for blood. Fairweather struck him from behind with a blunt object, probably a hammer. We discovered more blood in a downstairs bathroom. We think that's where she cut him up. I had the lab rush the tests. They came back this afternoon. Positive match to Jonathon Hayes.'

'Why not just shoot him? She had a gun.'

Gardella shook his head. 'That only works if the body is never found. I mean, if she just wanted to kill him then yes, a gun is the logical choice. But if the body was ever found, Fairweather wanted it to look like the wife did it. A body full of bullet holes would raise too many questions. Like, how does a housewife get access to a firearm? Fairweather didn't want that. She chose a weapon that would be available in any household. So far we haven't found it and we probably never will. It's almost certainly been disposed of.'

'If she was trying to set up the wife, why not murder Hayes at his own house?'

'I was wondering that too. I think the reason she didn't go that way was because plan A was to make it seem like Hayes had run off. Fairweather didn't want to leave pools of blood because she knew that would launch a homicide investigation. Think about it. Samara Hayes comes home on Monday, sees blood and phones the police. The cops come in, question the wife, find she's been out of town and there are a bunch of witnesses, bingo, she has a rock-solid alibi. So right there, the wife is ruled out. Fairweather didn't want to risk that. She wanted Samara Hayes to return home and wait for her husband to show up. This would create a window where she was alone with no witnesses.'

Harper thought this scenario through. It made sense, but there was another option that could have worked equally well.

'Fairweather could still do all of that simply by cleaning up. She could leave the scene in such a way so that no blood was visible, but there was still trace for the forensic team to find later.'

'True, but the longer you stay at a crime scene, the more chance you have of getting caught. It would've taken hours to clean up. In that time she was bound to leave a hair, a print or be spotted by a neighbour. Fairweather understood that eventually, we would go through the Hayes house with a fine-tooth comb. I think she was trying to avoid leaving any evidence. Remember, her primary goal was to make it seem like Hayes had walked out of the marriage. That's why she took the clothes and left his truck at the airport. But that was where she made her first big mistake.'

Harper detected growing excitement in Gardella's tone.

'By using the truck, she inadvertently laid a series of GPS breadcrumbs which led straight to the body. That changed everything. Now it was a murder investigation. Even then, Fairweather had an insurance policy. The affair. Combine that with the couple's financial problems, not to mention the life insurance policy, and you've got ample motive for the wife. Using the family rubbish bin was meant to incriminate the wife. If that fell through, Fairweather knew the Sharma lawsuit was another avenue of inquiry that would keep police busy. In any event, Fairweather assumed we would be sufficiently preoccupied and wouldn't focus on any other suspects.

'But her second mistake was to use her own rubbish bin. We also picked up blood in the Fairweather bin. It looks like she transported the body from her house using her own wheelie bin. At the Hayes residence she transferred the body into the Hayes' bin, loaded that into Jonathon's truck and drove it into the gorge and dumped it. To hide the fact she left her own bin at the Hayes residence she scratched off the serial number. Snowden was a crafty old bugger. All the ESR techs I spoke to had never heard of the technique he used to raise that number. They called it a stroke of genius. Amy Fairweather never counted on that. Without that number the primary crime scene would never have been found. We'd probably still be pissing in the wind.'

There was movement in the corridor. Gardella paused while two orderlies passed by pushing a trolley. Once they were out of earshot, he went on.

'We found out that the rubbish is collected every Thursday. Fairweather's bin would've been nearly empty when she swapped it. What little rubbish she did have, she put into the old style black rubbish bags and left them in her garage. In those bags we found the same masking tape used by the killer. We were able to match one end of the tape from the bin with the torn end from the roll. We also found a boarding pass from a Christchurch to Westport flight, dated the day after Hayes disappeared.'

'Any prints?' Harper asked.

'You bet. Fairweather's prints were all over the boarding pass. We caught her on CCTV at the airport as well. It means she was the one who dropped off the truck. But get this. We pulled a different set of prints off the masking tape.' Gardella let this last statement hang, offering nothing else in the way of explanation. Harper filled in the blanks.

'She had help. She would have needed help to lift the bin into the truck. Maybe even to cut up the body.'

Gardella raised both eyebrows and gave a slow nod. 'The name Li Qian ring a bell?'

'The mine manager. Did you find him?'

'I got shut down. Brass didn't want to know. They're happy to pin this on Fairweather. They're saying she and Hayes had been sleeping together. Their theory is that she got angry when Hayes called off the affair. They say she killed him out of rage or jealousy. They've got it all wrapped up in a nice little package. It's all bullshit of course. They just don't want me snooping around. They don't want a diplomatic incident.'

Harper lifted his head and looked past Gardella to the open door. The lights in the hall were low. The voices had gone silent. The drone of the hospital's air conditioning the only noise. Across the hall, Harper could see the foot of the guard stationed outside. His head fell back and his eyes closed.

'Did Snowden make it?' Harper asked.

The question was met with silence. Harper opened his eyes. The look on Gardella's face conveyed the bad news.

'I'm nervous about this, Dylan,' Gardella eventually said. 'They've got the screws on me real tight. I'm copping heat from places within New Zealand law enforcement that I never even knew existed. My apartment and car have been searched, my Wi-Fi keeps cutting out like someone's messing with the connection, and I suspect that I'm being followed. I'm not sure I'm safe anywhere.'

Harper felt like all the air had been sucked from the room. Amy Fairweather was the killer. That much was clear. She had murdered Jonathon Hayes because he had found out about the uranium. Now Fairweather was dead, the murder investigation would be shelved. The problem was, Fairweather was just the blunt instrument of a larger machine. That machine was trying to protect itself by removing anyone who knew too much. Snowden had known, but he was also dead. Harper's last hope was Hayes' USB drive.

'Did you find the USB I left it in the car?'

Gardella shook his head. 'We never found it. I went through the car myself. Your computer was there, but the hard drive was nuked. I had the Electronic Crime Lab look at it and they said someone had run a data destruction program. All the information was scrubbed. Not even the operating system survived.'

The last strand of hope was now gone. The only loose-end was Harper. He was the only one who had all the pieces. There were powerful individuals who could not afford to let that information see the light of day.

He looked at Gardella and summoned the strength to ask one more question. 'Is that guard there for my protection or my detention?'

Gardella's slate-grey eyes had turned ashen. He swallowed hard.

'Either way ... it's not looking good.'

Acknowledgements

I would like to thank the following people for their help and support in the writing of this novel.

My wife Melissa for her advice and reassurance and for reading my first draft and not telling me it was rubbish and encouraging me to keep working and improving. My two sons, Payton and Deacon, who amaze me every day with their boundless energy and who inspired me to try new things and rise to the challenge of writing my first novel. Thanks to Mary and Colin Warren for being my beta readers and pointing out all my mistakes. I'll always treasure the memories of sitting on your knees when I was little and learning to read by going through stories from the Westport News.

John Parsons who went through my manuscript with a fine-tooth comb and used his years of experience to make the story flow. Your expert advice and attention to detail greatly improved the writing and I am forever grateful. I hope you enjoyed the wine. To Deborah Newman my fantastic editor, you are amazing. Your suggestions and guide notes really helped me develop my style and establish my own unique voice.

Finally, to Craig Mckay, Elizabeth Sheppard, Rowan Carroll and Ian Williams from the New Zealand Police. You gave up your time to help a new author and you did it without question or favour. Your help was very much appreciated.

If you have enjoyed DEAD GROUND
here's a taste of Justin Warren's new book

THE LEWIS PASS

I step out of the car and into the night, my breath twisting in the streetlight, leather soles cuffing the wet footpath. I turn to shut the door but my taxi isn't waiting, the car moving before I've fully slammed it home. Can't say I blame the driver. I'd be scared of me too. Probably thought I was going to slit his throat or strangle him or beat him over the head with a tyre iron. Watched me in the rearview the entire journey, eyes wet with fear. But he was never in any real danger. It wasn't his turn. He gets to go home to a wife and kids and a cold beer and a warm bed and he'll not really appreciate any of it. Not until there is the threat of it all being taken away.

The tyre hiss fades into the suburban hush and I survey the damp darkness. Squat brick homes flank the long, curving street, their windows curtained and their lawns glistened with the cold night's sweat. I've spent a long while preparing for this moment. Imagining what it would feel like. Rehearsing what I would do. But nothing fully prepares you for when they finally set you free. I don't feel joy or relief or redemption. I just feel numb. Alone I stand, the sky pricked with a million broken promises, all winking down from above as if wishing me good luck.

I make for the other side of the road, collar raised against the chill. The driveway is slick and my feet slip on the gentle incline. Emptiness aches all around. My key hits the lock, sliding stiffly into the cylinder. The night sighs and I hold my breath.

The key won't turn.

Stuck.

Gritted teeth and gentle persuasion makes the mechanism relent, letting me into my own house. Its reluctance is understandable. I haven't been around for a while. Three years and fifteen days to be exact. Probably didn't recognise me. I step inside and ease shut the door and let out a long breath. First hurdle overcome. If they were going to kill me, I'd be dead by now. They would have been waiting just inside the door. But my blood's still pumping and I'm not full of holes which all gives me hope that I'll survive - for tonight at least.

But I'm tired. They held me seven hours longer than strictly necessary. Something about paperwork. That's what they say when they've run out of legitimate excuses. Even so, they couldn't keep me forever. Their influence doesn't reach that far.

I flick the lights. Nothing. Power's off. To be expected. I haven't paid the electric bill for thirty-six consecutive months so the power company were well within their rights. I make a mental note to sort it out tomorrow.

And the phone.

TV can wait.

I move along the corridor. There's an empty feeling, like last winter's chill has taken up residence in my absence. I'm wearing the same midnight-blue two-piece from sentencing day. The suit's as stiff as my leather Oxfords and doesn't fit anymore. I've lost eight kilograms since they locked me up.

The living room appears as I left it, two-seat sofa beside the bookcase, wall clock above the window, a framed print by Colin McCahon frozen on the wall and staring at me like it was expecting someone else. A coffee table squats between the sofa and the TV and surround sound speakers hide in the corners and very little of anything else fills the room. Just an empty husk that was once home to a man getting his life back on track.

A tall glass of water rests half-filled on the coffee table as if freshly poured and waiting. My eyes dart, looking for answers. Slowly, they come. I remember now. The last time I was here. Sitting on the sofa, glass in hand, waiting for my lawyer to pick me up and take me to court. It was the day of my sentencing and I had expected to be back. Told home detention was likely. A clean record and years of service would all would count in my favour. At least that's what my lawyer said. Useless prick. Never believe anyone who keeps repeating the words, "trust me," like it's some kind of mantra. Never think you can predict the future. Nothing is written in stone until they etch the epitaph on your grave.

I move across the room towards the sliding door. It rolls back smooth and I step into the kitchen. It's even colder in here. Silver moonlight falls through a dirty bay window onto shuttered cupboards and barren countertops and a six-seat dining room table that I've never fully used because I've never trusted that many people to have them all around one table at the same time. And that's all the moonlight should be falling upon. Except it isn't. A tall figure cuts a taut silhouette in the light.

The man doesn't move. I'm not sure if that's a good sign or not. An amateur intruder would be escaping out the kitchen ranchslider right about now. On the other hand, a pro would have already concluded his dirty business and I'd be face down on the floor losing body fluids and taking final breaths and wishing I'd been more careful. So whoever he is it seems he's here to talk. All right then. Let's talk.

'Who the fuck are you?' I ask.

Grey breath rises from the man, winding in lazy curls before dissolving into nothing.

'A friend,' he says, his voice as smooth as caramel coffee.

I shake my head. 'My friends have names,' I say. 'What's yours?'

Not a hint of movement to indicate he's registered the question. It's going to be a long night if he keeps this up. If he's here to kill me then his plan must be to watch me die of hypothermia.

'What's the matter?' I say. 'Shy?'

A soft chuckle reveals the white teeth of a relaxed grin. Judging from his shadow he's at least as tall as me, maybe six-three or six-four, lean and strong. An equal match if things get spicey. So long as he's not carrying, that is.

The man draws out a seat from the dining table and makes himself comfortable. 'Sit down,' he says.

I scan the room for hidden accomplices. A toaster hides in a dim alcove, the fridge stands still against the wall, and the microwave looks down from a shelf its digital clock, dead.

I say, 'Not until I get some answers.'

Another chuckle. 'You're just how my advisers described. They said you back down to no one. You're going to work out perfectly.' His voice as finely cultured as a late-night radio host. He picks up his hands and rests them on the table. My eyes are now better adjusted to the dark; I'm reasonably sure he's unarmed.

'Listen, mate. I'm tired and grumpy and if you don't tell me who you are, I'm going to throw you the fuck out.'

'You already know who I am.'

'Do I?'

'I'm the person who is going to wipe your slate clean. I'm DC Lawson.'

It takes a moment for the words to sink in. District Commander Lawson. One of the most powerful cops in the country. Only the commissioner and his deputy sit higher. I remember Lawson from when I worked homicide. Back then he wasn't the district commander.

He was some sort of special advisor. He would come in and assist whenever we had a big case. Anything with a lot of media.

The last time I saw him was when the Woolstone Coolstore exploded. Twelve men lost their lives and it made headlines around the world. Lawson flew in from Wellington to lead the investigative team. There were rumours the coolstore's owners were cutting corners and disabling sensors and breaching just about every safety protocol in the book. There was intense scrutiny from the public and much talk of a cover-up. It wasn't until the Christchurch Earthquake the following February that the media found something else to write about and Lawson faded back into his corner. As far as I know, no further progress has been made with a prosecution. So now he's DC. That means he's in charge of all the cops in the South Island. Still, it doesn't explain why he's sitting at my dining room table.

'What do you want with me?' I say.

'I have a proposition that you would do well to consider.'

'And what might that be?'

Lawson uses a foot to nudge out a chair. 'Take a seat. This is going to take a while.'

'You know what,' I sigh. 'I'm done listening to people who say they have my best intentions at heart. It's never really worked out that well for me.'

'Fair enough,' Lawson says. 'If that's what you want, I'll walk away and you can get on with the rest of your life. I'm sure there are plenty of jobs out there for a convicted drug dealer.'

'I was set up. Those drugs were planted.'

'You're preaching to the choir. I read the file. The case is full of holes. No prints, no drug paraphernalia, no evidence of a supply chain, no witnesses and no customers. Not to mention the question of why a homicide cop would move several K's of meth to a small town while investigating a missing person. But hey, you don't want my help. You'll just have to live with your conviction and hope for the best.'

I play it coy and take a breath to weigh my options. I have none. I mean, it's not like I've got anything else on my agenda for the foreseeable future.

Against my better judgement, I edge closer, careful to keep an eye on my uninvited guest. He makes no aggressive moves. Cautiously, I grasp the back of the chair and sit down. I'm just eight feet from Lawson, close enough to make out facial features and smell cheap cologne. He appears older than I remember, the furrows on his brow chiselled deep, eyes hooded, hair thinning. Moonlight frames the right side of his jaw. A jaw strong enough to shatter fists. A jaw with muscles that flex and strain like they're trying to send a message. The lines defining his mouth are dagger-sharp. I doubt a word has ever passed those lips without being perfectly formed.

'This better be good. I'm gonna be pissed if you waste my first evening of freedom.'

'I think you'll like what I have to say.'

'Yeah? I'll let you know.'

Lawson shifts his weight and every muscle in my body goes tense. He leans forward, laying elbows and forearms flat on the table like we're just two guys having a friendly chat over tea and biscuits.

'What happened to you was wrong,' Lawson begins, his voice matter of fact. 'The evidence was fabricated. It should never have gone to trial. Had I been in charge I would have made it a priority to have you cleared and back to work as soon as possible. My sources say you were once an excellent investigator. A rising star.'

I could remind him that I'm still an excellent investigator. But I don't. It's been a long day and the cold is beginning to bite. Starting an argument isn't going to get me any closer to where I want to be.

'I want to help you,' Lawson continues. 'I want to get your record cleared. I think I can get you back on the team. But you need to play ball. I need something from you. I need a job done. A job that will help solve a problem for both of us.'

Lawson pauses like he is expecting something. I'm not ready to give him anything. Not yet.

Made in the USA
Columbia, SC
07 December 2020